"Tell me exactly where you met this man."

Darcy stared at her mother. Then, shaking herself, she replied. "His name is Hunter Sloan, Mom. He coaches Meli's soccer team."

Hunter's eyes narrowed on Darcy. Why hadn't she told her mother that he was more than her daughter's coach? She began to speak again. "Mom, he's—"

But Marian's stiffened shoulders and gaping mouth silenced her. "Hunter Sloan," she said. "Are you the Hunter Sloan who grew up here in Hyde Point?"

"Yes, ma'am."

"I thought you'd moved away." Marian looked at Darcy questioningly.

"Yes, he moved away. But he came back this summer. What's the matter, Mom? How do you know Hunter?"

Her mother's lips thinned and her face hardened. "I know this man because when he was sixteen he stole my car."

Dear Reader,

Welcome to the second book of the SERENITY HOUSE series—a trilogy about women who spent part of their adolescence in a group home for troubled girls. As always with my series books, this one stands alone. But I hope you'll also read the others.

A *Place To Belong* is Darcy O'Malley's story. As a young girl, Darcy was wild and rebellious—out of control, her mother called it. As an adult—when the story opens—Darcy has become a responsible mother of two and the owner of the local day care in the town where she grew up. Everything seems to have fallen into place—and then the town's former bad boy, Hunter Sloan, returns home because he needs help with his troubled five-year-old son. Suddenly Darcy's well-ordered life is turned upside down.

Once again, this books deals with issues close to my heart: How a man can be a woman's friend before they fall in love and how he can help her become the person she was meant to be. How a father's love can transform a child's life. How female friendships—even under the most difficult situations—can sustain women. All of these things happen in A *Place To Belong*, where yet another Serenity House woman comes to terms with her past and takes control of her future.

Please write and let me know what you think. I answer all reader mail. Send letters to Kathryn Shay, P.O. Box 24288, Rochester, New York, 14624-0288. Or e-mail me at kshayweb@rochester.rr.com. Also visit my Web sites at http://www.kathrynshay.com and http://www.superauthors.com.

Kathryn Shay

Books by Kathryn Shay

HARLEQUIN SUPERROMANCE

A Place To Belong
Kathryn Shay

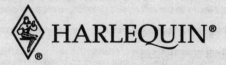

TORONTO • NEW YORK • LONDON
AMSTERDAM • PARIS • SYDNEY • HAMBURG
STOCKHOLM • ATHENS • TOKYO • MILAN • MADRID
PRAGUE • WARSAW • BUDAPEST • AUCKLAND

ISBN 0-373-71088-7

A PLACE TO BELONG

Visit us at www.eHarlequin.com

Printed in U.S.A.

To troubled teenagers everywhere—with the hope that they will find help to overcome the adversity in their lives, as do the women of Serenity House.

CAST OF CHARACTERS

Serenity House: A group home for teenage girls in Hyde Point, New York.

Jade Kendrick Anderson: Paige's sister, one of the original residents of Serenity House

Jewel Anderson: Jade's daughter

Lewis Beckman (Beck): Jewel's father

Porter Casewell: Resident of S.H.; baby-sits for Darcy's daughters

Ian Chandler: Obstetrician

Lynne Chandler: Ian's birth mother

Bart & Ada Cooper: Hunter's grandparents

Annabelle Crane: Police officer, one of the original residents of S.H.

Charly Smith Donovan: Social worker, original resident of S.H. Now runs S.H.

Nathan Hyde: Congressman, son of the town's founding father

Paige Kendrick Chandler: Pediatrician, original resident of S.H., married to Ian

Hannah Mitchum: Hunter's sister

Marian Shannon Mason: Darcy's mother

Jeremy Mason: Marian's husband

Elsa and Tom Moore: Ian's adoptive parents

Taylor Vaughn Morelli: One of the original S.H. residents

Nick Morelli: Taylor's husband

Darcy O'Malley: One of the original S.H. residents, now runs a day care

Meli and Claire O'Malley: Darcy's daughters

Nora Nolan: Founder and house mother of S.H.

Hunter Sloan: Local boy, friend of Dan Whitman's

Braden Sloan: Hunter's son

Dan Whitman: Police chief, fiancé of Nora Nolan

PROLOGUE

January 1987

NORA NOLAN ANSWERED the door at eight o'clock at night, her stomach in knots. This admittance to Serenity House would *not* be easy. On the porch, in the chilly January evening, she found her newest client, Darcy Shannon. "Hello, Darcy."

A go-to-hell teenage scowl met her greeting.

Darcy's mother, Marian Shannon Mason, glared at the girl, who was a petite five-foot-two with flame-red hair. "Say hello to Miss Nolan, Darcy Anne."

Still the silent sullenness.

"Well, come on in." Nora reached for the hot-pink suitcase Darcy carried, but the girl snatched it back. Her eyes—the color of wet grass—warned Nora not to invade her personal space.

Frozen for a moment, mother and daughter stood on the threshold of the newly opened home for troubled girls. Maybe they knew—as Nora did—that once they stepped through the doorway, their relationship would never be the same. A mother admitting she couldn't control her daughter damaged the trust between parent and child. Nora wasn't sure that trust could ever be regained. But at least Serenity House could help, which was why she'd fought to establish it in this rather conservative upstate New York town of Hyde Point.

Finally, Darcy and Mrs. Mason stepped inside.

Nora asked pleasantly, "Darcy, would you like to see your room?"

Darcy shook her head, sending her hair into her eyes. She clasped her leather jacket close to her chest. A pink sweater peeked out from beneath it.

"Straighten your shoulders and push your hair back," Mrs. Mason said.

Darcy's tongue clucked in resentment. Her gaze was distracted by someone on the stairs. Nora turned to find Paige Kendrick at the top of them.

"Darcy, this is Paige. She and her sister have been here a few weeks. Maybe she can show you your room. It's right next to hers."

Panic flooded Darcy's face. It was hard to believe this fragile-looking girl consistently stayed out all night, shoplifted, often refused to go to school and had recently been caught without any clothes by the police on top of Hyde Point Hill with an equally naked boy.

Paige trundled downstairs. "Hi, Darcy. I've seen you at school."

Darcy swallowed hard and eyed Paige's six-months-along pregnancy.

"There's three of us here. Me, my sister, Jade, and Charly Smith, who bakes great cookies."

"Well, good," Mrs. Mason said. "See, dear, you'll like it at Serenity House."

Nora refrained from rolling her eyes. Paige, however, wasn't so discreet. She gave Mrs. Mason an are-you-nuts-lady? look.

"So, I'll be going." The woman fidgeted with her purse. "I'll call you tomorrow, Darcy."

Darcy wouldn't look at her mother. Mrs. Mason didn't touch her daughter, simply said goodbye, nodded to Nora and opened the door. She had reached the porch before Darcy yelled, "Mom!" and bolted after her. In the darkness of late winter, Darcy threw herself at her mother, grasping her around the waist. "Please, don't leave me here." Hiccups. "I promise I'll be good. I'll change. I'll be what you want." Tears. "Just don't leave me in this place."

Paige moved close to Nora, and Nora put her arm around the girl.

They watched as Mrs. Mason placed her hands on Darcy's shoulders and pushed her away. "I can't, Darcy. You won't change. The authorities think this is the best. It's only for a few months until you learn some discipline."

"Please."

"No." The woman's voice was firm.

Darcy yanked herself away. "Fine. Forget about your own daughter. Go take care of other people's kids." Nora knew that Darcy was referring to the daycare that Mrs. Mason ran with her new husband, Jeremy Mason.

Angrily, Darcy brushed back her bangs and straightened her shoulders. "I'll never forgive you for this," she said in an icy voice.

Mrs. Mason paled. "Don't say that, Darcy."

The girl raised her chin. "I won't. Ever."

With quiet dignity, Darcy stepped back, entered Serenity House, and said to Paige, "You can show me my room now."

CHAPTER ONE

Fifteen years later

DARCY O'MALLEY GLANCED at her slim gold watch and smiled. "Better go, Mom. You'll miss your plane."

"Are you sure you can do this alone?" Marian Mason fussed with the books on the top shelf behind Darcy's desk. Her auburn hair was now sprinkled with gray, but she looked young and trim in a Chanel suit.

Darcy stifled the urge to tell her mother she'd been *doing this*—single-handedly running TenderTime Daycare—for almost a year. Technically, her mother and stepfather still owned it but they were easing themselves out of the day-to-day operation. "Yes, of course. We hired those two new aides just so you and Jeremy could get away." She smiled. "You need a rest."

So do you, girl. From good old Mom.

Forcefully, she silenced the voice of "the old Darcy" that sometimes escaped no matter how hard she tried to keep her hidden.

"All right, I'll go. We'll be away a month which means we'll be back mid-September. I'll phone, and we can fly back from the ship anytime." She hesitated. "Call David if you need anything. He's more than our lawyer."

With well-honed patience, Darcy stood. She was hop-

ing her mother would leave before Dan Whitman arrived. "Of course I will. I'll be seeing David, anyway."
She stepped out from behind her desk and hugged her mother. "Now, scoot."

Marian stared at Darcy. By the glow in her mother's eyes, Darcy knew that her white Ann Taylor suit, pale stockings and matching pumps met with Marian's approval. "Have I told you how proud I am of you, Darcy Anne? You've become such a good businesswoman. And you're raising two wonderful girls."

Despite her willing it back, a lump formed in Darcy's throat. "Thanks, Mom. Now go on that second honeymoon. TenderTime will be fine."

When Marian finally left, Darcy let out a deep breath. Since she'd returned to Hyde Point over two years ago, she'd established a truce with her mother, and now they shared a mutual respect that Darcy valued. But being around Marian could be stressful.

Because Marian the Librarian expects you to be like her.

Well, that was okay. Darcy *was* like her mother. Now.

Oh, God, spare me!

"Hel-lo."

Grateful for the distraction, Darcy looked up to see a smiling Dan Whitman in the doorway. Since his marriage last month to Nora Nolan, the founder—and savior—of Serenity House, the town police chief walked around with a perpetual smile on his face.

Darcy crossed to the door. "Hi, Dan. Nice to see you."

Dan stepped aside, revealing a man behind him. As Darcy hugged Dan, she got a brief glimpse of his companion's broad shoulders encased in a blue striped shirt, sleeves rolled up to reveal powerful arms. The guy's hair was almost black and his eyes were equally dark. Darcy had seen those high cheekbones before, though she couldn't remember where.

"Darcy, this is Hunter Sloan. Hunter, Darcy O'Malley. You met briefly at the wedding."

Ah, yes. Darcy remembered her conversation with Paige's sister when they'd spotted him in the crowd...

"Ah, too bad I've given up on bad boys." Darcy's words had ended on a sigh.

"How do you know he's a bad boy?" Jade had asked.

"Internal radar. It never dies. No matter how hard I've tried to smother it..."

"Hello, Mr. Sloan."

"Ma'am." His voice was rusty, as if seldom used.

Stepping back, Darcy invited the men in. "Let's sit here," she said, indicating the taupe leather sofas off to the side. She'd had them brought in to replace her mother's conference table.

The three sat. Pulling down the hem of her skirt, Darcy watched Hunter Sloan cross his jean-clad legs at his ankles. Scarred boots peeked out.

"Dan says you have a son, Mr. Sloan."

"Hunter." His face glowed at the mention of the child. "His name's Braden, Mrs. O'Malley."

"Darcy."

"I just moved back to Hyde Point and I gotta work. I need care for the boy." He said it as though he was admitting to a crime. Up close, he looked as if he might have admitted to several in his lifetime—his nose had a small I've-been-broken bump, he sported a scar just under the right side of his chin and a few more on his knuckles.

''We have a great program here at TenderTime. How old is Braden?''

''Five.''

Darcy caught vibes that told her something else was going on. She focused on Dan. ''Why this special meeting, Dan? We're pretty full here, but we have room for another kid.''

Dan said, ''Braden has some needs. Nora told us you've been integrating a program in your daycare for special kids. It's one of the reasons Hunter came back to Hyde Point.''

''What are Braden's needs?''

Hunter sat up and locked his hands together between his knees. ''Mostly he's a handful.''

''Has he always been a handful?''

''Always?''

''Since he was born? It makes a difference if this is new behavior or consistent.''

''I reckon always.''

Taken aback, she asked, ''You reckon? Don't you know?''

Darcy watched shadows play across Hunter's face. He was obviously about to say something painful. ''My son just came to live with me last month. I hadn't seen him since he was born.''

Immediately Darcy felt herself withdraw. She knew all about abandoning fathers. And husbands.

Dan reached out and squeezed Hunter's arm. ''Tell her everything, Hunter. She'll need to know in order to help Braden.''

''His mother and I got married to make Braden legitimate. We never lived together, and she didn't want me to see the boy after he was born.'' He gave a disgusted shake of his head. ''She'd already met somebody else and planned to marry as soon as we divorced. He didn't like me hangin' around.''

''Where do they live?''

''In Florida, where I've been living.''

That explained the hint of southern accent.

''Hunter sent money every month to take care of his son.'' Dan sounded defensive. He must have read her mind.

Darcy softened. ''Well, that's admirable of you. How is it that you have him now?''

Reluctantly, Hunter continued his story. ''Shelly's pregnant again for the third time. It's a hard pregnancy. She says she can't take care of Braden.''

Just like good old Mom, Darce. Only it happened to poor Braden at five instead of sixteen.

''She called outta the clear blue one morning and asked me to take him until she has this new kid.''

''Which is when?''

''A few months. Then she wants Braden back.''

''Does she see him at all?''

''No. She moved about two hundred miles from my house in the Keys. And then I came up here.'' He sighed. ''They talk on the phone, though.''

''When did all this happen?''

''Right after Dan's wedding. I've been tryin' to cope on my own in Florida, but nobody wants to watch the boy. Baby-sitters quit, daycares kick him out.'' The man's eyes glistened with pain. Even the thick lashes around them couldn't disguise it. ''And as I said, I have to work. I got me some kin here in Hyde Point—my grandparents. We're stayin' with them. They said they'd help take care of him. But they're older and, as I said, he's a handful.''

"Being uprooted from his mother must have been difficult."

A look of stark agony crossed Hunter's features. "Leavin' her was a nightmare. But that isn't the only reason he acts so bad. He's always been this way. It's one of the reasons Shelly gave him to me. Her husband was real glad to get rid of him for a while."

"Just what does Braden do?"

"In preschool, he couldn't sit still for story time. Apparently there were run-ins with the other kids. And he kicked the teacher, so they tossed him out. He was supposed to start kindergarten in September, but the teachers felt there'd be the same problems there, so they recommended his waiting a year."

"Not a bad idea."

"So," Dan said calmly. "Think you can handle Braden?"

Her mother's words came back to her...

Really, Darcy, why do you insist on integrating this program for troubled children?

Darcy's voice had gone cold. *Because troubled kids need good care, Mom. Or the rest of their lives can be ruined.*

Marian had gotten the message...

"I'd be happy to take Braden. I've just hired extra help for setting up this new program. We also have a room for four- and five-year-olds that would fit Braden perfectly. And a prekindergarten class which substitutes for public school four mornings a week starting in September." She smiled when Hunter's shoulders finally relaxed. "I'll personally keep an eye on him."

"You mean that?"

"Yes. Troubled kids are a speciality of mine."

For good reason.

Standing, she crossed to the file cabinet and withdrew some papers. "Here are several forms for you to fill out. Braden will need a physical. Paige Kendrick is the pediatrician I'd like you to see. She's working with me on this program. And she might have some insights into Braden's problems."

Hunter took the forms and nodded.

"So, when should he bring Braden in to visit the center?" Dan asked.

"Just a sec." Darcy checked the calendar that she'd brought from the desk. "How about tomorrow at nine? If you'd like, I can call Paige and see if she'll squeeze in a physical so Braden could start as soon as possible."

Hunter gave what might pass for a smile. "That'd be real good, Miss Darcy."

She cocked her head at the term.

"Sorry. The Southerner in me. Everybody down home uses Miss as a sign of respect. I been in the Carolinas and Florida over twenty years and picked up a lot of their way of talkin'."

"It's a nice phrase."

Dan stood. "Thanks, Darcy. Nora and I appreciate this."

As Hunter rose, and they made their way to the exit, Darcy asked, "How is the bride, Dan? I haven't seen her in a while."

"Busy with Quiet Waters." Now that Serenity House was being run by Charly Smith Donovan, Nora and Dan were spearheading a group home for boys. Which was one of the reasons he was retiring as police chief next year. "Hunter here's going to do the carpentry work."

"How nice." At the door, she said, "See you tomorrow, Hunter."

He nodded. "At nine." His dark gaze was grateful. "Thanks for goin' outta your way."

"No problem." Dan and Nora had been lifesavers to Darcy and girls like her. She was returning the favor.

Dan winked at her and said goodbye.

Thoughtful, she watched Dan put his hand on Hunter's back as they walked down the hall. She wondered what Hunter's story was. The guy obviously came with a truckload of baggage. The inner voice that bothered her more and more lately said, *Seems like a kindred spirit, Darce.*

Oh, fine, just what she needed in her life. A sexy bad boy with a heart of gold.

FOR HUNTER SLOAN, hell was spelled H-y-d-e P-o-i-n-t. Having left this godforsaken place when he was twenty, he'd vowed he'd never come back. He'd made a successful life in the Keys where he liked himself right fine, but coming back here did a number on his head. As he drove up to his grandparents' tidy little house on Second Street, the engine of his red Ford truck purred softly. The reason he'd returned to his boyhood town was tucked in that house, and he could only guess what havoc Braden had wreaked while his father had been at TenderTime with Dan.

Hyde Point. The town where Hunter had once again been subjected to people's biases. He hadn't missed the distaste of the pretty proprietor when Hunter told her he hadn't seen Braden since the kid was born. Those eyes had snapped some green fire. Hell, if he didn't know the circumstances, he'd be mad at himself, too. As he pulled to the curb and shut the engine off, he could still picture Shelly's face five years ago...

"You can't see him, Hunter. I appreciate your marrying me to give the baby a name, but I'm in love with somebody else. Hank said if I divorced you as soon as the baby comes, we'd still have a chance. But he doesn't want you hanging around…''

Oh, Hunter had put up a fuss, for all the good it had done him. In the end, he'd caved because Shelly said it was best for the boy. She never knew that she'd taken away from Hunter what he'd seen as the only really good thing he'd ever done. He never allowed anybody to see his feelings. It was easier—when they didn't get met—not to have gone public with them.

Getting out of the truck, he climbed the steps from the road to the house and found his grandfather near the porch.

"Hello, son." For some reason, his grandparents—the parents of the mother he never knew—didn't see him as backwater pond scum. His grandpa's job had meant they'd traveled a lot and hadn't been around when Hunter was growing up.

He smiled. "Hey, Pa." He scowled at the Weed Whacker in the old man's hands. "Told you I'd help you when I got back."

"I like weeding." Bart Cooper, still spry at seventy-eight, with grizzly white hair and kind brown eyes, looked up at him. "How'd it go?"

"Good. They're gonna take him."

Bart cleared his throat. "Wish we could keep him all day."

"Pa, *I* can't handle him all day. He tuckers *me* out."

"You do pretty good."

The front door opened and out loped a blur of gray fur. Bart shook his head. "Been hiding on the back porch, in the corner, since you left."

Hunter's chin snapped up. "Braden?"

The dog reached him and nuzzled Hunter's legs. Hunter knelt on one knee and nuzzled back.

"No, Tramp there."

"I told you, Pa, he's been abused. It was obvious when I found him beaten by the side of the road. He's mighty shy around people."

Bart harrumphed.

"Braden in the house?"

"Ma coaxed him outside. They're in the garden out back."

Not much kept his son's attention, and Braden rarely did anything he didn't want to without a fight, but he seemed to like being outside. He was also beginning to take a shine to his great-grandmother. "What's she got him doin'?"

"Picking the cherry tomatoes."

Hunter stood but left a hand on Tramp's head. "I'll go on back."

Bart nodded. Hunter got halfway around the gray-sided house, under the big trees, when he heard his grandpa call out, "Hunter?"

He looked up.

"Things gonna be okay, you know."

Summoning willpower he didn't know he had, Hunter didn't contradict his grandfather. "Sure, Pa, I know."

Making his way around back, Hunter thought about Darcy O'Malley. "She's got good breedin', Tramp," he said, scratching the dog's head. "Not like you and me."

Silent, the dog sidled into him.

"And she's a pretty little thing, isn't she?"

The dog gave what might pass for a growl.

Hunter caught sight of Braden in the garden and

stared at the kid as he approached him. "Sure hope Miss Darcy can handle that one." All fifty pounds of his son were covered with dirt. Hunter sighed at the thought of getting him into the shower, though it couldn't be as bad as the first bath had been...

"Not goin' in there," Braden had said, staring at the small bathtub in Hunter's bungalow.

"You're filthy as a greased pig, kid."

The boy's dark gaze—just like Hunter's—stared out angrily from under his shaggy brown hair. "Make me."

Hunter picked him up and dumped him, fully clothed, into the water. There ensued a battle, after which the entire bathroom was wetter than the deck of the *Titanic*.

Wide-eyed, Braden had scanned the mess and said, "Cool..."

"Hey, everybody."

At the sight of other people, Tramp edged behind Hunter. Braden looked up.

"Hi there, Hunter," his grandmother said.

"Hey," was all Braden mumbled. After almost a month, the kid still hadn't called him Dad. He didn't call Hunter anything. Braden's eyes focused on the dog. "Hey, Tramp. Come here, boy."

Tramp huddled farther behind Hunter. Braden met his father's gaze. Well, this was one thing he could give the kid. Slowly, Hunter crossed to the garden. When he reached his son, he knelt down, knowing Tramp would sit beside him.

Braden lifted a little hand. "Light, right?"

"Uh-huh. Very light, on his head."

"Why'd they beat him?" Braden asked, tentatively touching Tramp.

"I don't know, son. I never even found out who owned him."

Braden stiffened at the term, but the fact that Tramp allowed the petting was too much for him to pass up, so he stayed where he was and smiled. "Good dawggy. I won't hurt you, Tramp. I wouldn't ever."

A lump formed in Hunter's throat. "He'll come to know that, Brade. Soon." *Maybe you will, too.*

Braden shot Hunter a quick look, as if he'd spoken the words.

His grandmother wiped her eyes. At a chipper seventy-five, Ada Cooper's fondness for Hunter—and now his son—made her weepy. "Gettin' help with the tomatoes?" he asked, to ease the moment.

She nodded. "Yep. Braden here's my assistant."

Ducking his head, Braden looked away. Ada Cooper could melt a snowman. She'd had the same effect on Hunter when she and Bart had visited Hyde Point.

"How about some cookies, boys?"

"Can Tramp have one?" Braden asked.

"Don't see why not." Ada winked at Hunter. "They're your daddy's favorites."

"Chocolate chip?" Hunter felt his insides loosen up a bit.

"Mmm." She nodded to the house. "Let's go on in."

Braden and Hunter stood. "You're dirty, boy. Before we go—"

"He's fine. Just let him wash his hands and face at the well." Ada held out her basket. Hunter took it in one hand and reached his other out to Braden.

Braden frowned. Again a memory...

"Don't touch me. I don't know you."

"I'd like to change that."

"Don't touch me..."

Today, the kid seemed to consider taking his father's

hand. Well, that was an improvement. But Braden reached for Tramp's collar instead. The dog slipped away from the boy.

Hunter sighed. At one time, here in Hyde Point, rejection had been a matter of course. He'd forgotten how bad it felt. In Key West he had a few close friends. Some pretty good relationships with women who seemed to find him attractive. And his carpentry business had really taken off. But here…he was nothing again. He thought about the sophisticated woman at TenderTime. Though she looked like she'd been spoiled all her life, he hoped she knew something about rejection, because his son was going to need an understanding caregiver.

As the four of them walked to the kitchen, all Hunter could think was it was going to be a long few months.

CHAPTER TWO

"WHAT DO YOU THINK of the room, Braden?" Darcy reached out to rumple the boy's dark hair, but he jerked away. Okay. Darcy could remember not wanting anybody invading her personal space, either.

When Braden didn't answer, just stared mutely at the classroom for four- and five-year-olds not quite ready for school, Hunter leaned over and whispered, "Answer Miss Darcy, Brade."

The boy studied the walls, shrugged, then began to hop from one foot to the other. "Cool colors." His gaze catching on something, he took off a little too fast. Halfway to the rug in the middle of the room, he clipped another boy, who tumbled down to the floor. Braden just kept going.

Hunter rushed to the child and helped him up. "You okay, partner?"

The boy nodded. He pulled away and headed over to the area rug where Braden had dropped down.

Sighing, Hunter crossed back to Darcy. "He doesn't even realize what he does sometimes."

"Yes, I can see that." She smiled at the man, noting the shadows in his eyes. She nodded to the woman who was in charge of the room. Becky Lane was an experienced teacher. "Mr. Sloan and I are going to talk for a while. Braden will stay with you."

"We'll be fine."

Darcy said to Hunter, "Let's go to my office."

"All right." But he didn't move. Instead, he waited until Braden glanced over at him. "I'm going with Miss Darcy, son."

The boy's eyes narrowed.

"I'll be back in…" He looked to Darcy.

"About a half hour."

"Thirty minutes," Hunter said with an easy smile. He checked the clock. "When the big hand's on the six."

Braden watched him for another few beats, then turned back to the rug, which had a border of jumbo-size alphabet letters. He began tracing each one with his finger, humming as he performed the task.

On their way to the office Darcy said, "He thinks you might not come back."

"I know. Legacy from a mother who shuffled him off to me."

"Do you mind so much?"

Hunter stopped dead in his tracks. His black, rolled-up-at-the-sleeves shirt, along with his dark hair and eyes, made him look dangerous. "Mind? Of course not. Getting Braden is the best thing that ever happened to me."

The vehemence of his tone made Darcy step back.

"Sorry." His complexion reddened, and he looked away, jamming his hands in the back pockets of his black jeans. "I get addled 'bout that, I guess."

"It's nice to hear you care so much."

He swallowed hard, but said nothing more. This was a man not used to talking about his emotions.

They made their way to the office, and Darcy took a seat behind her desk. Hunter dropped into a chair across from her. She picked up the forms he'd filled out and scanned them for the routine information. Then she turned to the section of the application which she'd developed for troubled kids.

"Are my answers, um, legible?" Hunter asked. "I got used to doing everything by computer but I left mine in the Keys."

"Yes, I can read them." She smiled and peered over at him, noting he seemed like a kid in front of the principal. "You spent time on these."

"Why wouldn't I?"

"Some parents do a slapdash job on them."

"Parents should be more careful with their kids."

"I agree. Let's elaborate on some of these points." She looked at the checklist. "What are the signs of his restlessness?"

Hunter shifted in his seat, and his foot began to tap. "He fidgets. All the time. He tugs at his clothes as if he doesn't like having them on." Dark eyes narrowed. "And he doesn't sleep well. Seems to me he can't shut down, sometimes."

"How about distractability?"

"I try reading to him at night. I get halfway through the story and he's got his little trucks doing half gainers off the pillow."

Darcy smiled.

"I told you yesterday the school didn't want him to start because he can't sit still. He *disrupts* everybody." The last was said bitterly.

"It also says here he loses things, isn't organized."

"He's still a little tyke."

"Well, he should keep track of where he puts things. How does he do with chores?"

"If they're outside, he keeps track of them right fine."

"Tell me about that."

A restrained smile spread across Hunter's face. It startled her for a minute. "He loves being outdoors. Sleeps like a baby when I put up a tent and camp out there with him at night."

She smiled at the image.

"And his great-grandma and -grandpa take him outside to work in the garden and the yard. He loves to help out when he can dig in the dirt and grass."

Darcy covered a few more questions dealing with topics she and Paige had targeted to ask parents. Finally she said, "How about his self-esteem?"

Hunter's eyes turned bleak. "It's been stomped on. Big time."

"By the preschool in Florida?"

"Some. More by the fact that his mother sent him away." He glanced past her shoulder. "He cried every night for weeks when he first came to me, asking why she didn't want him." As if he couldn't help it, he added, "Damn near broke my heart."

"She couldn't handle him. There's a difference between that and not wanting him."

Fine, go take care of other people's children.

"Is there? Seems to me if she really loved him, wanted him, she'd have found a way to handle him, keep him, help him with his acting out." He sat up, leaned over and linked his hands between his knees. "Look, I'm not saying he isn't a handful. He drives me crazy. A lot. I'm just saying, if he was mine, I'd find a way to keep him."

"He is yours, Hunter."

"Not legally. She talked me out of staking legal claim. We never got any kind of custody document, but it's clear who he belongs to." Again he swallowed hard.

He stood and walked over to the window, played with the cords on the blinds. Was it nervous tension? After a moment, he came back to face her. "I'm not laying blame. I took the easy way out. I shouldn't have let her have him completely. I should've insisted on visiting rights. But now that he's with me, I'm gonna do the best I can for him."

"Giving up your job in Key West is a big thing."

"Carpenters are always in demand there. Especially on new boats. I can get work like that anytime."

"Oh, I thought..." She frowned down at the paper. "It says here you bartended."

"Yes, ma'am, I did. To earn money." He shrugged. "Guess I see myself as a carpenter."

"You bartended to send money for Braden, didn't you?"

"Yeah. He won't want for anything."

For some reason, Darcy had a flashback to the frantic phone call she'd made to Johnny O'Malley three years ago...

"Johnny, I can't support the girls on my waitress job. I need money from you for them."

"Sugar, I can barely put food on my own table. And I just lost my job—"

"Again?"

"Miss Darcy?" Hunter's voice broke into her thoughts. "Did I say something to offend you?"

"No, I'm sorry. My mind wandered a bit."

Briefly, Hunter wondered what had brought that hot look to Darcy O'Malley's eyes again. She'd doused it quick, but it had been there. Those eyes were accented today by the dress she wore; it was the color of spring grass in the morning.

The phone rang, interrupting his unusual thoughts.

Darcy answered. "TenderTime Daycare. Darcy O'Malley."

A pause. "Thanks for getting back to me so soon, Paige." She waited. "Um, yes, Mr. Sloan's right here." She covered the mouthpiece. "It's Paige Kendrick. She can squeeze Braden's physical in tomorrow at eight-thirty before her other appointments. Can you make it?"

If I cancel a job go-see at the Boxwood Inn. "Yep, I can."

As Darcy set up the appointment, Hunter wondered at the connection she had with a doctor who'd squeeze in a physical. Must be they did a lot of work together for the daycare. Hell, maybe they'd gone to boarding school together.

"You'll like Paige." Darcy's voice interrupted his rumination after she'd hung up.

"Is she good with kids like Braden?"

Darcy's smile beamed from her face. "She's good with all kids, but especially little guys like Braden." She cocked her head. "We've all got his best interest at heart."

Hunter remembered the teachers, and cops—except for Dan Whitman—and population in general of good old Hyde Point. "Must be things have really changed in this town."

"Changed?"

"Hyde Point didn't used to care about trouble-makers."

"No," Darcy said soberly. "They didn't."

Something about her tone…

"However, there are a lot of people here now who wield power and do care about troubled kids."

He just lifted an eyebrow.

"Congressman Nathan Hyde's putting up a lot of the money for Quiet Waters."

"Yeah? I'm going to see about doing some work for him on a house he bought."

"Well, his family foundation does good things for the community. And Nathan seems to want to help troubled kids."

"The schools any better than they used to be?"

Darcy hid a smile. "The high school got rid of Mrs. Rising and Mr. Miller years ago."

"Thank the good Lord." He thought a minute. "You grow up here?"

"Afraid so."

"You were probably in all advanced classes."

She laughed. "No, I had my share of the teachers who got the bad kids and hated them."

He didn't believe it for a minute.

She held up the papers. "I think I have all we need here. And since his physical's tomorrow, Braden can come straight to TenderTime after he sees Paige."

"Should we ease him into it? Maybe just a few hours tomorrow?"

"I was just about to suggest that."

He stood. "Good. I'll bring him by after the physical, and then pick him up before lunch."

"All right."

She stood and walked with him toward the door. He sighed before he could stop himself. "I hope this works for him. He *needs* something to finally go right."

"It will." She reached out and grasped his arm. His first impulse was to step back, but it felt good to have her small hand on him. She was so petite, so delicate. He wasn't a big guy, but he towered over her. Looking down, he noticed a fancy ring on the third finger of her left hand. He couldn't tell if it was a wedding band.

Not that it mattered. He was completely out of his league with this delicate flower who'd probably been coddled and coaxed through life, whereas his upbringing had made him as tough as those weeds in his pa's yard.

"I mean it, Hunter," she said. "I know what I'm doing here. TenderTime will be good for Braden."

"I'm real glad you think that." He straightened. "Thanks for taking him. For caring."

"You're welcome."

He left the office, feeling just a little bit better.

When he reached the 4/5 room, his sense of well-being fled right out the window.

He found his son sitting on a chair off to the side, his face ashen. The teacher, cradling a boy on her lap, looked up as Hunter entered. "Mr. Sloan, Braden had a little accident."

Hunter's heart began to gallop in his chest. "Is he all right?"

"Yes, but Tommy isn't." She nodded to the boy in her lap.

"He knocked me down," the kid said around fingers stuffed into his mouth.

"Braden says it was an accident."

Hunter dragged in a deep breath and crossed to his son.

"THANKS, MRS. O'MALLEY. I appreciate the ride." Porter Casewell, a five-month resident of Serenity House, smiled shyly at Darcy. Her chestnut-brown eyes, which matched her long hair, echoed the sentiment. "And the chance you're giving me."

Darcy returned the smile as she pulled into the drive-way of the carriage house on her mother's estate where she lived. About a thousand square feet, the small structure's quaint wood-and-stucco exterior, as well as the carefully decorated interior, was perfect for her and her daughters. "You're welcome. We all need people to believe in us, Porter."

The seventeen-year-old girl shrugged her thin shoulders. "My mom said she was surprised you'd let me near your daycare, let alone your own kids."

Her heart twisting in her chest, Darcy faced Porter across the seat of her sturdy new Taurus. "You've been clean for a year, right?"

Porter nodded.

Darcy knew, intimately, how hard it was to kick destructive habits. "And Mrs. Donovan says you're getting A's in school. Nora Whitman told me you practically run Serenity House. Seems like your mom doesn't know the person you've become."

The girl's eyes misted briefly. The twist in Darcy's heart tightened.

How can she do this to me, Nora? She's my mother.

She doesn't really know you, Darcy. She doesn't know what's behind all that rebellion.

"Sometimes, people closest to you can't see past the veneer, Porter. They're afraid."

"Lois and George Casewell aren't afraid of anything. It isn't in their genes."

A common understanding passed between the two. Darcy squeezed Porter's arm and they exited the car. Just as they reached the house, the door flew open.

Darcy gasped. "Oh, no, Meli, what did you do?"

Seven-year-old Melanie Anne O'Malley smiled out

from behind a face and shirt covered with chocolate. "We're making brownies. Claire let me mix."

Darcy stiffened. "You didn't turn on the oven while I went to pick up Porter, did you?"

"Nah-uh."

Claire, ten going on thirty, appeared behind Meli. "Mama, we'd never do that. You said a million times not to."

Yeah, well, a little rebellion might do this one good.

For once Darcy agreed with the voice inside her. Not about the stove, of course.

Meli's green eyes danced. "Dr. Kendrick said we can swim in her pool tonight."

Darcy glanced at Porter.

"I was on the swim team in my old school, Mrs. O'Malley."

"And Dr. Kendrick will be home," Claire put in, her voice hopeful. "Dr. Chandler, too, and Scalpel."

Smiling at the thought of how Paige joked she'd married both Ian and his dog in the small, private ceremony this month, Darcy glanced at her watch. "It's fine with me. I need to shower before David picks me up. Stay and say hello to him, then you can go swim."

Claire stepped back and turned away. Meli wasn't nearly as tactful. "Aw, Mama!"

"No lip, ladies. Clean up, then get your suits on. He's due in ten minutes and I want you to say hello."

Porter grasped each girl's hand. "We'll take care of the kitchen. When we're done, it'll be time to go swimming."

Ten minutes later, Darcy exited her tiny bedroom just as the doorbell rang. She could hear the three girls laughing in the kitchen. "I'll get it," she called out, fastening hammered gold earrings, checking her hastily done braid and smoothing down her navy linen dress.

She opened the door to David Carrington. Blue eyes crinkled in a face that was made more boyish by his curly brown hair. But he gave her a very adult male perusal. "This was worth waiting for."

She smiled up at him. "Why, thank you, David."

"Nice dress."

Boring, the little voice in Darcy's head said. At one time—when she was Porter's age—she wouldn't have been caught dead in this kind of outfit.

The girls drifted out from the kitchen. "Well, here are the other lovely ladies. Hello Melanie, Claire."

"Mr. Carrington." Claire stayed near the doorway until Porter came out, then sidled close to her.

Meli marched right over to David. "Hi, Mr. Carrington." She peered up at her mother. "Can we go now?"

"Mind your manners, Mel." Darcy ignored Meli's pout. She introduced Porter to David, then said to her daughters, "Go ahead. And do as Porter says. I'll be home by ten."

The three girls hurried out, closing the door behind them. "Let me get a shawl and my purse. I'll be right back."

David snagged her arm. Drawing her close, he smiled down at her. "This first." His mouth pressed to hers gently, as always. His lips were warm and firm.

"There, that's better. I've been thinking about doing that all day, Mrs. O'Malley."

"Hmm." She kissed his cheek. She'd been thinking about Braden Sloan and his mysterious father all day.

As they drove to the country club, David said, "New sitter?"

"Yes."

"Does she live up here?"

"Why?" Darcy asked.

"Because I'll give her a ride home. Save you a trip."

"How sweet. No, thanks, though. Charly Donovan's picking her up at ten."

"Charly? The woman who took over Serenity House?"

"Yes." Darcy felt his reaction more than saw it, and cursed her loose tongue. She was so comfortable with hiring girls from Serenity House she rarely thought to keep their background quiet.

"Your sitter's from that place?"

Ambushed by his critical tone, Darcy's throat closed up. "Porter's there for a few months while she works things out with her parents," she said.

"Are you sure your girls are safe with her?"

"Nora says she's very reliable and trustworthy."

"Reliable and trustworthy young women don't end up in group homes for troubled girls."

"I appreciate your concern, David, but I'm capable of determining who's good enough to watch my children."

He squeezed her knee. She moved away. "I'm sorry, I didn't mean to interfere. I care about Melanie and Claire." He shot her an ingratiating smile. "And you."

Her shoulders lost some of their starch. "I appreciate your concern. But it felt like criticism."

Touchy tonight, aren't we, Darce? Is it because Mr. Brooks Brothers doesn't know you were a bad girl?

"I'm sorry," David repeated. "Let's not ruin the evening. I've been looking forward to this time with you."

She returned his smile, albeit weakly. "Fine by me. Tell me about the world of tax law."

David groaned. "I don't want to put you to sleep."
Even he thinks he's boring.

Despite her irreverent thought, she enjoyed David's stories. Her mood had brightened considerably by the time they entered Hyde Point Country Club and bumped into Nora and Dan in the lobby.

"Darcy," Nora said, hugging her. "It's been too long."

"You look like a million bucks, Mrs. Whitman."

Nora leaned into Dan. "Marriage agrees with me."

"With us," Dan said, hugging Nora.

David greeted the Whitmans, then a club member walked by and drew him aside.

Dan said, "Did you meet with the Sloans this morning?"

"Yes. Braden's adorable."

Nora's smile beamed from ear to ear. "Only you, Darcy, would say that about Braden. Most people would call him impossible."

"Paige is giving him a physical. She'll help me determine what kind of help he needs."

"What did you think of Hunter?" Dan asked.

He's certainly not boring.

"He seems very nice. A little shy."

Dan chuckled. "The terror of Hyde Point would die if he heard you say that."

"Was he that bad when he was here?"

"He had a wild streak that nobody could control."

"Nobody but you, darling." Gazing up at her husband, Nora added, "Dan scooped him out of more doorways and off more park benches than I can count. Most times Dan gave that poor boy a place to sleep, too."

"What about his home?"

"Tipper Sloan and Hunter didn't agree on much."

Dan's face hardened. "The man's answer was to use his fists, and when Hunter got old enough, he just left the house for days at a time."

"How awful."

Nora tucked back a wayward strand of hair that had escaped from Darcy's braid. "There are all kinds of abuse, sweetie. Speaking of which, how's Porter doing?"

"She's wonderful. I love her and the girls think she walks on water."

"Hello, everybody."

Darcy turned to find Nathan Hyde and his fiancée, Barbara Benton, had entered the club. Tall, lanky and at ease in his Armani suit, Nathan embraced Dan. Dan Whitman had been a surrogate brother to Nathan all his life. She knew he'd been particularly supportive when Nathan's wife had been killed in a tragic car accident five years ago. "How's it going, Nate?" Dan asked.

"Fine." After greeting everyone, Nathan said to Dan, "I'm meeting with that carpenter you suggested tomorrow morning."

"We were just talking about Hunter. He does great work."

Barbara rolled her eyes. "For Nathan's pet project. Really, darling, I don't know what exactly you expect to do with that house."

When Nathan saw Darcy's questioning look, he said, "I bought the old Winslow place. I'm redoing the interior now."

"Much of it himself, which is something else I can't comprehend. Especially not in an election year."

"Wow!" Darcy brightened at the thought of the Victorian house on Magnolia Street. "We always said it looked like George Bailey's house in *It's a Wonderful Life.*"

"We?" Barbara asked.

"Some of the girls I was friends with as a teenager. Anabelle Crane particularly loved that place."

Nathan stilled, and Dan stiffened. David returned, breaking the oddly charged moment. "Sorry. They've asked me to run for the board of directors of the country club."

Nathan said, "Great. You can help shape things up around here."

Darcy scanned the ornate lobby of Hyde Point Country Club. An uncomfortable feeling stole over her. It was exacerbated by the little voice inside her.

You don't belong here, girl.

Determined, Darcy raised her chin. She *did* belong here. She'd spent the last two years of her life becoming someone who would fit into places like this. Stifling that nagging nuisance inside her, she took David's arm, bade her company goodbye and followed him to dinner.

NORA EXCUSED HERSELF from the post-dinner discussion with Nathan, Barbara and Dan when she noticed that Darcy—who'd left her table five minutes ago—had not returned. Nora found her former charge at the window of the ladies' room, staring out at the lighted greens. She looked lovely in her chic navy dress and tidy hair, but very unlike the girl Nora had known years ago.

"Darcy, are you all right?"

Darcy pivoted. "Nora. Hi. Of course I'm all right."

"I noticed you left the table. You've been in here a while."

"I'm fine."

God, Nora hated those words. After Darcy's mother had left her at Serenity House, that had become the girl's mantra. *I'm fine,* she'd said when Nora found her crying on the swings in the playground. *I'm fine,* she'd said when her mother never came to visit. *I'm fine,* she'd said when Marian extended Darcy's stay at Serenity House from two months, to four, to the final seven months she'd spent there.

"Come on, sit down, sweetie."

"I should get back to David."

"He's occupied. Somebody from the club came over to talk to him." They sat on the ornate divan. "Do you like going out with David, Darce?"

"Yes, of course. Why?"

"You seem unhappy lately."

"Do I?"

She grasped Darcy's hand. Fifteen years ago, after weeks of trying, Nora had finally coaxed Darcy to open up. When she'd returned to Hyde Point, they'd gotten close again. "Tell me."

A long sigh escaped. "I'm feeling hemmed in, I guess."

"By David?"

"Yeah. And by my mother." Her eyes narrowed. "By the person I've become."

"You've become a lovely young woman."

Darcy threw her an impish smile. "You're prejudiced."

"Maybe. But, you know, you didn't have to do a complete 180-degree turnaround. I liked the young girl you were, too."

"That's what Jade told me." Darcy smiled wistfully. "Remember how we used to fight?"

"Yes. I treated more than a couple of scratches."

Darcy stared down at her clipped, unpolished nails. "Who was that girl, Nora?"

"You, sweetie."

"No, not me." She looked up, her eyes liquid pools of concern. "I miss her sometimes."

"Then let her out once in a while."

"Marian the Librarian would have a fit."

"She'll survive." And too bad if she didn't. Though Marian had mellowed over the years, the woman was still more concerned with appearances than with her daughter's well-being. She deserved the moniker—Marian the Librarian—from *The Music Man.* She was every bit as prim and proper as the main character from that show.

Darcy stood. "It's not an option. If I let out the old Darcy, I'd probably turn back into bum gum."

Nora chuckled at the term Jade had applied to the young Darcy's penchant for attracting bad boys. "I don't know about that."

"I've got to get back to David."

"All right. Don't be a stranger, though, okay? Come visit Dan and me."

"Sure. I will." She kissed Nora's cheek. "You always make me feel better."

Together, the women left the ladies' room. Though Darcy had perked up, Nora felt the opposite. She was worried about the young woman who was trying to be so perfect. It wasn't good for her or for her girls.

"I DON'T *WANNA* STAY HERE." Dressed in navy shorts and a gray shirt—that Hunter had had to wrestle him into this morning—Braden's bottom lip quivered at the door to the 4/5 room at TenderTime. They had just come from the physical with Dr. Kendrick.

Kneeling, Hunter reined in his immediate impulse, which was to haul the kid to his chest and tell him nothing would ever hurt him again. "Brade," he said in the gentle tone the boy seemed to react to best. "I gotta work to support us. We talked about this."

"Why can't I stay with Grandma and Grandpa?"

Because you're such a handful. Hunter braced an arm on his knee. "You know they're old. And they're not used to having us around. We agreed you'd stay there afternoons and come here mornings."

"Grandma and Grandpa don't want me. Just like Mom."

Hunter had a flash of memory…Braden, when he'd first come to live with Hunter, diving into his bed, screaming, "She doesn't want me. Why doesn't she want me?"

Somehow Hunter got around the lump in his throat. "Are you kidding? Grandpa Bart's chompin' at the bit to take you to the creek and fish today. But we gotta watch out for them, too. Keep them from doing too much. I need you to help me in that, son."

"'Kay."

"I'll be back by noon."

Braden's expression said he'd believe that when he saw it. Hunter stood. His son just looked at him. *Aw, the hell with it.* He bent down again and tugged Braden to him, giving the boy a big bear hug. Again, as on the other occasions when Hunter chanced physical contact, Braden stiffened. But a little less than the last time. Maybe half as much. Well, it was progress. The teacher came over, smiled at Braden and invited him into the room.

Hunter waved goodbye and managed to get out the door before he broke down. Leaning against the wall, eyes closed, he chided himself. *Get a grip, Sloan. You got things to do. Braden'll be fine.*

"Hunter, are you all right?"

Damn. He opened his eyes to find Darcy O'Malley staring at him. In a pretty yellow sundress, she looked like a fresh summer daisy. When she cocked her head, he saw a yellow ribbon around the knot of hair at the back of her neck.

"I'm..." He had to clear his throat. "I'm fine."

Folding her hands over her chest, there was a glint of understanding in her green eyes. "Did he cry?"

"Nope. Near to, though."

"Did you?" At Hunter's skeptical look, she added, "Hey, parents like you cry all the time dropping kids off. I often play shrink."

His smile was weak. "I never left him with strangers."

"It hurts, the first time."

His face colored. He hadn't been this embarrassed since he'd been caught with his pants down...literally...in the girls' locker room in tenth grade. "I'm okay."

Again her slight hand went to his arm. It squeezed this time. "Sure you are, tough guy."

He pushed away from the wall. "I'm gettin' outta here before I embarrass myself."

She sobered immediately. "I think men who show their emotions are attractive, Hunter." Her face, dotted with several summer freckles, reddened immediately. And those grass-colored eyes widened.

Hunter felt a laugh bubble up from inside him. "Well, now, Miss Darcy, that's real nice to hear. It sure takes the edge off the morning." Nodding, he said goodbye and sauntered down the hall.

Don't that beat all, he thought as he exited TenderTime and turned right. The pretty lady thought he was attractive. Damn if he didn't start to whistle, too.

His good humor died when, three doors down, he found himself standing in front of Hannah's Place, the local diner. It was a cute little shop, with green striped awnings and outdoor tables set up on the sidewalk for summer dining. Peering inside, he saw that the breakfast crowd had thinned out. *What the hell,* Hunter thought. She was here. He had a few minutes. He opened the door, jangling the little bell. At the sound, the woman behind the counter pivoted; she wore a big smile on her face.

When her gaze landed on him, the smile, and the light in her eyes died. "Oh," was all she said.

"Hello, Hannah."

His sister's spine stiffened. "Hunter." She wiped her hands on her apron. She'd dressed casually for work in jeans and a blue T-shirt. "I heard you were back."

"Is that so?"

He knew she had. Pa had told her, when he'd had breakfast in her restaurant last week. Before Hunter had come to town, Hannah had visited her grandparents frequently at their home. Now—more than likely to avoid her brother—Hannah invited them to her home or to the diner. Hunter tried to quell the sarcasm that rose naturally to his lips whenever he was around Hannah—but failed, as usual. "Nice of you to come by and say hello."

Her spine went poker stiff now, and she lifted her chin. "Why pretend there's any love lost between us?"

"Why, indeed." He put his hand on the door; then he remembered his son and decided to give it one more shot for Braden. "You got a nephew in town. Your kids got a cousin."

"Yes, I heard about that, too. Is he as bad as you were, Hunter?"

His grip tightened on the handle. Hannah's face, her senior year in high school—he was only a freshman— swam before him. The cops had come and handcuffed him and were leading him out the front door. She stood by the lockers, in her red-and-white cheerleading uniform, her face ashen. She had reason, he reckoned, to hate him.

But not his son. "Braden has some problems, as you seem to know, but he's nothing like I was."

"Thank God," was all Hannah said.

He tried to short-circuit the pain. But like an electric charge, it shot through him, detonating anger, setting off feelings of inferiority. He left the diner, any comeback on his lips killed by the ache in his heart.

Outside, he could breathe better. He tried to focus on something pleasant. Darcy O'Malley's compliment. *I think men who show their feelings are attractive…* Her words about his son. *I know what I'm doing here. TenderTime will be good for Braden.* By the time he'd made his way to his truck and driven to Magnolia Street, he felt better. Deliberately, he pushed Hannah out of his mind.

The Winslow place loomed before him. Set back from the road about two hundred yards, it had a huge lawn, peaked roofs, even a turret off to the side in another wing. The structure had weathered to a pretty gray. From the freshly painted shutters and gleaming windows, it seemed the outdoor work was just about done.

On the front porch, Hunter rang the bell. Chimes pealed. He rang twice more before the door opened.

Nathan Hyde looked like a peon. His jeans were splattered with plaster, and his hair held traces of a battle with the Sheetrock. "Hunter, hi." He went to hold out his hand and laughed. "Sorry, I'm a mess."

"Hard work'll do that to you."

"Nothing wrong with that. Come on in."

The foyer was enormous. A winding staircase spun upward as far as Hunter could see. A huge parlor was off to the left, sporting a brick fireplace. "This house is great, isn't it?" Hunter said.

"Well, it's getting there. It was abandoned for years."

"I know. We used to break in here as kids." Hunter shook his head. "Probably shouldn't have told you that."

"Hey, I sowed some wild oats in my time."

Not like me, Congressman. But he kept the observation to himself. Though they were close to the same age—forty—Hyde wouldn't know about the extent of Hunter's exploits because he'd gone away to a prep school, while Hunter had attended Hyde Point High.

"The kitchen's this way. It's where I need a craftsman like you." That comment, along with Darcy's, made Hannah's words sting less.

At the end of a corridor sprawled a kitchen that was half as big as the whole downstairs of the house where Hunter had grown up. The room had been ripped apart. A new black iron stove had been installed, and he could see where a huge fridge and other appliances would be placed. The Sheetrock was almost finished, so the wiring must be in.

"This is a gem," Hunter said, scanning the interior.

"I know, it's my favorite room."

Hunter glanced out the window. "Mine'd be that turret. The walls are curved, if I remember right."

Nathan got a faraway look on his face. "I knew someone once who loved that tower." Shaking himself, he nodded to the kitchen. "I ripped out all the old cupboards and the floor here. I want you to build new ones."

"The only floors I've done are teak. On boats."

"I was thinking oak."

"Go light. It'll gleam like pure gold when the suns streaks through that bank of windows."

"What about the cabinets?"

Hunter walked around. He eyed the ceiling heights, the broadness of the openings. It felt good to be in his element, where he knew stuff. "I'd go oak there, too. Maybe a few shades darker than the floor." He thought of something else. "No, wait. I'd put in multicolored strips on the floor. Maybe even design a pattern in it. You can pick up the dominant shade in the floor with the cabinet fronts."

"Would you do a soffit at the top?"

"I wouldn't. I'd leave it open for pots and pans or even just decoration."

Nathan smiled. "You're the man for the job, Hunter. What do you say?"

Hunter sighed. It was a lot of work. "I got a son I need to be with." And he was going to volunteer his services at Quiet Waters, though Dan thought they'd be paying him.

Nathan leaned against the wall and crossed his arms. "Enjoy your kid. They grow up faster than you can imagine."

"Yeah. You got kids?"

"One. She'll be a sophomore at Cornell. Seems like yesterday she started kindergarten."

"I just brought Braden to daycare for the first time."

"Ripped your heart out, did it?"

Hunter snorted. "I can't believe it. One little boy, staring up at me with those big eyes. I was mush in fifty seconds flat."

Nathan shook his head. "I wanted to die when Kaeley went to kindergarten. She trotted into the school without batting an eyelash." He grinned. "I hate to tell you this, Hunter, but it doesn't get any easier. When I took her to college for the first time, I bawled all the way home."

Hunter smiled. Then shifted. He didn't talk like this with anybody, especially a guy. Especially the town's fair-haired boy. Their differences had not escaped him. Nathan Hyde was the kind of man Darcy O'Malley would go for. Hunter wondered if she was married to somebody like him.

"So, what do you think, Sloan? Want to take on the cupboards and the floor? I'll pay somebody else to install them. You build them and be in charge."

"Why you doin' this, Hyde? You don't know me."

"I saw your portfolio of work."

"Yeah, but still."

"And Dan Whitman's like a brother to me. He says you're good, you are."

"Dan's a great guy." Who had smoothed Hunter's way back into town a whole lot more than Hunter had realized. "Okay, I'll take the job."

"Great." Nathan smiled at him. "And bring that boy around sometime. I'd like to meet him."

"You're on." Hunter said goodbye and headed for the door.

Once outside, he leaned against the railing. Damn this town. It always did put him on a roller coaster. But this time around, he thought, looking back to Hyde's house, and thinking about TenderTime Daycare, it seemed to have a few more peaks than valleys.

CHAPTER THREE

THE HYDE POINT FALL SOCCER League began in mid-August. It was a sight to behold. Beneath a hazy-hot summer sky, a large group of children twelve and under gathered at Meadows Park on Saturday morning for the kickoff. Divided into teams by age, the kids were about to begin a pennant race to see who would come up the winner by mid-October.

Running late, Darcy herded Meli, already dressed in goalie gear, to the designated field. Claire had come along as cheerleader and carried water bottles and a blanket to sit on. "Over there, honey, near the pavilion, is where you're supposed to meet the five-to-seven team you're assigned to."

"Babies," seven-year-old Meli muttered under her breath.

Darcy hid a grin. When they reached the field, there was a crowd of parents gathered around an orange-shirted official. He held a clipboard and wore a grim expression.

"All right," the guy said. "Now, I've got some bad news for you. Moe Baker, who always coached this team, got transferred to Colorado for work. And I've been calling around for a replacement. Seems like no one's interested."

Meli dropped the ball. "What?" she said. "No coach?"

"'Fraid not, missy. I talked to some of your parents and nobody wants the job, either. This team might have to drop out of the division."

A parent asked, "Can't you split up the kids and put them onto the other teams?"

The guy shook his head. "No. You're the second to lose a coach and we just divided one group of kids. Now, we've reached the limit of players per team."

A pretty woman with silvery-blond hair and the longest legs Darcy had ever seen stepped forward. "I played in college. I could be an assistant, but I can't coach the whole thing."

"A girl coach?" a boy next to them griped.

"Great. That's a start," the official said. "Anybody out there I didn't get in touch with? Any volunteers to head up the team?"

Darcy held her breath. Meli was looking forward to this sports season so much and she needed the physical outlet.

After a moment, a deep voice said, "I can coach."

The crowd shifted, giving Darcy a clear view of Hunter Sloan.

"And you are?"

"Sloan. My boy Braden and I just moved to town last week."

"Could be why I didn't reach you." The official eyed Hunter. "You had any experience?"

"I played when I was younger. I follow professional soccer."

He played when he was young? At the high school?

"Got any experience with kids?"

"Some. And I know the drills for practice. What I'm not up to snuff on, I can read about. Talk to the other coaches about."

"Hell, if he knows the rules and wants to do it, let him coach," a parent said.

"Don't need no Pelé," somebody else commented.

"Fine." The official conceded easily. "Come on, I'll take your information."

After a short talk, Hunter accepted the red COACH baseball cap and settled it on his head. His dark hair peeked out at his temples and curled at his neck. The bright color highlighted his cheeks. "Need somebody to mind our dog, though," he said, nodding to the mutt that Braden held by a leash.

When nobody volunteered, Meli prodded Darcy's arm. "Mama."

"I'll look after him," she said.

Doing a double take, Hunter waited a minute, then jogged over. "Hey." In the morning sun, his dark eyes twinkled like nighttime stars. "Got myself into something, I reckon."

"It was nice of you to volunteer." Suddenly, Darcy wished she'd worn an outfit other than the brief cutoffs she'd hastily donned with the ragged James Taylor T-shirt. But she'd gotten up late and grabbed the first things in her drawer.

Hunter held out the leash. "Sure you want to do this?"

"Uh-huh. He doesn't bite, does he?"

"He doesn't do anything."

"Not true." Braden grasped the leash. She noticed that the dog sat away from the boy. When Braden went to pet him, the animal crouched in closer to Hunter. Only then did he allow Braden's touch.

"Go play, guys. Claire and I will watch your dog."

"I haven't met your daughters."

"I'm Meli, Coach." Darcy's youngest stretched out

her hand. Hunter shook it and gave her an amused smile.

"This is Claire," Darcy said, nodding at her older daughter who stared up at Hunter with owl eyes.

He knelt down on one knee, despite the fact that it was obvious the other parents were getting restless. "Hello, Miss Claire."

She smiled at the form of address.

"Think you can watch my dawg, here?" Hunter said with added southern flavor.

"What's his name?"

"Tramp," Braden told her.

What else? Darcy thought and took the dog's leash. As Hunter headed to the center of the field, she studied the mutt. He looked just like the dog in Disney's *Lady and the Tramp*. It had always been one of Darcy's favorite movies.

She glanced up when she heard, "Okay, ladies and gentlemen, gather round." Hunter stood with his hands on his jeaned hips. From under his black T-shirt, muscles bulged.

A woman behind Darcy quipped, "Hmm, looks like soccer practice just got a lot more interesting."

The woman's friend laughed.

"Go get 'em, Meli," Darcy yelled and dropped down on the blanket Claire had spread out. Tramp sat as far away from them as possible, watching Hunter and Braden.

Braden didn't take his eyes off his father, except when he turned to check on Darcy and the dog. Once, when she met his gaze, he gave her a reluctant smile. She'd made a point of visiting the 4/5 room yesterday morning. Though he'd seemed wary of her, she'd managed to find some common ground with him when she took him onto the computer to learn about dogs.

Drills began. Hunter obviously knew his stuff. And his quiet manner commanded respect. The other parents seemed impressed, as did Julie Jacobs, the soccer mom who'd volunteered to help coach. She kept going up to Hunter, touching his arm, making contact. Darcy scowled as she watched the byplay.

"What's the matter, Mom?"

"Nothing, honey."

"You looked mad."

"Did I?" She glanced around. "Didn't you bring your books?"

"I'm all done with them."

"Already? We just went to the library Wednesday night."

Claire shrugged.

"You'll be bored."

"I like watching Meli play." She eyed the dog. "He isn't happy."

"Who, honey?"

"Tramp."

"Hunter says he doesn't bite. You could try to pet him."

"He doesn't want to be petted."

"How do you know?"

"I can tell."

After a half hour, Claire got restless. She didn't complain—she *never* complained—but she flopped on her back, stared up at the sky and sighed. Darcy noticed Hunter glancing in their direction several times. He must be worried about the dog, from whom there hadn't been a peep.

"Can I do your hair?" Claire asked.

Darcy sighed. She should get it cut, she thought, touching the knot she'd hastily tied it in. But there was some reason she didn't.

It's the last thing left of the old Darcy.

Ignoring the thought, she let Claire go to work.

At eleven, Hunter ended practice. He called his team into a huddle and talked to them briefly. "Good work, kids. I can tell you all like the sport and I hope you were having fun. That's the most important thing."

"Winning is."

He looked into the impish face of Meli O'Malley. "Well, Miss Meli, I don't agree with that. Having fun is."

"I think so, too." Braden stood up tall next to Hunter. If he didn't know better, he'd think his son was proud of him.

"Next practice is Monday night at six. See you then."

The leggy blond assistant approached him. "We need your phone number, Coach, for the parent sheets. In case somebody's sick, or going to miss a game."

He took the clipboard, scribbled his information and nodded absently. Then he, Meli and Braden headed for Darcy, who was sprawled on the blanket in a pair of drive-me-crazy shorts. When he neared her, though, his mouth gaped at something other than the enticing view of her legs. "Damn, where did all that hair come from?"

The girls' eyes widened at the curse. "Oops, sorry, ladies. But Miss Darcy, where you been hidin' all those curly locks?" All those luscious, touch-me curly locks that flamed a thousand different colors in bright rays of the morning sun.

"She puts it in a bun to be…" Meli's face scrunched up. "What's the word you used, Mama?"

"Demure," Claire filled in.

"Yeah." Meli rolled her eyes, flipped back her messy braid. "Just like Claire."

Claire flushed. Hunter said immediately, "The knot looks nice, but this…" He caught himself. What the hell was he doing? "It's, um, downright nice too."

Darcy smiled self-consciously. As she stood, her hair fell forward over her shoulders to cover her breasts. Geez, it was nearly waist length. "You did a great job, Coach."

Out of the corner of his eye, Hunter saw Braden smile.

"Thanks." Taking advantage, he reached out and ruffled his son's hair. "Champ here's been holding out on me. He's done gone and got to be an expert ball handler." He smiled at Meli. "You, too, little lady."

Meli grinned.

Hunter looked over to see Claire studying the dog. "You don't play soccer, Miss Claire?"

She shook her head but didn't meet his gaze.

Meli moved in close to her sister. "She could. She's got long legs and she's fast. She just doesn't want to."

"Shouldn't play ball if you're not gonna have fun."

When Meli wrinkled her nose, Hunter couldn't resist tweaking it. She scowled.

He laughed.

The dog barked.

Then all three kids giggled, too.

When he glanced over, Darcy's green eyes were alight with amusement. She looked young. And healthy. And desirable.

Hell, Hunter thought, turning away. He had to get out of this town.

DARCY MET UP with Hunter at the Elsa Moore Center at nine o'clock Monday morning. They'd arranged to meet Paige here to discuss Braden. As they were shown into the office Paige shared with her husband, Ian, Hunter turned to Darcy. "Why are we meeting here? Is it because of the money?" The center was for young mothers who couldn't afford medical care for themselves or their children. "I can pay for Braden."

She was surprised by the vehemence of his tone. "No, it has nothing to do with your ability to pay. Paige has a private practice but only works there part-time. She spends most of her time at the center, so it was just easier to meet here."

Hunter's shoulders visibly relaxed under his denim work shirt. He crossed to the window and stared out, giving her a great view of the back of his tight jeans.

Yum-my.

Ignoring her wayward thought and Hunter's backside, Darcy said, "You made a pretty good coach Saturday morning."

"I bought some books." He slid the cord of the blinds through his fingers. "I been readin' up all weekend so I don't embarrass myself or the kids."

"The kids are grateful for your help." She smiled. "So are their parents."

"Three moms called me this weekend."

Darcy wasn't surprised. She'd heard the women discussing him. *Hmm, looks like soccer practice just got a lot more interesting.* "Everybody wants their kids to be able to play. Meli would be heartbroken if the team was disbanded."

"Meli's a talented little player." He smiled at her. "Does she get it from her mother?"

"Me? I'm athletically challenged. I don't know a softball from a baseball."

He hesitated, then said, "How about her dad? Is he good at sports?"

He's good at chasing skirts and tipping beer bottles. "No, I don't know where she gets it."

"Is he too busy to coach her team?"

"No, he—"

"Hi, Darce. Sorry I'm late."

Darcy turned to find Paige entering the office, pushing a double stroller with two sound-asleep babies in it. A striking woman with soft-brown hair and sharp blue eyes, Paige looked down at the children, her expression wondrous. Darcy remembered what it was like to be in awe of her own newborns.

"I'm sorry about this," Paige said, "but Ian was supposed to be home to watch them this morning and he got held up at the hospital."

Darcy crossed to the babies and bent down. Little eyelashes fluttered over their cheeks, and the boy, Sammy, sucked his fingers. "Oh, Paige, they're beautiful."

"I know. I can't believe..." Her eyes got misty. "Don't mind me. Both Ian and I are running on no sleep."

Darcy said, "I remember what it was like."

Paige glanced up and noticed Hunter. "Hi," she said. "You must be Braden's dad." She wheeled the babies off to the side, parked the stroller and crossed to Hunter. "I'm Paige Kendrick."

He shook her hand. "Hunter Sloan. Looks like congratulations are in order."

"A wedding and babies in the space of two weeks," Darcy commented.

Hunter tried to stifle his surprise. As she sat at her desk, Paige smiled over at him. "We're adopting them, but we've got custody for foster care for now. I'm in love, big time."

With the kids and with a hunk of a husband who would walk on hot coals for her. Darcy wondered what it would feel like to have a man care about her like that. Johnny O'Malley and the rest of the bums she'd taken up with had never felt so deeply for her.

"We should get right to this," Paige said, holding up a folder. "No telling how long double trouble over there will sleep."

Hunter took a seat next to Darcy. Paige addressed him directly. "I've spent a little time with Braden. I think your son exhibits several characteristics of attention deficit/hyperactivity disorder. Do you know what that is?"

"No. I don't have much experience with kids."

"It's a syndrome where, simply put, kids, and adults, too, have trouble attending to a task. They're fidgety, and can't sit still. They can't focus enough to do what they're supposed to do. In school, they provide distractions for other kids because of their impulsivity."

He scowled and took a deep breath. "I hate labels. You sure about this?"

"No, it's just a possible diagnosis." Paige darted a brief glance to Darcy. "I hate labels, too. We're all hurt by them."

"All right. Suppose he has this thing. What is it exactly?"

"The condition, ironically, was first diagnosed by a man named Dr. George Still, in 1902. Until recently, we called it ADD—Attention Deficit Disorder. These days we distinguish between ADD and ADHD. In the latter, the *h* stands for hyperactivity. It's a delay in the maturing process of the brain. The part that controls attention. As a child grows, the brain centers for attention function on a lower, less mature level.''

''Does it ever mature?''

''Sometimes symptoms of ADHD diminish with time. More often, a person just learns to compensate.''

''How do you get it?''

''It's something kids are born with.''

''You mean I gave it to him?''

''No, no, it's genetically passed on. Sometimes a parent has it. Oftentimes not. It's just in the child's genes. At least that's the thinking now.''

''What can you do about it?''

''That's a good question. But we're getting ahead of ourselves here. First, we need to do some screening to determine if Braden really has ADHD.''

''Isn't there a medical test?''

''No. The process starts with a case history, medical exam and a description of the child and his behavior. We'll need an evaluation by your son's regular pediatrician, his mother and his school or daycare worker. Some of those people will be asked to fill out a rating scale to identify behaviors.'' She cocked her head. ''You just moved here, didn't you?''

''Yes, temporarily.''

''Well, we'll need his records from…where were you?''

''I live in Florida, so does his mother.''

She looked puzzled. Hunter glanced at Darcy. She nodded her support, and Hunter explained his situation.

Hearing it again, so starkly put, Darcy's heart broke for Braden, and for Hunter, too.

If he was mine, I'd find a way to keep him with me.

Johnny O'Malley certainly hadn't felt the same about his girls.

But Darcy did. She and Hunter had something in common.

Hmm. Bad boy. Bad girl. Yep, Darce, you do.

When Hunter finished, Paige said simply, "Well, that's quite a story. How about if you get me the addresses of your ex-wife, Braden's preschool and his doctor down there. I'll send them official forms to fill out. After I receive the information from them and from you, I'll probably speak to them in a phone conference. At that point we can determine what course of action to take."

Hunter's face was blank but a muscle leaped in his jaw.

Paige finished, "That's about all we can do at this point. Unless you have more questions."

"No, not right now."

A nurse appeared at the door. "Paige, Ian's not here and there's a state inspector in the front office wanting to talk to the operators of the center."

"About what?"

"He won't tell us lowly nurses."

Paige glanced at the sleeping babies. "I—"

Darcy said, "Go ahead, I'll watch them."

"Are you sure? There's nothing like both of them crying at once and having only one pair of hands available." She rolled her eyes. "They have the lungs of opera singers."

"I run a daycare, Paige."

"Oh, right."

Paige stood, said goodbye and scooted out of the office.

"I don't know how she does it," Darcy said. "I—"

A banshee's wail went up from the stroller. Hunter startled. Darcy said, "Oh dear," when the other baby also began to cry. Maternal instinct kicked in. Darcy flew to the carriage and picked up the nearest twin. "There you go, little one. Shh."

The baby cried even louder. "He won't stop while the other one's crying." She glanced at Hunter. "Would you mind?"

Hunter stood, a look of pure male horror on his face. "Darcy, I don't have a clue what to do with a baby."

Wail, wail.

"I think picking her up would be enough."

"I, um…"

"Come on, Hunter. Live a little. I'd guess Braden on his best day is a tougher challenge than one-month-old Suzy."

"*One* month? Oh, God."

Louder wails.

"Hunter…"

"What the hell." He crossed to the carriage, bent over and scooped up the baby. Awkwardly he held Suzy in front of him, then his panicked gaze darted to Darcy.

"Just cradle her up against your chest and support her head. Like this." She indicated how she was holding Sammy.

With a grim scowl, he brought the baby close to him. Suzy nestled into his shoulder and quieted. In moments, Sammy stopped crying, too. Hunter's eyes rounded in surprise. Then his shoulders relaxed and he adjusted the baby more naturally. Without being told, he began to rub her back.

"You never got a chance to do this with Braden, did you?" Darcy asked.

"Nope. I wasn't welcome." He seemed to breathe in the baby. "She smells great."

"She likes you."

"Glad somebody does."

"Braden adores you, Hunter." Darcy swayed back and forth while she talked.

"Braden acts like he hates my guts most of the time."

"You're the nearest target. He can't take his anger and frustration out on his mother, so he's doing it to you."

"You think?" When Suzy squirmed, he began to walk her. "Shelly called last night. Braden wouldn't talk to her."

"Do you blame him?"

"No, I know about a mother's abandonment."

"Me, too." Damn, Darcy hadn't felt that swell of anger toward Marian in years.

"What do you mean?"

"Oh, just stuff from the daycare." As Hunter walked back and forth, Darcy took a seat in the chair. She cuddled Sammy, surreptitiously watching the somber man soothe the tiny baby. His face was creased with concentration, and he looked as if he were off in some unpleasant place.

She wondered what demons he harbored.

THE FIELD WAS EMPTY when Hunter, Braden and Tramp arrived Monday night for practice. "Wanna kick the ball around with me, Champ?" Hunter asked his son.

Though his eyes flared briefly with pleasure at the nickname, Braden shook his head. He was pouting because Hunter had made him eat vegetables tonight.

When Braden pushed the green beans—which the kid *liked,* for God's sake—off his plate, Hunter sent him to his room until practice. Hunter guessed the boy was still smarting about his mother's phone call, but Hunter couldn't let the bad behavior go. He wondered if Darcy would have any advice about how he should be handling this stuff.

Taking the field by himself, Hunter ran the length of it and dribbled the ball, but his mind was on Tender-Time's pretty proprietor. She'd been real easy on the eyes this morning, looking so natural holding that baby, almost Madonna-like, except for the flaming-red hair which, when she wore it down, belonged in a bordello not a church. He wondered again if she was married. He still didn't know whether or not the ruby-encrusted band she wore was a fancy wedding ring. What was her husband like? As the warm summer wind blew around him, he dribbled faster. Why the hell was he thinking about her anyway? Ruthlessly, he reminded himself of where he'd learned to play soccer, to dribble the ball at breakneck speed, take risky shots, dive into the goal. It was at Industry School for Boys, a juvenile detention center near Rochester. That memory brought home the fact that Darcy was way out of his league. Which was a good thing because Hunter wasn't about to form any attachments in Hyde Point. It was bad enough he was loving every minute of being with his grandparents. And he was beginning to wonder how he'd ever let Braden go in a few months. There was no need to complicate things any further.

His gaze caught on something red off to the side. Claire O'Malley. Her hair was down tonight, spilling around her shoulders and onto her back. Meli, coming up behind her, had her locks in two pigtails, the kind little boys just loved to tug on. Where was Mom? And what would *her* hair look like tonight? She'd worn it scraped back this morning, along with a prim suit that made her look all trussed up like some antebellum maiden.

Darcy came into view. She wore those half slacks, half shorts things; they stopped about midcalf and were white. With the pants, she sported a peach-colored top that was…demure. He was disappointed to see her hair pulled back, but then a rope-thick braid fell over her shoulder as she came toward him. Threaded through it was a peach ribbon. She stood on the edge of the field watching him as he kicked and ran, kicked and ran. He wondered why she was here early, so he jogged over to find out.

She grinned when he came up close. Her eyes glowed with feminine approval. "You look good out there."

Her freckles were more pronounced tonight, as if she'd gotten some sun today. Her green eyes sparkled like emeralds. "I'm trying to increase my stamina." He gave her an easy smile. "You're early."

"I wanted Meli to run around a bit before practice." She glanced over to where Braden and Meli and Claire stood with Tramp, who was tied to a post.

"Is not!" Braden said loudly.

"Is too!" This from Meli.

"Uh-oh. Meli's in a rotten mood. I made her clean her room before we came."

Hunter rolled his eyes. "I'm in the doghouse, too. I made Braden eat his veggies."

"How dare you!"

Smiling weakly, Hunter watched his son. "Everything's a struggle with him."

"Everything's a struggle with all kids."

"Miss Claire doesn't look like she's ever given anybody a speck of trouble."

"She used to. Before…" Darcy trailed off.

"Before what?"

A blush crept up out of the scoop of her peach-colored top. "Nothing."

He could tell that wasn't true from the shadows in her eyes. *Let it go,* he warned himself. "Hey, you know all my deep dark secrets. Not that you'd have any," he hastened to add.

Her eyes lost a bit of their sparkle. "I have plenty. This one is about Claire's father."

"He doesn't take an interest in their activities?"

"He's not around, Hunter. We've been divorced for five years." She swallowed hard. "They never see him."

"I'm sorry. It must hurt them."

"Meli copes better with it. She'll scream and cry and get mad. There's never a complaint out of Claire."

Hunter found himself reaching out to squeeze Darcy's arm. It was a big mistake. Her skin, lightly freckled there, too, was petal soft. He stepped back as if he'd been burned.

Darcy coughed. "I'll, um, watch Tramp again."

"Oh, thanks." Hunter glanced around him. When had all the other parents begun arriving? Damn it to hell, he hadn't even heard them.

Darcy headed over to the kids, talked to Claire and set out the blanket near where Tramp was tied. Yanking his gaze away, Hunter hightailed it back out to the field.

During practice, he kept glancing their way. At one point, Darcy handed Claire a bag and the girl drew out a ball and two other things he couldn't identify. Claire placed them in front of Tramp. The dog looked down but didn't take the bait. For the next half hour, he caught glimpses of the little girl's attempts to attract Tramp to the toys. She rolled the ball back and forth. She picked up another thing and waved it in front of him. Near the end of the practice, Tramp lay down on all fours and finally nosed one of the toys. Then he grabbed it with his teeth and began to chew.

Hunter saw Claire tug on Darcy's arm excitedly. Darcy gave them both a huge smile that turned Hunter's insides to mush and his lower body into anything but.

Picking up his clipboard, he started to make notes. Hell, he hated to write without a computer. He'd always had trouble with handwriting; in school it had been one of his shortcomings. He needed a secretary. Hearing a squeal from the sidelines, he looked up to see Claire petting Tramp, and the dog allowing it.

Hmm. Maybe he could do something for the shy little girl, return the favor Darcy was doing for Braden.

When they were done practicing for the night, Hunter jogged over to Darcy and Claire. "Hey, thanks for bringing toys to Tramp."

"Our pleasure. Claire likes him."

"Guess Miss Claire wouldn't be interested in helpin' me out, then."

Instantly Claire's head snapped up. Just as quickly she sidled close to her mom.

"What would you want her to do?" Darcy asked, sneaking an arm around her daughter.

"Well, I need help recording stuff. Team lineup. Stats on who scores, who assists. But it's gotta be somebody good at arithmetic."

"Claire's great in math," Darcy said. "She helps Meli out all the time."

"Don't suppose you'd consider forsaking Tramp here to help me?"

Claire's eyes were wide circles in her face.

"I'm desperate, Miss Claire."

The girl watched him from behind her mother. Then

she took a tentative step to the side. Finally she raised her chin. "Do...do you really need help?"

"Cross my heart and hope to die."

She giggled.

"I need an expert statistician. You maybe wanna try out the job? If you don't like it you can quit."

Youthful enthusiasm finally won out. "Oh, I'd like it. A lot. It'd be almost like playing." Her eyes glittered. "Would I get to wear a shirt and hat?"

"Yes, ma'am. We got a deal?" He stuck out his hand.

Claire stared at him for a long time, then gingerly shook his hand. "I'm gonna go tell Meli and Braden."

When Claire scampered away, Darcy turned to Hunter. On her face was a mixture of shock and gratitude. Her voice was shaky when she said, "Thank you so much for doing that. She's always on the outside looking in. This will make her feel included."

"Well, I know what *that's* like." Hunter glanced Claire's way. "She's such a sweet little thing. I'm glad she decided to do it."

"How can I thank you for this?"

He had a few X-rated ideas, starting with a huge bed, a dark room and perfumed sheets.

Hunter drew in a breath, mumbled, "No thanks necessary," and turned away. He was afraid he'd say or do something really stupid. Even though she wasn't married, this woman was off limits.

CHAPTER FOUR

DARCY LAZED BACK in the old claw-footed bathtub and stared up at the beams overhead. The bathroom, like everything else in the carriage house, was small and compact, but at least the high ceilings gave her breathing room. From every shelf and surface, vanilla-scented candles flickered in the dimness. Sighing deeply, she closed her eyes, grateful for the peace and quiet. It was Friday night and both girls, miraculously, had sleepovers with friends. It happened so rarely that Darcy had an evening to herself, she didn't quite know what to do with the time.

Lifting her leg out of the water, she feathered the soap down her skin, chiding herself for the expensive bubble bath she'd purchased in a weak moment. She could have bought the girls an extra pair of sneakers with the money.

Tie yourself to the post. Flay your skin for spending money on yourself. You're pathetic.

She didn't know why the old Darcy was sneaking out so much lately. For the past three years, she'd effectively banished the imp who'd spent money on makeup and clothes and frills without blinking an eye. But lately...

Her gaze rested on the scar on her leg. Another remnant of the girl she used to be. She shook her head.

Fingering the six-inch thin white line, she could still see her boyfriend, Jackie Junior, flirting with a girl at a bar outside of town. Darcy had followed him out the door, where she suspected he was going to meet up with the chick...

"What the hell do you think you're doing?" she'd asked Jackie in the semidark alley that smelled like raw sewage.

"Just gettin' myself a little air."

Then the girl came around the corner.

"Yeah, sure," Darcy said disgustedly.

"Gonna fight for me, doll?" he'd asked, lighting up a cigarette and leaning insolently against the wall.

Darcy had faced him, taken a drag on his smoke, and was just about to tell him to do something anatomically impossible, when she'd been jumped from behind.

Glass broke, and a slicing pain pierced her leg. Three girls were on her. The next thing she remembered was being rushed to the hospital for stitches on her leg, a sprained wrist and a beauty of a shiner.

She'd been sixteen...

Shuddering now, she climbed out of the tub and reached for a towel. "See, Darcy Anne, you're so much better off now. No men to complicate things. No danger lurking around corners."

No excitement.

Well, that was true, but it was worth the trade-off, wasn't it?

Wrapping herself in a big towel, she left the bathroom and crossed to her bedroom and stood in front of the closet. What to put on? She was sick of the suits, tailored slacks and shirts that hung like uniforms in neat straight rows. Briefly she wondered how her taste in clothes had changed so much. Once in a while, the girls—Claire particularly—mentioned how she used to dress, but Darcy rarely thought about it now.

She'd created another image for herself, one that fit the conservative businesswoman and proper daughter she'd become. An image that, tonight, she'd just as soon shed. Digging through her clothes, she found some items buried in the back of the closet. Jeans. Mahogany-colored leather pants and vest. A jumpsuit swirled with varying shades of green that Darcy had been unable to part with.

What the hell? Nobody was here. She wasn't going anywhere. "I wonder if it still fits?" she asked aloud.

It did, though it was tight on top, a visible result of having babies. Slipping into sandals, she tugged the knot out of her hair and let it ripple down her back.

Damn, where did all that hair come from? Hunter Sloan had asked.

Trying not to think about his comment, or the man himself, she brushed her hair till it shone, then dabbed on some coral lipstick. She almost looked like the old Darcy.

"Which you'll never be again." Nor did she want to be. But she'd enjoy the clothes and the freedom of having her hair down for tonight. She'd almost reached the kitchen to fix something for supper when the phone rang.

Grabbing it off the wall, she crooked the receiver on her shoulder. "Hello."

"Darcy? It's Mother."

She opened the fridge. "Hi, Mom. How's the cruise?"

"Bumpy. Jeremy's been seasick."

"Oh, I'm sorry to hear that."

After some chitchat, Darcy waited for her mother to come to the reason for the call. "I wanted to ask you about some expenditures at TenderTime," Marian finally said.

"Expenditures? How would you know about any money matters from the business?"

"David's been faxing financial reports to the ship."

"Excuse me?"

"David Carrington. Our attorney. Jeremy asked for the statements to be sent to the ship."

"Why?"

Her mother hesitated. "We wanted to stay in touch with the daycare while we were gone."

"For a month? Did you think I'd bankrupt the place in a *month?*"

"Really, Darcy, no need to take that tone with me."

Staring into the open refrigerator, Darcy struggled to quell the anger rising inside her. What did she have to do to get her mother to trust her? She'd changed her whole lifestyle when she'd moved back to Hyde Point. She'd become an upstanding citizen. She worked like a slave to make TenderTime an innovative, competitive daycare.

She'd become respectable.

Yet her mother was checking the finances of TenderTime from thousands of miles away.

"Darcy, dear, I can tell you're upset."

Reining in her emotion, Darcy said, "I didn't realize you'd be checking up on me like this. That you didn't trust me."

"We do trust you." A long pause. "But money is always a concern at facilities like ours."

Well, that was true. *Grin and bear it,* her adult self warned. "What did you want to discuss about the figures, Mother?"

"Mostly these expenditures for the new aides. You have two people on the payroll for this program you're dabbling in with Paige Chandler."

Kendrick. It was Paige Kendrick. Paige had kept her own name, but Marian wouldn't understand that. "Yes, Mother, I told you about that."

"It's a great deal of money."

"The aides are certified teachers."

"Do we need certified teachers for the problem children?"

"Obviously I think so."

"Hmm. Jeremy's concerned."

"About the money, or accepting troubled kids?"

"Well, both."

"I see." Her tone was glacial, she couldn't help it. This program was important to her. She thought of Braden Sloan and how she was going to help him.

Marian might be prissy, but she was swift on the uptake. "Look, dear, we'll discuss all this when I get back. I just wanted some clarification. And to touch base with you."

"Well, if David sends you any more disturbing faxes, feel free to call and question my judgment."

An even longer pause. "Really, Darcy Anne, you don't have to get snippy."

No, she didn't. It wouldn't help, anyway.

The doorbell rang. Thank God. "Someone's at the door. I've got to go."

A beleaguered sigh. One Darcy had heard when Marian had found pot in her room, each time Marian had

had to pick her up at the police station, when Marian had talked to the PINS—Pupils in Need of Supervision—people. Darcy didn't miss the irony of hearing that sigh again, after so long, simply because she wanted to help troubled kids like the one she'd been. "I'll phone again, dear. When you're in a better mood."

"Goodbye, Mother."

Darcy hung up and swore viciously at the phone. The bell rang again, and, gathering her calm, she crossed the room and swung open the door.

"Oh, sorry," she heard from the small porch. "I thought Darcy O'Malley lived here."

Darcy smiled at her friend Jade, who'd come to town for Nora Nolan's wedding and decided to stay. "Yeah, well, the new and improved Darcy's disappeared for tonight. Mommy and kiddies aren't around."

Jade's pretty eyebrows arched. "Hey, Red, that's good to hear. I told you I missed the old Darce."

When Jade and Darcy had been at Serenity House they'd fought miserably. Jade, like Darcy, had thought her stay was only temporary, but her parents had died in an accident, and Jade and her sister had remained at Serenity House until Paige had turned eighteen.

Reaching out red-tipped fingers, Jade flicked Darcy's hair. "This looks great. It's even longer." She smiled. "I hate you for it."

Darcy eyed Jade's mass of blond curls, heart-shaped face and green eyes, a darker green than Darcy's, the color of evergreen trees. "Yeah, you're such a plain Jane."

"Well," Jade said, throwing back those curls, "this plain Jane wondered if you wanted to go get something to eat with her."

"Where's Jewel?" Jade had a three-year-old daughter.

"With Paige and the twins. Man, I don't know how my sister does so much. She wanted her niece to stay over tonight."

"Come on in."

Jade entered the carriage house. She'd been here before but Darcy saw her scan the main room. "Ever read *A Doll's House* by Ibsen?"

Darcy rolled her eyes. "Yeah, sure, in my spare time."

"No, we read it in high school, in Mrs. Stanwyck's class."

"I used to bring in *Cosmopolitan* and sneak that out during reading time."

Jade laughed. "This story was about a woman in the 1800s whose husband treated her like a plaything. He kept her in clothes and a house and gave her three kids, but she was really just a toy to him."

Darcy glanced at the phone. "Okay, I get the parallel." She swore again. "This is my mother's doll's house and I'm her doll." She blew out a breath. "Does that make Meli and Claire grand-dolls?"

Sitting on the edge of the sofa, Jade dropped the taunting veneer. "What's the problem, Darce?"

She tossed back her head. "Marian the Librarian called." She filled Jade in on the rest of the conversation.

"You could leave TenderTime. Get another job. Everybody *respects* you now. You'd have no problem finding other work."

"Yeah, well, tonight that respect is cold comfort."

She scanned Jade's tight white capri pants and cropped emerald top. "Where do you want to go? I'm game."

"How about we stop at Hannah's Place to eat then head on over to Rascal's."

"Rascal's? The bar on Main Street?"

"They got a great band after nine. They play cool music. We could dance our little tootsies off."

"My mother would die if she heard I was dancing at a bar on a Friday night again."

Jade stared at her.

Darcy stared back.

Then they burst out laughing. Jade held up her hand and Darcy gave her a high five.

Darcy said, "You're on, kid. Let me get my purse."

"STOP JUMPING on the bed, Braden. Right now." Though he tried to keep his voice low, Hunter could feel the steam coming out of his ears. He'd been chasing the kid all over the house since after dinner; the worst part was that Braden's antics had upset his grandparents, who couldn't calm him down and felt bad.

Jump. Jump. "Don't *wanna* stop."

"I'm gonna tell you one more time. Stop jumping."

From under a heavy swatch of hair, dark eyes threw him a what're-ya-gonna-do-about-it look. It was the last straw. Hunter dived onto the bed and caught Braden in the knees. The boy toppled to the mattress and gasped for breath. Well, knocking the wind out of him had shut him up, anyway. But put fear into his eyes. The expression was one Hunter had seen in the mirror in his own youth. A gut-sick feeling cramped his stomach as he remembered his father's fists.

He gentled his grip on Braden, but still held the boy down. "I'd never hurt you, son, I promise."

Braden's look was so solemn, so doubting, that an insidious fear rose inside Hunter. "Has anybody ever hit you, Braden?"

Still nothing. But Braden's little fingers crept to his mouth.

Oh, please, God, no, don't let the same thing have happened to my boy.

Despite the fact Braden didn't like to be hugged, Hunter stretched out on the bed and dragged the kid to his chest. He wrapped his son up as tightly as Braden would allow. "My daddy used to hit me when I was little, Brade. It was awful. I'd never do that to you. I'll kill anybody who does. Who did."

Braden stiffened. "M-m-mom spanked me."

"I don't mean that, Champ. I mean beat on you."

Once again, nothing. Hunter tried to remember what Shelly's husband looked like. If he recalled right, Hank Michaels was the size of a lumberjack. "Did Hank ever hurt you?"

Braden's shake of the head was quick. Too quick. Hunter drew back. "Brade, you can tell me anything. I promise, I'll never let anything or anybody hurt you again."

Braden's eyes shone with a pain too old and too deep for a child of his age. Still with his fingers in his mouth, Braden said, "Don't want you to go."

"I'm not going away, son. Is that what this is all about? That you're afraid I'll leave you?" Like your mother.

The kid's eyes got even bleaker. "T'night."

"You don't want me to leave you *tonight?*"

Braden nodded. Hunter pulled him close again. "I got a job a couple of nights a week to bartend, son. We need the money to live."

Braden was quiet. Then he said, "I won't eat much. Don't need no new toys."

His son's words tore him up. How did he tell Braden he couldn't afford the fees at TenderTime unless he did something more lucrative than building a few kitchen cabinets?

"Listen to me. I'm going to work tonight and Wednesday night. I'll leave when you're asleep and be back by the time you wake up. That's a promise, Brade."

Just for a second the kid burrowed into him and whimpered a bit. Hunter's heart swelled in his chest at the voluntary gesture. "Hush now. Grandma Ada and Grandpa Bart will be right here. I know you like them. And they love you."

Reluctantly, Braden nodded.

Checking his watch, Hunter said, "How about if I stay right here until you fall asleep."

"'Kay."

Hunter snapped off a lamp, leaving the night-light to cast a dim shadow around the room. Smoothing down Braden's light pj top, Hunter prayed the boy fell asleep soon. He only had a half hour to get to his job.

BECAUSE BRADEN HAD TAKEN a long time to zonk out, Hunter found himself speeding toward town on the motorcycle he'd brought up from Florida in the back of his truck. A few minutes on the road and he saw red lights flashing behind him. Shit! Pulling over to the shoulder, he was hit by a sense of déjà vu so strong, it almost leveled him. The cops of Hyde Point were after Hunter Sloan again. "Come on," he yelled, throwing his arms up in the air at a deity he really didn't believe in. "Gimme a break."

He was still fuming when he slid behind the bar twenty minutes late for his first night on the job at Rascal's. It stung to hear the owner, Manny "The Rascal" Lando, quip, "Don't look good to be late the first night, Sloan."

Hunter tried to ignore the two strikes against him tonight in this goddamn town as he began to serve drinks. Instead, he recalled how he'd been a reliable employee in the Keys, how he'd been a good bartender and a successful carpenter who had more work than he could handle. It was Hyde Point that stripped him of his confidence as easily as turpentine taking off paint.

Behind the bar, he scanned the area. The room was a good size, with a long mahogany bar, several tables and chairs to the right, and a huge dance floor with a band set up to start at nine. The place was dim and crowded with the over-thirty population.

"You new in town, handsome?" a brunette at the end of the bar asked when he served her a manhattan. She winked saucily at him.

He smiled, knowing the bartender drill. "Not nearly new enough, doll baby." He smiled. "Y'all from here?" He indicated her group of friends.

"Oh, a southern accent." She cooed. "How sexy."

He was making small talk with the women, when he glanced down the other end and saw a blonde signal for his attention. He went to wait on her. Her forest-green eyes reflected amusement. "Hi, Hunter."

"Now, I know I don't know you, sweetheart. I'd remember if we'd met before."

"But we did meet, briefly, at Nora and Dan's wedding. I'm Jade Anderson, Paige Kendrick's sister."

"Oh, hey." He smiled genuinely now. "Paige has been helping my son."

"She's a good doctor."

He cocked his head. "What can I get you?"

"I'll have a chardonnay. My friend's in the ladies' room, but she's going to live a little and have beer." Jade said the last with amusement. He didn't get the private joke, but fixed their order.

"On me," he said easily. "For Dr. Kendrick's sister and her..." His voice trailed off as Jade's "friend" approached the bar and took a stool.

Hunter Sloan wasn't easily shocked, but the vision before him literally poleaxed him. He wouldn't have recognized Darcy O'Malley if he hadn't seen her hair unbound at the soccer game. It hung tonight in waves down to her waist and sparkled like fine ruby wine. It covered a sexy sleeveless outfit, not her usual Wall Street style.

Jade said, "Hunter Sloan, this is Darcy—"

"We know each other." Darcy grinned at him. "Hi, Hunter."

"Miss Darcy." He barely got the words out.

"Hunter bought us a drink," Jade said.

"That's nice. Thanks." She picked up her beer and sipped. "Hmm. I haven't had a beer in years."

"Well, that oughtta be illegal," Hunter teased.

The women laughed.

"So, you ready to dance, Red?"

Darcy chuckled. "Sure." She explained to Hunter.

"Friday night's organized dance night—the macarena, line dances, the electric slide. And a ton of others."

"They even do the chicken dance," Jade added.

"Oh, be still my heart," he said drolly.

The familiar strains of a country line dance came from the band. "Let's go, kiddo. Before you lose your nerve."

"Watch our drinks?" Darcy asked.

He nodded.

The floor wasn't crowded yet so he had a clear view of the women out there moving and shaking. Darcy's outfit was a one-piece silky-looking thing that hit her in all the right places when she moved. It made a man's hands itch to touch her. As the song progressed, Hunter found he had to turn away. Her *dancing* was having an unmistakable effect on his body.

He made his way to the end of the bar. The women he'd talked to earlier weren't dancing. They were still checking him out. So he smiled at them and tried to flirt.

But his eyes kept straying to a certain little redhead on the dance floor. It didn't take the men in the establishment long to pounce. Jade and Darcy were like fine jewels in a coal mine. The male population of Hyde Point kept them busy for a long time. Long enough for Hunter to regain his composure. After several dances— a few twists, one macarena and a cross between swing and the jitterbug, along with other dances he didn't recognize—Darcy approached the bar alone. She sank down and sipped her beer.

Hunter told himself not to go to her. His history meant she was out of his reach...

Okay, mister, off the bike. Gimme your license and registration...

Sloan? the older cop had asked. *Your daddy Tipper Sloan? Christ, he was a bastard...*

And yet, Hunter made his way down the bar. "Need anything?" His voice was hoarse.

"Got any oxygen?" she joked. Her face was flushed from the exertion. He noticed her neck, exposed above the scoop, pink and pretty.

"You kept up good out there."

"I'm out of practice. I haven't danced like this in ages."

"Why?"

She looked at him, and the flush deepened. "It's not who I am anymore."

"What's that mean?"

She shook her head, sending waves of burnished red flying. "Nothing." She shifted in her seat. "Claire hasn't stopped talking about you, and how she's going to be your assistant."

Hunter thought about the shy little girl, who was almost as pretty as her mother. "I'm a lucky man," he said.

"How's Braden?"

Studying her for a minute, Hunter finally said, "He threw a huge fit because I was going out tonight."

"I'm kind of surprised to see you here myself. You seem to want to spend all the time you can with him."

He wouldn't have her thinking bad about his role as a daddy. "I do, but I, um, need the money."

Green eyes—lighter and more sparkly than Jade's—widened. "Hunter, if the daycare expense is the reason you've taken a second job, there's assistance money available.''

His insides went ice cold. "I can pay for my son's care.''

"I didn't mean—''

"Darcy, is that you?'' A man in a pinstriped suit and tie came up behind her.

Reluctantly she turned around. "David, hello. What are you doing here?''

"Our firm's dinner just finished and the guys wanted to stop for a beer. I tried to call you but there was no answer so I came here with them.'' Hunter took in the guy's styled hair and perfect clothes. They made him think about his black T-shirt and jeans and the fact that he needed a haircut.

Like father like son, the cop had told Hunter tonight.

The man's gaze turned hot as he scanned Darcy from head to toe. "You look different.''

Darcy touched her hair self-consciously. "I, um, wasn't planning to go out. Jade came over, so I left as I was.''

Again his eyes raked her. "The outfit's a little…''

Tight across the breasts. Hunter had noticed, too. It looked great.

Darcy tugged at the top. She seemed embarrassed for some reason. "This is old…I…''

A slow song began to play. The guy grasped her hand. "Come on, I'll shelter you from all the covetous male eyes here.''

She glanced away. Briefly Hunter met her gaze. Her annoyance was clear, yet she put her hand in the man's. Hunter was still watching them when Jade returned to the bar. "Where's Darce?''

"Appears like the man in her life arrived." Ignoring the bump in his chest, he nodded to the dance floor where the guy held Darcy close.

"Oh, God, David Carrington."

He tried not to care. "Yeah?"

"Esquire. Big-time attorney in Hyde Point."

Jade's tone alerted him. "You don't like him."

"I don't like anybody Marian the Librarian approves of."

"You lost me."

"Darcy's mother. We call her…never mind. Anyway, her mother thinks they're perfect together."

"You don't."

"Are you crazy? He'd bore me to death."

Hunter smiled at the beautiful woman before him. "I like you, Jade Anderson."

She smiled up at him with mischief in her eyes. "I like you, too, Hunter Sloan." She waited a minute. "I think Darcy likes you, too. She's talked about you a lot tonight."

He'd raised a cola to his lips and sputtered it all over his black T-shirt. "You kiddin' me?"

Jade studied him. "It was nice what you did for Claire."

"I like Miss Claire."

"How about Darcy? Do you like her, too?"

Hunter had had a lot of experience dodging these kinds of bullets. "She's a great person. She's been super with my kid."

"My daughter, too. I have a three-year-old who goes to TenderTime when I help out at Hannah's Place."

Hunter stiffened. "You work at the diner?"

"Part-time. I need more hours somewhere, though."

She scanned the bar. "I used to be a pretty good bartender in New York."

"Yeah?"

"You like working here?"

"I don't know, this is my first night."

A man came up behind Jade. "Wanna dance, gorgeous?"

She swiveled around. "Why not? See ya, Hunter."

For a half hour, he watched Darcy and David; he saw her frown several times, especially when the lawyer apparently didn't want to do the fancy dances, and dragged her off the floor. When the band took a break, Jade returned to the bar, and Darcy made her way over when Carrington headed to the men's room. "Damn it."

Hunter was standing down a few feet, but could hear them if he strained.

"What?" Jade asked.

"He doesn't like my being here with you. He thinks my outfit's too wild. He said I should cut my hair."

Hunter dropped the glass he was washing and it smashed into the sink. Darcy glanced up. He was staring at her hair, but tore his gaze away and began to clean up his mess.

Jade's voice was hot. "Darce, that's stupid. Your hair's stunning. You *look* stunning tonight."

She sank onto the stool. "He's right, this isn't the real me. I'm playacting because my mother's out of town." She shook her head. "I'm behaving like I did when we were young."

Jade opened her mouth to speak again.

"No, don't say anything. I'm going to leave with David now. I should never have come here."

Jade frowned when Darcy got up. As she moved away from the bar, Hunter watched her; she looked over her shoulder about a foot away from him. "Nice to see you again, Hunter."

She turned her back to him, then he called out, "Hey, Miss Darcy."

Pivoting, she smiled at the name.

"Come here a minute."

She covered the few steps to the bar.

Leaning over the wide mahogany surface of a stool, he grabbed a fistful of her hair. It felt like raw silk and smelled like heaven. "I'm no fancy lawyer, darlin'," he said in his thickest southern accent, "but it doesn't take Einstein to figure out that this is about the sexiest thing I've ever seen. Don't let anybody talk you into cuttin' it. It'd be a mortal sin."

Her eyes lit. She smiled broadly. "Thanks, Hunter. I needed to hear that." And she sashayed away, the cute-as-hell jumpsuit hugging her even cuter fanny.

CHAPTER FIVE

BY MONDAY MORNING, Darcy had convinced herself that her behavior on Friday night was an aberration and had nothing to do with who she really was now. She went through the day with ruthless efficiency and decorum, lunching with the mayor at the country club about a committee he wanted her to head, and conducting a seminar on working mothers for the Women's Auxiliary Guild. She'd been trying to get onto the Internet all day to do some research, but hadn't had a block of time to do it.

At five, before she got online, she called Meli and Claire at home. During the summer, they spent some of their days at TenderTime, some at various camps they enjoyed, and some at home when Marian was there. Darcy didn't like leaving them by themselves, though Claire contended that at almost eleven, she was old enough to baby-sit. Today, Porter Casewell had spent the day with the girls.

Reliable and trustworthy young women don't end up in group homes for troubled girls.

Oh, dear, was she wrong there, too? Was David right?

Stop it, Darce. Be a martyr if you want, but I won't let you put down the Serenity House girls.

Meli answered breathlessly. "Mama, where *are* you?"

"I'm at work, honey. Mrs. Johnson said she'd drive

you to practice.'' Sara Johnson was a teammate of Meli's and the youngest Johnson girl went to TenderTime. The two single mothers often carpooled.

A long silence on the other end. ''There's a scrimmage tonight, Mama. I'm gonna be goalie.''

Damn, Darcy had forgotten. ''All right. I'll get there as soon as I can.''

''Can't you drive me?''

''Mel, that's not necessary. It's all arranged for you to be picked up. I'll meet you there.''

Meli grumbled something and hung up the phone.

Darcy called back and got Porter. ''I'm sorry, Mrs. O'Malley. Meli won't come to the phone.''

Another thing she'd have to deal with today, Darcy thought as she hung up. Leaning back in her office chair, she closed her eyes against the headache beginning to pound at her temples. How could things get out of hand so quickly? Just a few days ago, her life was on track and everybody was happy.

Everybody but you.

''Oh, shut up,'' she told the voice in her head as she switched on her computer. While she waited for a search engine to find her sites, she thought about the weekend, specifically Friday night. A vision of Hunter Sloan's eyes perusing her with very male appreciation was juxtaposed to David's disapproval.

Yeah, until he got you alone. What's the old saying? Be a lady in the parlor and a whore in the bedroom?

The thought made her nauseous. David's attention had been uncharacteristically ardent when he'd driven her home. At the door, he'd swept her into his arms and kissed her with more passion than he'd ever shown before. His hands had also wandered into new territory.

And all Darcy could think of was Hunter Sloan leaning over the bar, fisting *his* hand in her hair, telling her it'd be a sin to cut it. She skimmed her fingers along her throat. What would those callused, carpenter's hands feel like on her body? David's had felt soft and…unappealing. So she'd pulled away.

He hadn't been pleased…

"What is it, Darcy? We've been seeing each other for months. I want to take this to the next level." He nodded to the house. "And your kids are gone for the night."

"I'm not ready for that yet."

"You sure as hell look ready."

"What does that mean?"

"Nothing." He stepped back. "If I'm out of line, I'm sorry. You took me by surprise in that outfit, with your hair down."

"You seemed to disapprove at Rascal's."

He'd grinned boyishly. "We're not at Rascal's anymore. You can be a bad girl here, if you want."

The term had sobered her. She'd pleaded exhaustion and left him standing on the doorstep, confused and more than a little annoyed…

Darcy scanned the list that had come up on-screen and she clicked into a daycare site she'd visited before. She wanted to see what kinds of success the programs she'd based hers on were having these days. She'd researched this area thoroughly, though she'd only found a few places that offered the special kind of care TenderTime did. Nobody wanted to watch kids like Braden in daycare because they were too disruptive. Nobody wanted to spend the money to get the right people to do it.

Do we need certified teachers for the problem children?

She was printing off some moving letters from parents when she caught sight of the clock. Damn it. She wondered what time Meli's scrimmage was scheduled for. *Please, not at six,* she prayed to whomever as she hurriedly left the office and drove too fast to the field. The night was hot, and she knew she'd swelter in the eighty-degree August evening in the prim ankle-length dress she wore. She considered going home to change, but it would take too much time. She should at least have ditched her panty hose, she thought, as she arrived at the field and made her way across the grass.

The shouts coming from the sidelines told her the match had begun. She neared the play and saw Hunter, wearing a red shirt and cap, on the sidelines. Next to him was Claire, also in a cap and T-shirt, holding a clipboard to her chest. Claire had mentioned Hunter a million times since he'd asked her to be his assistant.

Oh, dear, who was watching Tramp? Darcy had forgotten she'd volunteered for the job. She scanned the area, and found the dog next to an older couple. She recognized them as Bart and Ada Cooper, Hunter's grandparents. Everybody had made it to the scrimmage but her.

Feeling guilty about her parental negligence and a thousand other things, she zeroed in on Meli, standing tall and confident in the goal. The goalie shirt hung down to her knees and the headgear obscured her face. Darcy knew her small features would be tense with concentration.

Just as Darcy reached the sidelines, the other team dribbled toward Meli's goal. Her daughter crouched, ready to spring in either direction for a goal kick. Shouts rose from the parents; Darcy's gaze went to Hunter, who followed the play down the field, trailed by Claire.

Then it all seemed to happen in slow motion. Meli whipped off her helmet—a definite breach of safety—as the other players neared the goal. A boy obviously big for his age booted the ball toward the net. Meli read it correctly and lunged to the left.

Right into the steel goalpost.

"Oh my God," Darcy cried as she raced in two-inch heels to the goalie box. Dimly aware that the official was blowing the whistle, and all the other kids were sitting, she tore through the grass, her heels snagging in it. She kicked her shoes off halfway there to run faster.

By the time she got to Meli, Hunter had reached her, too, along with the other coach.

Meli was sprawled out on the ground on her back, not moving.

HUNTER'S HEART thundered in his chest as he dropped down next to the little girl lying immobilized on the ground. Ordering himself to stay calm, he tapped her gently on the cheek. "Meli, sweetheart, wake up."

No response.

He heard noises in the background, was vaguely aware of Darcy at the goal. "Stay back," he said to everybody, desperately trying to recall the first-aid course he'd taken when things had gotten rough in a few of the joints where he'd bartended.

Don't move or elevate the head.

He bent over Meli.

Make sure the victim is breathing.

Relief swept through him as he saw her chest rise and fall noticeably.

Check pulse.

Placing two fingers on her neck, he got a slow tha-rump. Thank God. But she still wasn't awake.

Whipping out the cell phone he'd bought just to bring to the field, he looked up. The first person he saw was his grandfather, his hand on Braden's shoulder. He tossed Bart the phone. "Call 911, Pa."

A moan from beside him. He looked over at Darcy, who'd gone chalk white, and was kneeling next to him. He squeezed her arm. "She's breathing just fine, Darce."

"Is she?"

"Yeah. And she's got a strong, steady pulse."

Darcy's eyes sought his frantically. "Then why isn't she awake?"

"I don't know. The ambulance will be here soon."

When Meli moaned, and her head lolled to the side, Hunter glanced up at his assistant coach. "Get me towels or blankets to immobilize her head."

"God, she could have—" Darcy cut herself off. "Can I hold her hand?"

"Yeah, that'd be real nice." Hunter took the towels offered him and rolled them up on either side of Meli's head. "There you go, little one."

He brushed the hair out of Meli's eyes, wondering why the hell she'd taken off the helmet. She'd been mad as a hornet about wearing it, but still...

"I don't wanna wear this," she'd whined when he gave her the gear.

"Got to, Miss Meli. You need protection." At her mutinous look, he said, "I got a mind to take you outta the goal if you don't."

She'd mumbled under her breath. He could tell, from only a month with Braden, that Meli was upset and it wasn't about helmets. Surly, Meli had plopped the helmet on her head. "It's too big."

He'd adjusted the strap, tweaked her nose and hustled

back to the line, chuckling at what a pistol she was. He never thought to warn her to keep the gear on...

A small noise brought him back to reality. Claire was crying softly. Hunter leaned over and squeezed her shoulder. He wasn't one for platitudes, but he couldn't let this go. "She's gonna be all right, Miss Claire. I promise."

Huge hazel eyes filled with gratitude. "Okay."

In the distance, sirens wailed. Thank God. The wait seemed never-ending, but the medics finally arrived. Two female ambulance crew leaped out with a stretcher and raced over.

Darcy and Claire stood, as did Hunter, when the EMTs reached Meli. Quickly Hunter filled them in on what had happened. They went to work on Meli, immobilizing her neck with a head brace and securing her body on the board. Darcy gripped Claire's hand as she watched. Her eyes were dry but she was mercilessly biting her lip. Once again, Hunter squeezed her arm. "She'll be all right."

Darcy glanced at Claire. "Of course she will." Once Meli was on the stretcher, she said to the attendants, "We can ride with her, right?"

"Of course."

Solemn and silent, Claire clung to her mother's hand and looked to Hunter. So did Darcy.

"I'll follow you there. We'll need a car to take Miss Meli home in."

After the ambulance drove away, Hunter crossed to his family. Though Braden didn't touch him, he stared up at Hunter with fear on his young face. Hunter went down on one knee. "Meli's gonna be all right, Champ. She'll have a big goose egg, but she'll be all right." At Braden's unchanged expression, he said, "I'm gonna get in her face about taking the helmet off, though, soon as she's better."

Braden smiled weakly and moved close to Tramp. Hunter stood and said to his grandfather, "I'm going to the hospital. Can you take Braden home?"

"Sure. Grandma and I walked here." The park was only two blocks from their house. "Braden can escort us back."

Wildly Braden shook his head. "Wanna go with *you.*"

Oh, Lord. He knelt down again. "You can't come to the hospital, Brade. It'll be hours before I get out of there."

"Don't care." Hunter recognized the signs of Braden digging in his heels. The kid could be as stubborn as a country mule.

"I'm sorry, Brade. This is my call. You can't come."

Mutinous eyes stared at him.

Ada Cooper came to Hunter's aid. "Hey there, young man. Remember that peach cobbler we made? I'll heat it up in the microwave just like you like it, and you, me and Grandpa'll have a snack on the back porch while we wait for your daddy."

"Tramp, too," Bart put in.

Hunter thanked God for his grandparents.

Braden finally left with the older couple and Hunter headed to the parking lot. Halfway there, he tripped on something in the grass. Shoes. He'd noticed Darcy was barefoot, so he bent over and picked up the expensive leather pumps. Holding them tight, he hurried to the truck.

FEAR AND GUILT curdled Darcy's stomach as she sat in the waiting room with Claire, forcing herself to stay calm, trying to pray, refusing to think of Meli's little body so still. Her daughter hadn't regained consciousness on the short ride to Hyde Point Hospital, and the emergency-room personnel had whisked her away once they'd arrived here. Darcy probably could have gone into the treatment room, but Claire couldn't have gone with her. Torn between her two children, there was really no choice.

Gripping her hand like a frightened toddler, Claire had latched onto Darcy and not let go. They sat side by side on ugly orange vinyl chairs, when Hunter Sloan flew into the waiting area, still wearing his baseball cap and red shirt, just like Claire. He crossed to them. "Any news?"

Shaking her head, Darcy swallowed back emotion.

He went to sit down near Darcy. But he saw Claire's face and took the chair next to her, instead. Circling her shoulders with his arm, he said, "You okay, Miss Claire?"

"I'm scared."

"It's okay to be scared." He leaned over and whispered, "Ya know, I got knocked out by a ball once. Hit me square in the head."

"Really?" Claire's trust in him was clear from just that one word.

"Honest. I was fine. I have a feeling your sister's head is as hard as mine."

Darcy was astonished when Claire laughed, and snuggled against Hunter. Not only was Darcy comforted by his presence, but he'd taken on some of the burden of reassuring Claire.

They sat in silence for a while, until Paige trundled through the doors. Dressed in shorts and a T-shirt, her bathing suit peeked out from under her clothes. "I'm here, Darce."

Darcy stood, and Paige hugged her. When they drew back, Paige asked, "You okay?"

"Yes. Go see about Mel, please."

"I will." Paige ruffled Claire's hair. "Your sister will be all right, honey."

Claire didn't smile. "I know," she said. "Hunter says so." When Paige left, Darcy sat down again and heard Claire mumble, "...should've left it on."

"What did you say, sweetie?"

Her daughter peered up at her. "Coach told Mel to put the helmet on. She did, but took it off." Tears welled then. "Why'd she take it off, Mama?"

"You know Mel, Claire. She's got a mind of her own." Darcy faced Hunter. "Thanks."

"I wish I'd done more." For the first time she noticed he was holding something. He held them out.

"Oh, God, my shoes. I wasn't even aware..." She glanced down. Her stockings were torn, and her feet filthy.

"You could go clean up. I'll stay with Miss Claire."

Shaking her head, Darcy leaned over and slipped on her shoes. "No, it's okay."

Fifteen minutes later Paige came out of the treatment area, and Darcy could see that her friend was smiling. "Mel's awake. She's going to be fine, but she has a concussion."

Darcy wavered and felt a strong hand steady her back. "Easy," Hunter whispered.

Closing her eyes, she let herself lean into him for a minute. *Thank you, God.* Claire, however, started to cry. Bending down, Darcy took her child into her arms and held her close. "Go ahead and cry, baby. It's okay.

Everything's okay.'' Her voice cracked. ''Your sister is going to be fine. Just fine.''

When Claire quieted, Darcy stood. ''Can we see her?''

''Sure. I'll take you back.'' Paige smiled at Hunter. ''You, too, Coach. Meli's asking for you.''

''Me? Why?''

''Something you were right about. Come on, let's all go back. She really is fine.''

The three of them went through the treatment door and down the corridor to a cubicle sectioned off by curtains. Behind them, flanked by a couple of doctors, Meli lay on a cotlike bed. Darcy's breathing hitched when she saw the plum-size bump at Meli's temple, but otherwise the child *did* seem fine. ''Hi, Mama.''

''Hi, yourself.'' Leaning over, Darcy kissed Meli's head. Her throat was closed up, but she smiled down at her daughter. ''Does it hurt, honey?''

''Uh-huh.''

Hunter, who was holding Claire's hand, urged her to the bed. He stood behind her, his hands on her shoulders. ''See, Claire, your sister's fine.''

''Coach says you got a hard head,'' Claire told Meli tearfully.

Chuckles around the room. Meli's gaze turned to Hunter. She said, shyly, ''Hey, Coach.''

''Hey, Miss Meli. How you doin'?''

Meli frowned. ''I'm sorry.''

Leaning over, he gently ruffled her hair. ''Apology accepted, so long as you give me your Scout's honor you'll wear that helmet every time you step in the goal.''

''I promise.'' She looked at Darcy. ''Am I gonna be punished?''

"We'll talk about that later."

Paige introduced them to the emergency personnel. Darcy asked, "Can I take her home?"

"Actually, we'd rather you didn't."

Her heartbeat escalated. "Why?"

Paige said, "Relax. We're not keeping anything from you. It's not uncommon to keep a child this young overnight after a trauma to the head." Paige squeezed Darcy's arm. "She's only seven, honey."

Darcy searched Paige's eyes for the truth. She saw it. "I can stay with her, can't I?" She looked down at Claire. "Though Claire shouldn't…"

"Of course you can." Paige smiled at Claire. "Maybe Claire would like to come home and stay with me and Ian tonight. I could use some help with my two little monsters."

Despite the gravity of the situation, Claire smiled. She loved Sammy and Suzy. Still, she hesitated. "I should stay with Mama."

"No, honey, that's not a good idea." Darcy looked at Paige. "Thanks. I appreciate this."

Paige said, "You should go home and change, though. Get some clean things for Meli to wear home tomorrow."

"I will."

"Claire and I can wait here with Meli while you do that, then I'll take this young lady with me."

A nurse came in and pulled Darcy aside to sign the admittance papers, then she crossed back to the bed where Hunter was talking softly to Meli and Claire.

"I'm going to check you into a room, sweetie, then go home and get some stuff for us. Clothes."

"Get Tickles for me." Meli wouldn't sleep without her stuffed bear.

Darcy chuckled.

Hunter smiled. "I'll wait till Miss Meli's settled."

"You don't have to do that."

"You left your car at the field, Mama," Claire said.

"I'll drop you off," he said easily.

Their eyes met over the bed, and she felt a warmth sift through her. "Thanks," she said softly.

IT WAS TWILIGHT by the time Hunter pulled up next to Darcy's sedan in the parking lot of Meadows Park. From across the bench seat of his truck, she looked over at him. "Thanks for the ride, Hunter."

He watched her for a minute. She'd been mostly silent on the way, responding to his stumbling attempts at conversation with one-syllable words. "You don't have to pretend with me, Darce. Your hands are shaking."

She swallowed hard. "I'm okay."

"You'll feel better if you let it out." He knew the reaction. Cool during a crisis. Breakdown after. He didn't want her behind the wheel of her car when that happened.

She straightened. "No, no, I'm fine."

Her rejection kicked into his old insecurities and he felt himself withdraw. But she fumbled with the seat belt when she tried to unfasten it and he had to reach over her to release it.

"Thanks again." Giving him the phoniest grin he'd ever seen, she added, "For the ride. For taking care of Meli. And for comforting Claire. She really listened to you."

"I'm real fond of both your girls. I'm glad I could help."

Darcy opened the door and got out. Slowly she made

her way around the bed of his truck to her car. He watched her through the rearview mirror. Her back was rigid and her shoulders were stiff. When she reached the driver's side of her Taurus, she fished in her purse for the key. Then she looked up, and her gaze traveled past the hood to the soccer goal.

She stilled. Was she seeing her child hit the goalpost? Witnessing the incident had scared Hunter silly. He could only imagine what it had done to Darcy. How would he have felt if Braden had gotten hurt?

Shaking herself, Darcy looked down at the door. He heard the keys jingle, then they fell from her hand; her shoulders began to shake. She dropped down by the side of the car and didn't stand back up.

Hunter whipped open the door, bounded out of the truck and circled around her car. She was kneeling in the gravel, her head buried in her hands. The quiet, restrained sobs coming from her almost broke his heart.

He squatted down behind her and placed a hand on her shoulder. It was so slim, so delicate. "Darce."

She shook her head.

"Darcy." Both hands grasped her, rubbed up and down her arms.

The sobs increased.

He didn't have much experience with crying women, and had stayed away from emotional situations all his life. But he couldn't just ignore this. So he eased onto his knees and drew her to him. Again he was surprised by the delicacy of her frame, her slightness. Awkwardly, he enveloped her in a kind of cocoon. His lips near her hair, he said, "It's okay, darlin', let it out."

She began to cry harder. She tried to bury her face farther in her hands and her whole body shook violently.

Acting on instinct and the need to comfort, he angled around and plunked his butt down on the gravel, his back propped up against her car. Then he pulled her onto his lap. She went as easily as a child would. Drawing her to his chest, he enfolded her in his arms and placed his hand on her head. He was at a loss for words, so he just held her.

The sobs got worse before she calmed. But by degrees, she stopped crying, sniffled, hiccuped; all the while, she kept her face buried in his chest. Knees raised, she cuddled onto his lap as though she belonged there.

After a moment, she turned her head and rested her cheek on his shoulder. "I'm sorry."

"Don't be. It's been building all night."

"I have to be strong. For the girls."

"Nobody's here but you and me. You can be strong in a few minutes."

He felt her relax against him. "I can't remember the last time I did this."

"Everybody needs a good cry."

She gave a gentle snort. "Yeah, sure, I'll bet you do this regularly."

"I've come close a time or two."

She drew back. It had gotten darker since they'd pulled in and the light from the parking lamps was far away enough to cast her in shadow. Clumsily, he reached around and pulled a handkerchief out of his pocket. She took it, mopped her face and blew her nose. Then she met his gaze. "I'm a mess."

Right at that moment he thought she was as pretty as a Carolina sunset. Only one thing would make her more so. Without censoring his reaction, he reached up to her hair. Slowly, he released the pins, unfurled the knot and fanned the long locks over her shoulders and back. "There," he said, his voice gritty. "That's better."

"Better?"

"Hmm." He let his fingers get lost in the strands. "The knot was too tight. It'll give you a headache."

"You like my hair down," she said softly.

"Oh, yeah. Do I ever."

Tilting her head, she said, "You're an interesting guy, Hunter Sloan. And very nice. Sensitive."

"I doubt that's an adjective too many people in Hyde Point would apply to me."

"The people of Hyde Point don't always understand character."

He angled his head. "Now how'd a girl like you know that?"

"I know." He waited for her to say more, but all she said was, "Look, I have to go."

"Yeah, I guess you do," he said, disappointed.

She scrambled to her feet. He groped around before he got up, found her keys and stood. Like a courtly gentleman—oh, brother—he unlocked her door.

She hesitated before she got into the car and looked at him. In the light from the lamps, her eyes were liquid green, like some ancient potion. "Thanks, Hunter."

He tilted her a smile. "You're welcome."

Then she surprised the hell out of him by reaching up and winding her arms around his neck. His arms closed around her; their bodies met naturally, as if they'd done this before.

And in the dim parking lot of Meadows Park, Hunter realized that if he let her, this woman could mean something to him.

Not good.

But he couldn't help himself from hugging her back.

From watching her as she drew away, got into her car, started the engine and drove off.

Hands in his pockets, he stared at her Taurus until the taillights disappeared.

CHAPTER SIX

QUIET WATERS was located about a mile from Serenity House, up on a hill, in East Hyde Point. The sun sparkled off the huge pond that gave the soon-to-be boys' home its name. Birds chirped cheerily in the surrounding oaks and maples; the whole area smelled like flowers and trees. Nora Whitman listened to Hunter and Dan discussing the blueprints for the framed-in structure. Hunter's oddly silent dog, Tramp, hadn't once left his side in the hour they'd been touring the place.

"See, right here," Hunter said in the voice that was somehow always world-weary and that clutched at Nora's heart. Maybe because she knew he'd been a troubled kid, like her Serenity House girls, and no one, except Dan, had tried to help him. Well, that's why they were opening Quiet Waters. "The boys' closets," Hunter continued, "should be for more than just clothes."

"They look like entertainment centers." Dan's low rumble flowed through Nora's system like aged brandy.

Hunter chuckled. "Not quite. But the guys who'll come here need some space of their own." He hesitated. "Speaking of which, I wanted to talk to you about the bathrooms."

"What about them? I had the architect redesign their placement after you took a look at the plans I sent to you in Florida."

"Come on, I'll show you what I mean."

"Honey, come with us." Dan touched her arm.

"Sure." Pivoting, Nora saw Hunter pat Tramp's head, and the dog stood at attention. She followed the men and mutt to the first boys' suite. Hunter had suggested that each set of rooms have its own bathroom. Though Hunter's suggestion increased the building cost, Dan and Nora had found the extra money because Hunter's privacy arguments had made sense.

Standing in the six-by-six space, Hunter lost the reserve and self-deprecation that he always seemed to exhibit and gestured enthusiastically to the right. "The toilet over there should be enclosed. Just a wall and door would do it. I'd be glad to put in the Sheetrock and doors myself if the builders frame it that way."

"You're already doing too much," Dan grumbled. "And I'm still pissed as hell that you won't let me pay you."

His hand absently scratching the dog's head, Hunter's dark eyes sparkled with genuine, if rare, warmth. "Yeah, well, this place is being built on grants and donations, so consider this my contribution."

"Still, I—"

Nora touched Dan's arm. "Dan." She sensed this was important to Hunter's pride, and the few times she'd been with the guy, she'd suspected that his pride had been badly battered by the residents of Hyde Point.

Dan caught her undertone of warning. "All right. I'll let it go. But only if you bring Braden to dinner at our house soon." Dan went to pet the dog, but it moved out of reach. "And Tramp, too. We've got a fenced-in yard."

A father's grin softened Hunter's features. "You sure

you want that? My boy's not nearly as well mannered as Tramp here. Especially at the dinner table."

"I'm sure. Darcy brought Meli and Claire over last night and the girls were full of stories about you and Braden." Dan smiled. "Claire couldn't stop talking about how she's helping you with the soccer stats. I think you've won a little girl's heart there."

"Claire's a treasure. I just can't understand how her daddy…" Hunter shook his head. "Never mind," he said and turned away. Ostensibly, he was checking out the studs, but Nora saw that his back had stiffened. "I haven't seen Miss Meli since the accident. Doc said she couldn't play soccer for a week."

"Yes, and she's driving her mother nuts." Nora chuckled. "She reminds me of a younger Darcy."

Hunter's head snapped around. "Is that so? I'd have reckoned Darcy was more like Claire."

"No, not back then." And, in Nora's view, she was too much like Claire now. Both needed loosening up.

Hunter's gaze locked on Nora. "How do you know Darcy so well, Miss Nora?"

Uh-oh. "Mmm, this is a small town. I've lived here all my life. And some of the Serenity House girls work at the daycare."

His dark eyebrows furrowed. "It's great that she'd give the girls a chance. Especially since she's got nothing in common with them."

Nora wasn't surprised Hunter didn't know Darcy's background, and she wouldn't reveal it. "Darcy's a complicated woman. She understands a lot more than people give her credit for." She smiled. "Now, I want to go look at the kitchen. It's all framed out, but I need your advice on the cabinetry. It won't be fancy like the one you're doing at Nathan's place, but I want the best possible use of space. These boys are going to learn to cook!''

Hunter gave her a little salute, said, ''Yes, ma'am,'' and followed her to the kitchen area in the front of the structure, the dog close at his heels.

Later, as Dan walked Hunter to his car, Nora made notes on the kitchen design, but her thoughts were on Hunter Sloan. She liked him a lot. And there was something in his tone when he spoke about Darcy...

Strong arms circled her waist. ''So, what do you think, Mrs. Whitman? Are you gonna be happy running this place for a while with me?''

''I'd be happy anywhere you are, Chief Whitman.''

He dipped his hand inside her shirt, gave her a quick and tender squeeze, then drew back. She turned around to find him leaning against the counter. ''So, what do you make of Hunter?'' he asked.

''Well, one thing is clear. You care about him as much as you do about Anabelle Crane.''

''I heard from Anabelle, by the way. She just got promoted to detective.'' He scowled, his handsome features worried. ''She'll be involved in even more dangerous undercover work.''

''She can take care of herself. She had a good cop to teach her.''

''I was hoping she'd move back here. Of course, with Nathan still living in town part of the time...'' He trailed off and scowled.

''What is it?''

''I'm worried about Nathan. Something's going on with him. I can't go into what just yet.''

''I'm sorry to hear that. But he hurt Anabelle, Dan.'' Nathan and Anabelle had been involved when she'd worked for him ten years ago. It had ended badly and had caused her to leave the Hydes' employment suddenly. In the intervening years, Nathan's marriage had worsened, and then Olivia Hyde had died in a car accident. And since Anabelle left, there was a pervasive sadness about the man. Still, she blamed Nathan for hurting a young and impressionable Anabelle. "It's hard to forget what he did."

"I know, honey. Let's drop it." He glanced at the door. "Hunter asked me more questions about Darcy."

"Really?"

"I have a feeling he's got a hankerin' for red hair."

"A hankerin'?" She crossed to Dan, and snuggled into his wide chest. At fifty-five, he was still fit and trim. "You turning southern on me, cowboy?"

"Hmm. You think it's sexy?"

"Yep."

"Show me."

"I will. Let's make a stop at home."

"You're on, love."

At the framed-in front door, she hesitated. "Hunter's in town only temporarily, isn't he, Dan?"

"Yes." Dan tugged at her hand to hurry her along.

"I wouldn't want Darcy to get involved with him, and then have him take off. She's got a history of that happening to her, you know."

"I know. But the vibes are there. At least from Hunter."

"From her, too. I could tell by the way she asked after him last night." Nora scowled as they traversed the front yard. "And the girls like him. Especially Claire. That might not be good, if he's going to leave Hyde Point."

They reached the car. "He *will* leave, Nora. This town's been hard on him, and there are still strong traces of its bias today." He sighed. "All we can do is watch over Darcy and the girls, and be there for them." He kissed her right there on the road. "Now, be quiet, woman, so we can get home and deal with our own love life."

She slid into the car. "Yes, dear."

BUTTERFLIES ZIPPED around in Darcy's stomach as she made her way to the Elsa Moore Center. Her hand settled briefly on her middle; she wondered if the peach dress looked good on her. She'd changed her outfit three times for this meeting with Paige and Hunter.

Hunter.

It's okay, darlin', let it out.

He'd held her on his lap, for God's sake, on the pavement of the Meadows parking lot exactly a week ago today after Meli had been hurt. His muscular arms had soothed her as he simply accepted what she was feeling.

And something else, Darcy baby. He'd felt like a real honest-to-goodness man hugging you.

Even the taunting of her pesky inner voice couldn't mar her mood. By rights, she thought as she pulled into a parking space and hurried out of the car, she should at least be self-conscious. She hadn't seen Hunter since that night. She'd taken a few days off to stay with Meli—who'd been like a bear with a wounded paw—and then she'd had an off-site seminar for the next two days. She'd arranged for Claire to go to the practices with Porter Casewell, and when her daughter came home, she was full of stories about Hunter and Tramp and Braden.

But instead of feeling shy on this end-of-August morning, Darcy was looking forward to seeing Hunter again. His easy acceptance of her need to let out her feelings and not be strong for a little while was better than getting the Citizen of the Year award.

At the center, the receptionist directed Darcy to go to the conference room, where Paige was waiting for her. She knocked, and took a deep breath when told to enter.

Hunter wasn't there. Paige sat at the end of the table with her husband, Ian, and his mother, Lynne, flanking her. Darcy knew Ian was adopted, and that his work with Lynne—his biological mother—in their Internet agency that matched adopted kids and their biological parents was an important part of his life. She also knew it had been hard for Paige to accept Ian's interest in her, since she'd given up a child when she was seventeen and living in Serenity House.

Darcy said, "I'm sorry, the receptionist said to come here."

Paige looked up. It was obvious she'd been crying. "No, it's all right. We're done."

Ian smiled. "Hello, Darcy. You know my mother, right?"

A well-groomed blonde, with the same interesting eyes as Ian, stood. "Hi, Darcy." Picking up her purse, Lynne leaned over and hugged Paige. "I'm so proud of you dear. I promise, this will be good."

Weakly, Paige gave her a smile. "I know, I want to do it."

Standing too, Ian drew Paige out of the chair. In typical, brash Ian-style, he took his wife in his arms, whispered something in her ear, then gave her a lush kiss worthy of an on-screen clinch. "I love you."

Paige drew away. "I love you, too." She shook back her hair. "Now scoot."

For a second, Darcy was hit by a bolt of jealousy so

potent it stunned her. She wanted what Paige and Ian had. She'd never had that kind of relationship—where a man was obviously your best friend as well as your lover. For three years, she'd convinced herself she didn't need it. But right now, she wanted that kind of closeness more than anything in the world.

Nobody's here but you and me. You can be strong in a few minutes. A vision of Hunter's muscular arms embracing her took away her breath. She was barely able to say goodbye to Ian and Lynne as they left.

Paige sighed deeply after them. "Sorry. That man gets me so emotional sometimes."

"I'm sorry I interrupted."

"No, it's okay. I wanted to tell you about this anyway."

Darcy cocked her head.

"I've decided to look for the daughter I gave up for adoption."

"Wow!" Impulsively, Darcy crossed to Paige and hugged her. "This is great."

Vulnerability flashed in Paige's eyes when she drew back. "I know. It's just scary." She nodded after Ian. "We've been for counseling. And Lynne has been a great help, talking with me for hours about doing the search."

Darcy took Paige's hands. "Oh, honey, I'm so happy for you."

"Thanks." She glanced at the clock and assumed her doctor persona. "I told the nurse to have you meet me here, but I was so rattled about my decision, I forgot the materials for the meeting. I'll go to my office and get them."

Darcy was perusing the wall of photographs of moms and their babies that the center had treated, and thinking about all Paige had been through, and how happy she was now, when she heard, "Mornin', Miss Darcy."

Her heart gave a funny little lurch at the low masculine baritone. Turning, she found Hunter in the doorway. Though there was nothing unusual about what he was wearing, he looked different. It took her a minute to realize that he was relaxed, lazing against the door frame, his arm braced against it. Weight-lifter muscles bulged beneath the cotton of his shirt. And his dark eyes glowed.

"Morning, Hunter."

His grin was lazy, too. She smiled back. It looked as if their little episode in the parking lot had broken down some barriers for him, too. "Thanks for meetin' me here."

"I'm anxious to hear Paige's recommendation for Braden. How is he?"

"Good. And Miss Meli?"

"Grouchy. Thank goodness she can come back to practice tomorrow. She's hoping to play in the game Wednesday."

"And Claire?"

"She's thrilled to be your assistant. She talks about you all the time."

"I like her." He gave Darcy a once-over. "How's Miss Claire's mama?"

"Better than the last time I saw you. I should apologize."

"What? For being human?"

"No, for blubbering all over you."

"Well now, Miz Darcy—" the accent got noticeably thicker and made Darcy's insides feel like Jell-O "—it was my pleasure."

"Seriously, I was a mess."

He crossed into the room to stand before her. Up close, she got a whiff of some spicy aftershave. "Your kid got hurt, so that's understandable. And hey, I don't get to play knight in shining armor very often."

"You play it well."

"Thank you, ma'am."

Paige entered the room. "Hi, Hunter. Sorry, I'm a little rattled today. You're going to think I'm always late."

"No, ma'am," Hunter said, glancing back at Darcy. "It gave Darcy and me a chance to catch up."

They sat at the conference table. Hunter took the chair right next to Darcy, and Paige sat across from them. Hunter's shoulders were broad and nearly touched Darcy's. She found his masculine presence both comforting and exciting.

Paige opened a manila folder and took out some papers. "I have the forms on Braden, Hunter," she said, all doctor now. "And I've met with our psychologist, Elliot Emerson, to review the behavioral surveys. He was also in on the conference call with Braden's doctor in Florida."

She felt Hunter tense next to her, saw the muscles in his bare arm beneath the rolled-up sleeve bunch. From underneath the table, she could sense his foot tapping.

"And? Has he got this ADD or ADHD thing?"

"We think so, Hunter. The results of the surveys and the anecdotal responses indicate he has enough of the symptoms from the *Diagnostic and Statistical Manual of Mental Disorders* to qualify as ADHD."

Hunter swallowed hard.

"There's more. His doctor in Florida told me he was glad to hear you were pursuing the possibility of

ADHD. He'd suggested to Braden's mother several times that Braden should have an evaluation like this."

"What?"

"Why didn't she follow up?" Darcy asked.

"The doctor thought she was amenable, but her husband didn't believe in this kind of thing. Apparently the guy said it was some psychological mumbo jumbo and Braden just needed a firm hand."

Hunter gripped the edge of the table. "A firm hand? Did he…did the doctor suspect…"

When he didn't finish, Paige said, "No, Hunter, I asked about that. Cal Smith seems very competent. If he suspected any kind of abuse, he'd have followed up on it."

Darcy glanced at Hunter. His eyes were volatile. "But you're saying a doctor suggested some treatment for my kid—how long ago?"

"Twelve months."

"A year ago, and Shelly didn't do anything about it?"

"That's right."

Throwing back the chair, Hunter stood and crossed to the window. He tapped his fingertips nervously on the panes of glass. Paige and Darcy exchanged a worried look. After a moment, Darcy rose and crossed to Hunter. She touched his arm. "Hunter, are you all right?"

He pivoted, more composed now. "Yeah. Sorry. I just…how could she not try to help the boy? It's so obvious he has problems."

"What's important is what *you* do," Darcy told him.

Raking his hand through his hair, he said, "Yeah, you're right."

They returned to the table and sat down. "All right, what can I do?" Hunter asked.

Paige took out a sheet of paper from the file. "I've assembled a list of Web sites that have the best current information on ADHD. I give it to all the parents of my patients who may be suffering from this malady. I'd like you to visit the sites, learn as much as you can about the condition. Read the case studies and the letters from parents. The material will review a lot of what we already discussed."

Hunter said, "I don't understand. Isn't there something you can do for ADHD right away?"

"Many patients go on drugs like Ritalin or Dexedrine. They're stimulants to increase the child's focus. But the drugs are controversial because of their side effects. Other camps say teaching compensatory social skills and behavior modification combined with a change in diet works best. I'd like you to make an informed decision on this."

"Don't you have a recommendation, Paige?" Darcy asked.

"I'll tell Hunter my thoughts after he's read the material. Given Braden's age and the fact that he's recently been uprooted, I think there's a lot to consider here."

Hunter glanced down at the list. "I'll do this right away."

"Take a few days. It's tough reading, and you'll want time to assimilate it." She smiled. "Besides, I'll be out of the office for a bit. I've got some personal business to take care of."

"Fine."

Paige stood. "Hunter, we're here to help you with this," she told him. "You're not alone."

Hunter studied Paige Kendrick; she had no idea how

laughable what she said was. He'd been alone all his life, except for maybe Dan Whitman. But he'd be damned if his son would be left on his own. "I appreciate that, Paige," he said soberly. "And all the time you took for my boy."

"I'm glad I can help." She glanced at the clock. "I have an appointment. I'll see you soon."

"Can we stay here a sec?" Darcy asked. "I want to talk to Hunter."

"Sure. See you later." Paige closed the door on her way out.

Darcy turned to him, cool and competent in a sleeveless dress the color of peaches. "You're upset."

"I'm fine."

She gave him a sideways glance. "It's not fair to be dishonest with the woman who bared her soul on the pavement of a parking lot a week ago."

He grinned. "Yeah, okay. I'm mad as hell. How could Shelly not do what the doctor said, Darce?"

"Parenting is complicated. She had another child, and got pregnant a few months later with a third. Maybe she wasn't feeling up to it."

His eyes glittered like onyx. "That's a stupid excuse."

"All right. Her husband probably wouldn't let her."

"Damn him. And her."

"As I said, what's important is what you do now for Braden."

"I guess. But I've only got him for a few months. What if Shelly won't follow through?"

"If you don't do anything now, there won't be anything to follow through on, will there?"

"No. I reckon not." He glanced at the list. "Do you know if the Hyde Point library has Internet access?"

"Yes, I imagine so. Don't you have a computer at your grandparents' house?"

His smile was affectionate. "No, Bart and Ada haven't entered the technological age. And I left my own machine in my bungalow in the Keys."

"You can use the computers at TenderTime."

"I wouldn't want to impose."

"It wouldn't be imposing. We have several in the kids' rooms, and my office has a huge unit. It's fast. You could get into the sites quickly and print the articles if you want."

He cocked his head. "That's real nice of you to offer, Miss Darcy."

"I'd like to return your kindness from last week when Meli got hurt."

"Now how can I refuse that?"

"You can't."

"When would be a good time?"

"Well, you could give yourself an hour before you're supposed to pick up Braden." She frowned. "The only problem is that the office is sometimes a zoo during the workday." She smiled. "Could you come later tonight? I'm doing some summer file cleaning after we close. Porter's watching the girls—they're having a sleep-over—so I can tackle that nasty job."

"I could come tonight."

"It's a date, then."

The words hung heavily in the air. He glanced uncomfortably at his watch. "I'm due at Hyde's in ten minutes. I'll see you later."

"Sure."

He watched her. "Thanks, Miss Darcy."

"You're welcome, Mr. Sloan."

TENDERTIME'S STATE-OF-THE-ART computer hummed like a well-tuned car in front of Hunter; the machine was a beauty, but Hunter's mind kept straying to the *beauty* in the small filing room beside the office, who was singing along with a Beatles CD.

He'd bitten back a grin when he'd arrived and found her in those same cutoff shorts she'd worn to a soccer practice. She was easy on the eyes on any given day, but with her red braid dangling down her back like a fiery rope she looked as cute as Daisy Mae from Li'l Abner. When he told her so, she'd giggled like a girl. But there was nothing girlish about her body in those down-home clothes.

Needing to get his mind off her, he forced himself to focus on the articles. He planned to skim them and print what looked important. That way he wouldn't have to stay here too long.

"Hey, Ju-u-de..."

Not that he minded being here.

Quickly, he scanned the first article.

Three to five percent of all children have ADD or ADHD, almost two million American children.

More boys than girls are affected.

So far, not so good.

He got to the symptoms...*hitting playmates for no reason...inability to focus...inattention, hyperactivity and impulsivity are the hallmarks of the disorder.*

Paige had told him all this, but he printed the information to reread at home.

He was into his third article when something caught his attention. *Other research shows that some attention disorders run in families.* Though his heartbeat quickened, he reminded himself that Paige had also told him the syndrome was genetically transmitted. But this was different. *Most children who have ADD/ADHD have at least one close relative who also has the disorder. One-third of all fathers with ADD/ADHD have children with it. Many times with identical twins, if one has the malady, so does the other.*

Hunter started to sweat. Could he...no, wait, he wouldn't jump to conclusions. "Just read," he told himself. *ADD/ADHD children can suffer from oppositional defiant disorder. They can be stubborn, have outbursts of temper or act belligerent. In school they are seen as troublemakers.*

It sounded like Braden. But the description was familiar for another reason. Hunter's high-school science teacher's favorite adjective for him had been "belligerent." His gym teacher had called him the worst troublemaker in the school.

"No, please," he whispered and read on.

The next paragraph. *Adults with ADD/ADHD often feel restless, easily bored, and seek novelty. They are often unable to establish intimate relationships with a member of the opposite sex.*

Hunter stared blindly at the screen. That was him.

"Hunter, are you all right?"

Looking up, he saw Darcy standing in front of him. He stood up abruptly. "I gotta go."

"Why?"

"I gotta go. Look, thanks for—"

"Hunter, you just got here."

"No, I can't, I don't—"

He headed for the door, hearing her call from behind. But he couldn't stop. Once on the street, he tried to remember where he'd parked his car. Down the road a piece. In front of Hannah's Place. He headed left.

Nothing registered until he felt a tug on his arm. "Hunter, wait."

He stopped and turned around. Darcy. "I—"

"Tell me what's going on."

"It's nothing. I just gotta get out of here."

"Come back inside. We can talk."

"No, I—" He yanked himself away, spun around and plowed into someone on the street.

The person said, "Watch it—oh, well!"

Hunter stared into the face of his sister.

Old accusations came blustering back through his consciousness. *You're a chip off the old block... You're just like him...*

He couldn't handle Hannah's contempt tonight. He just couldn't.

She looked past him. "Darcy, is that you? What are you..." Her expression turned pitying. It sliced Hunter in half. "Are you with *him?*" When Darcy said nothing more, Hannah added, "I'm shocked."

Hunter felt his stomach hollow out at the despising tone of his sister's voice. He took off across the street, once again hearing Darcy call his name. There was a park in the center of town. He'd spent time smoking and drinking in it as a teen. Breaking into a jog, feeling like the loser he'd been then, he headed toward the entrance, needing some time alone. He reached it quickly and made his way to the center, where there was a gazebo. Though only eight-thirty, it was getting dark and the trees shadowed him even more. He dropped down onto a bench and stared out into the night.

That was where Darcy found him, his shoulders slumped. She had no idea what had happened but she intended to find out. "Hunter?"

His head snapped around. She couldn't see his eyes,

they were shadowed in the darkness. "I'd like to be alone."

She had a feeling everybody left this man alone.

"Not on your life." She sat down beside him. "Tell me what upset you."

"You wouldn't understand. Not a woman like you." He started to stand. "I'm goin'."

She pulled him down. "What do you mean 'a woman like me'?"

He stared at her. Then cautiously, he lifted his hand and his knuckles brushed her cheek. His touch was velvety soft and very sexy. "You're good, Darcy. You've lived a fine life, made something of yourself. You can't possibly understand a guy like me."

Now there's an irony, her inner voice said.

He dropped his arm and glanced up at the sky. "Hannah's shock over the fact that you were with me is warranted."

"What is Hannah to you?" Darcy asked.

"My sister."

"Your *sister?*"

"Yeah, so she knows what I really am. Now, let me go before I cause any more trouble."

"No." Facing him, she said, "Do you remember when you asked me how I knew Nora Whitman?"

"Yeah, but..."

"When I was sixteen, my mother put me into the newly opened Serenity House."

"What?"

"I was one of the original residents."

"You?"

"Uh-huh."

"Why?"

"Well, it probably had something to do with carousing in bars around town, staying out all night, dating the absolute wildest boys in school.''

''I don't believe it.''

''Believe it. Jade called me bum gum...I even married a bum, Johnny O'Malley.''

He shook his head.

''So, don't you tell me, Hunter Sloan, that I don't understand how you grew up. I do. Now, what just happened?''

He watched her for a long time, then finally said, ''I don't know where to start.''

''Start with the computer.''

He ran a hand over his face. ''I gave this thing...this ADHD...to Braden.''

''Hunter, Paige *said* it was congenital. That doesn't mean that it's your fault.''

''She may have said that, but one of those articles I read was about adults with ADHD who've had it from childhood. It stated outright that ADHD tends to run in families. One-third of fathers with this thing have children with it. Usually all ADHD sufferers have one close relative with the disorder.''

''But that doesn't mean you had it.''

The look he gave her was so grave, it broke her heart. ''When I was young, I was just like they described, Darce. Like living in a kaleidoscope of sound and images. Everything shiftin' in my head. I never could concentrate. So I acted up. The articles call it oppositional defiance disorder. I picked fights, bullied kids, taunted teachers. I had ADHD. I know I did. Even in my adult life, I've been restless, easily bored. I went—go—after novelties and excitement like they're an addiction. Just like the articles said.''

Darcy was still.

Because it all made sense. She remembered his playing with the blinds, fidgeting when he'd been sitting too long, needing to move. But instead of the revelation turning her off, it sparked anger inside her. He'd been a troublemaker because of his ADHD and had never been helped.

"And," he said, disgusted, "I gave it to my son."

His anguish drew her from her thoughts. "Look, if Braden needed glasses, or allergy shots, or had diabetes, would you think that was your fault?"

He didn't say anything.

"Be honest."

"Probably not. That'd be an accident of nature."

"Well, then..."

Sighing heavily, he sank back against the bench. Something else occurred to her. Reaching over, she took his hand in hers. He stilled, then laced their fingers. "That's not all that's got you upset, is it?"

Slowly he shook his head.

"Tell me."

"It's selfish."

"Nobody's here but you and me. You can be unselfish in a few minutes," she said, parroting his comments to her that night she cried in his arms.

He raised his face to the sky. "All those years, all those years, I just thought I was *bad*. Inside. When really..."

"When really you had a documented disorder."

"Yeah. Looks that way."

"And nobody helped you with it."

Again, the shake of his head. "The school. My family." His face darkened. "Everyone just wrote me off. Especially Hannah. I got in some pretty big trouble and embarrassed her at school and around town. Apparently I still do.''

Darcy squeezed his hand. ''I'm so sorry.''

''Maybe I could have made something of myself if somebody had helped me manage this.''

Her throat aching with emotion, she said, ''I think you turned out mighty fine.''

He smiled. Then took in a breath. ''I won't let people ignore this with Braden.'' He straightened. ''Even if I only have him for a few more months. I'm gonna help him and force Shelly to follow through when I give him back.''

''There you go.''

''I want to read those other articles. They talk about treatment.''

''Now, that's more like it. Let's go back to the office.'' She stood. But he held on to her hand and tugged her back down. ''Darce?''

She looked over at him. Some of the tension was gone, softening his angular features. She watched his lips. For a brief moment, she wondered if they'd be soft or insistent. Warm or hot. Urgent or...

''You got a strange look on your face. What're you thinking?''

''You don't want to know, Hunter.'' Her voice was a whisper.

He leaned over. Brushed his lips on her forehead. She heard a chuckle, was so close she could feel his chest rumble. ''Hard to believe you were almost as bad as me, darlin'.''

But right at that moment it wasn't hard for *her* to believe it. Hunter Sloan made her think of doing all kinds of bad things again.

With him.

CHAPTER SEVEN

"WHO WOULDA THOUGHT?" Jade said archly as she dangled her feet in Paige's pool on one of the clearest days of the summer. Her irreverent gaze swept over the other four women—all original residents of Serenity House. "We look like the Junior League."

Charly Donovan, holding Taylor Morelli's youngest child in the shade of an umbrella table, snorted. "Yeah, sure. That zebra bikini you're wearing would give the Junior League a heart attack."

From the shallow end of the pool, Jewel, Jade's three-year-old, pulled her fingers out of her mouth. "Don't you like Mommy's bathing suit?" Since she wore one identical to it, Charly frowned. "Oh, sweetie, no, I love it. I was just teasing Mommy."

"Beck teases Mommy," Jewel said, smiling.

Paige sat on the steps inside the pool, dunking little Sammy's feet in the aquamarine water. His squeals echoed in the quiet afternoon. She gave her sister a sideways glance. "I'll just bet."

Claire, who mirrored Paige's actions with Suzy, asked, "Who's Beck?"

"A friend of ours." Jade gave Paige a be-quiet look.

Darcy intervened. This was tense territory between the sisters, as Beck was Jewel's father and married to someone else. "Think Meli and your two boys are okay downstairs in the rec room, Taylor?" she asked.

Looking tired, Taylor smiled and closed her eyes. "Yes. Jacob's as responsible as his father. He's only ten, but he'll watch over the other two." She sighed and nestled into the padded chaise, pretty in her pink flowered suit. "This is great. Thanks for having us here, Paige."

"Hey, we girls have to stick together." The five women, who now lived locally, had made a pact at Nora's wedding to try to get together once a month. They'd promised to call Anabelle in Seattle to include her long distance. Today they had gathered at Paige's house, which was right across from where Darcy lived.

Darcy sat in partial sun, wearing a sensible black Speedo, rubbing lotion on her fair skin. She watched each of her former house sisters enjoy a pleasant afternoon by Paige's pool. *When I was sixteen, my mother put me into the newly opened Serenity House.*

She could still see Hunter's dark-as-night eyes widen with surprise at her confession. They had been hazy with hurt when his sister dissed him on the street; they'd been incredibly sad when he described how he felt about Braden's ADHD. And just before he'd brushed his knuckles down her cheek and kissed her forehead, those eyes had glowed with desire. *It's hard to believe you were as bad as I was, darlin'.*

"Earth to Darcy," Jade said, splashing her with water. The drops prickled her hot skin. "Claire's talking to you."

Darcy saw that while she'd been daydreaming, Paige's twins had been dried off and set in their portable cribs under a tree. Claire and Jewel had gotten out of the water, donned robes, and stood before her hand in hand. "I'm going down to the playroom with Meli and the boys," Claire said. "I'll watch Jewel."

"Okay, sweetie."

Claire hesitated. "Mama, can Jacob and Jed come to my birthday party, with Braden and Jewel?"

"If Taylor says it's okay." Darcy wondered why Claire didn't want a birthday party with other eleven-year-olds. Instead, she wanted to invite the children of Darcy's friends.

When Claire and Jewel left, Jade hopped into the water, but turned around and braced her arms on the rim of the pool. Her green eyes gleamed with trouble-in-the-making. "Hey, Red, if Braden Sloan comes to Claire's birthday party, will Hunky Hunter come with him?"

Darcy felt a flush creep up her cheeks. "I couldn't say."

"No? Seems like you've been spending a lot of time with the guy."

Having done a few laps, Paige surfaced next to Jade. "What are we talking about?"

"Hunky Hunter."

"Mmm, he is yum."

Darcy rolled her eyes. "Weren't we going to call Anabelle?"

Clasping the baby to her demure one-piece navy suit, Charly glanced at her watch. "Not for a bit yet. So, Hunter Sloan's yummy?"

"Who *is* he?" Taylor asked, yawning.

Trying to detour the conversation—and with genuine concern for her friend—Darcy asked, "Aren't you sleeping well, Taylor?"

"Not right now. It comes and goes."

"Still having the nightmares?" Paige wore her doctor's expression. All of them worried about Taylor, who'd come to Serenity House with amnesia and had never regained her memory.

"Off and on. Nick wants me to see a psychologist again, but I tried that, and it didn't work."

"I think you should go," Paige said. "I, um, had personal experience with one lately."

Taylor sat up, and Charly leaned forward. Jade touched Paige's arm.

"I'm going to search for my daughter. I'm finally ready to do it."

As they oohed and aahed over Paige's decision, Darcy was grateful the spotlight was off Hunter. Yummy Hunter.

"Jade has some news, too," Paige said when she finished her story.

The women listened attentively.

"I got a job at Rascal's. Bartending a couple of nights a week."

"Who's going to watch Jewel?" Darcy wanted to know.

"My landlady, Mrs. Stanwyck." The woman had been Jade's English teacher in high school and Jewel and Jade had recently moved into her duplex. "Jewel will be in bed by the time I leave, so it shouldn't be too much of a problem. I'd feel bad about imposing, except that Mrs. S. is really lonely since she retired and she seems to love having us there."

"So, you're going to be working with Hunter?" Paige asked.

Oh, brother, Darcy thought.

Jade darted a mischievous glance at Darcy. "Yep. I'm thinking of asking him out."

She tried not to take the bait. Jade had always teased

her about boys. Always flirted with her boyfriends. Not that Hunter was her boyfriend or anything.

Okay, Darce. Whatever you say. But I remember how close he got the other night.

"He's only in town for a few months," Darcy said evenly. "I wouldn't get too involved with him if I were you." She frowned. Saying the words out loud made them real. For her and for Claire. Ever since Hunter had asked her to help out with the soccer team, Claire thought he hung the moon. And, not for the first time, Darcy worried about how much Claire liked Hunter, how often she talked about him, how she looked at him during practices, how she even took to Tramp. Oh, God, Darcy hoped Claire wasn't getting attached to another man, like her father, who'd be out of their lives all too soon.

"I don't need months," Jade quipped. "I'd settle for a few weeks with Hunter."

"It would probably ruin you for other men," Paige joked.

For a minute, Darcy pictured Jade entwined with a naked Hunter on a king-size bed. Because the thought hurt, she stood. "I'm getting more lemonade. Anybody want some?"

When she returned from the kitchen, she sat under the umbrella with Charly. "How's Porter doing?"

"Great." Charly smoothed down the baby's feathery hair. Little Isabella had fallen asleep in Charly's lap. "You're a good influence on Porter."

Darcy remembered her own babies and how she'd wanted another after Meli. "Hard to believe, isn't it?"

"Not for me. I always thought God gave us troubles in our youth so we could help others later on."

"Well, that's certainly true about you."

"Don't put yourself down, Darce. You, too."

Darcy sighed.

"Something wrong?"

"Nah." She looked around. "This is perfect here, isn't it?"

Towel-drying her hair, Jade joined them at the table. "Hey, nothing less than perfect for our Paige."

Paige came up behind her sister and headlocked her. "Man, you're in rare form today. Why are you picking on everybody?"

"It's going to be a full moon tonight. I can't help it."

Paige glanced over at Taylor, who'd fallen asleep in the chaise. "She's not okay, is she?"

"It must be a terrible thing not to know where you came from," Charly said. "What you were like for the first seventeen years of your life."

"Sometimes I wish I couldn't remember what I was like then." Darcy heard the yearning in her own voice.

"There's your problem, Darce." Jade turned serious. "You spend all your time trying to squash your feelings, and not having enough fun."

"I have fun. David and I go out to a lot of fun places."

"Bor-ing," Jade commented, just like the little voice in Darcy's head.

Paige picked up the cordless phone sitting on the table. "I'm calling Anabelle before World War Three breaks out."

A few minutes later, Paige spoke into the mouthpiece, "Hey, Detective." She listened, chuckled. "So, who are you playing these days?" Anabelle was an undercover cop. "I know, I know you can't tell me."

Each woman spoke with Anabelle. When Darcy took her turn, she said, "Hi, kiddo. How are you?"

"Sleepy."

"We wake you up?"

"Uh-huh."

"Sorry."

"No, it's okay. I wish I was there with you. So, what's new in Hyde Point?"

"Oh, something is. Remember the old Winslow place?"

Anabelle cleared her throat on the other end. "Yeah."

"Nathan Hyde's..." She remembered, too late, what Anabelle had told them at the lake before Nora's wedding. "Oh, geez, honey, I'm sorry, I forgot what you said about him that night at the lake."

"No, it's okay. What's Nathan up to?"

"He bought the house. He's remodeling the whole thing, inside and out."

"With Hunky Hunter," Jade yelled through cupped hands.

Darcy said, "I wonder why he bought it."

"Who knows." Anabelle's voice had gone neutral. "So, tell me about the girls."

Darcy sighed and cursed her loose tongue. Sometimes she did revert to that young girl, who never thought before she spoke. And often it had negative consequences.

She thought of Hunter Sloan. Of Claire's feelings for him. Of her own. Speaking of negative consequences...

HUNTER TRIED to stay calm. *Go, kid,* he cheered mentally. He wanted so much for his son to be a success, and if his guess was right, sports just might be Braden's vehicle.

Practically holding his breath, he watched as the boy dribbled the soccer ball down the field. In a quick fake, Braden darted to the left, still in control of the ball, and headed toward the goal. With the skill of a pro, he slowed and booted in a perfect shot. The team and the spectators erupted just as the ref blew the whistle to signal the end of the game.

Braden leaped into the air, threw his small arms up and shouted, "Yes!" Then he turned and scanned the crowd, his gaze landing on Hunter. Braden grinned and ran toward the sidelines. Without warning, he threw himself at Hunter. Catching the boy in midflight, Hunter was speechless as he held on to his son in the very first physical contact Braden had ever initiated. "I did it! I did it!" Braden yelled.

Somehow finding his voice, Hunter managed to say, "You sure did, Champ," and held on. It was at that moment that Hunter fell in love for the very first time. With his own son.

Kids and adults crowded around, breaking the moment. Hunter tucked it away, deep in his heart, to take out, examine and enjoy later. Standing, he turned and, from a few yards back, he saw Darcy watching him from the crowd. She was with the teenager she'd introduced as Porter, the girls' baby-sitter. Smiling, she nodded at Braden, and the connection between them crackled through the mild end-of-summer night. He knew she wasn't smiling about the win.

Surrounded by parents, he reveled in the camaraderie, so foreign to him. "Great job, Coach... Did you see that kid fly... Good idea, Sloan, to put the goalie up..."

Two mothers approached him. Both hugged him, as

did his assistant coach, Julie. "Way to go, Hunter," she said.

"Hey, Braden saved the day." He caught sight of red-as-flame hair over his shoulder. Meli was staring narrow-eyed at the fuss. "And the rest of the team deserves credit. Meli O'Malley had three great saves, and Sara Johnson scored, too."

"The teams usually go to Fuzzy's for ice cream after a game. Come with us, Hunter," Julie suggested.

"Sure. My treat."

"Mmm. Not this time. We want to…treat you." It took him a minute to realize she was flirting.

As the kids dispersed, he turned and found Darcy had come to the sidelines. Claire held Tramp's leash now, and he noticed the dog was closer to her than he usually got to people.

Hunter winked at the little girl. "Looks like you got a friend there, Miss Claire."

Claire blushed. He turned to her mother. Darcy wore those half pants, half shorts again, this time with a top the color of orange Popsicles. "Nice job, Coach."

"Thanks." Pushing back his red baseball cap, Hunter noticed that Darcy had gotten some sun. He wondered what she'd done today. He'd wondered about her all day, after what she'd told him last night.

It probably had something to do with carousing in bars around town, staying out all night, dating the absolute wildest boys in school.

His hands curled. She'd felt like pure gold leaning in close to his body, holding on to him. Her scent—something light and flowery—had combined with the summer-night smell of newly mowed grass and rich loam, and had stayed with him long after he'd gotten home.

Something had happened between them on the bench

in the gazebo. Some bridge had been crossed. He hadn't slept well, pondering it, knowing it was a bad idea to think too much about this woman, but unable to stop himself. He was drawn to her like a magnet and couldn't seem to stop the momentum.

The crowd dispersed, and everybody piled into their respective cars.

On the way to the ice-cream store, Braden said, "I did good, huh?"

Reaching back, he ruffled the kid's hair. Braden did *not* flinch this time. "Yeah, son, you did."

"I never did good in sports before."

"Did you play in Florida?"

"I started on a team. Hank made me quit 'cause he didn't want Mom gone so much."

Son of a bitch! "I'm sorry to hear that. You're a natural."

"Can I call Mom tonight and tell her about the game?"

The kid missed his mother, Hunter knew that. Even though half of the time Braden wouldn't talk to Shelly when she called—dutifully—three times a week.

This morning, after he'd dropped Braden at daycare, Hunter had phoned *her*. She'd sounded tired—another reminder of the baby she carried.

"Is everything okay with Braden?" she'd asked immediately.

"No, Shelly, it's not. What the hell is this about his doctor recommending some tests for ADHD and you sayin' no to it?"

She was silent a long time. "Hank says ADHD's just an excuse for behaving bad."

"Oh, and Hank knows more than the doctors?"

"He says his boss at the plant told him."

"Sound medical advice on that front." There was a guilty silence. "Well, I'm gonna pursue it."

"Okay." Something about her tone.

"Shelly, is there anything you're not tellin' me about Hank and Braden?"

"No, they get along great."

And I'm a monkey's uncle.

"What are you going to do for Braden?" she asked, changing the subject.

"There's a lot of choices. For all of 'em, you're gonna have to keep up whatever I do when I give him back."

"I'll try."

"That's not good enough."

"Look, I gotta go. Tell Braden I love him."

Yeah, sure…

When Hunter pulled his truck into the parking lot of Fuzzy's Famous Ice-Cream Parlor, almost everybody was there. The line snaked around the lot, the kids hopped about excitedly and the parents chattered. Braden bolted out of the truck with Tramp and headed to the crowd. Hunter saw Claire, who'd been watching the road—for them?—cross to Braden and take the dog's leash from him. In a good mood, and distracted by the accolades, Braden willingly handed over Tramp's leash.

Hunter approached her. "Hey, Miss Claire, you don't have to baby-sit Tramp anymore."

"I want to." Her eyes widened. "It's all right, isn't it?"

"It's just fine. He likes you." He ruffled Claire's hair. "I'm much obliged."

Again the girl blushed, then led Tramp to a playground off to the side. When they reached it, Claire picked up a stick. She threw it. Hunter was shocked to see the dog scamper after it.

He joined the line. Darcy was a few places ahead with Porter. He noticed how the white cotton hugged Darcy's bottom real nice and the pretty little top caressed her bare shoulders. Those had been kissed by the sun, too. Just then, she turned around and caught him staring. Her face flushed. "Hi, Coach."

"Hey, Miss Darcy." He nodded to Meli. "Hey, Mel. You had great saves," he said again.

She smiled. But frowned at Braden. Uh-oh.

After everybody was served their ice cream, the parents gathered at picnic tables near the playground. Hunter let the soft croon of voices—first about the game, then about starting school, about kids in general—bathe him in its warmth. Never in his life, as a kid or an adult, had he been part of normal talk like this. He was shocked at how comforting it was.

Darcy sat two tables down, but her glances kept coming his way.

His went her way, too. He wondered if she was feeling what he felt about last night.

When twilight fell, many of the parents drifted away. "Can we stay?" Braden asked. "I wanna swing."

"Sure."

He took off with a boy, Josh, from the team. Hunter caught sight of Claire with the dog by the jungle gym now. He rose and crossed to her. "Want me to take Tramp so you can go play?"

She glanced at the other kids. "It's okay. I like being with Tramp." She peered up at him shyly, and dug her toe in the dirt. "Coach?"

"Yeah?"

"Mama said I could ask Braden to my birthday party on Saturday."

"I know. He's excited about coming."

She reached out and petted Tramp. The dog raised his head for closer contact.

Now, don't that beat all.

Claire said, "Um, I was…"

Hunter watched the little girl carefully. She was embarrassed by something. He knelt down on one knee. "Something wrong, darlin'?"

"No. I just thought, maybe, if you weren't doing anything, maybe you and Tramp could come to my party, too. Mama said Dr. Kendrick and Dr. Chandler are coming. And the Morellis. And Jade, with Jewel. So there'll be adults there."

A soft sweep of emotion coursed through Hunter. It took him a minute to realize what he felt was pleasure. "Why, I'd be honored to come to your birthday party, Miss Claire. Now let me see, you're gonna be sixteen, right?"

She giggled. "No, eleven."

"You sure 'bout that?"

"Uh-huh."

"If you say so." He looked up to see that Darcy had come over with Porter.

"Hi, guys."

Hunter stood.

Claire grinned widely. "Coach said he can come to my party."

Darcy's face shadowed, but she smiled. "Great."

"I'm gonna tell Meli and Braden." Claire looked at Porter. "Wanna come?"

"Sure," the pretty dark-haired teen murmured.

Darcy and Hunter watched the two girls scamper away.

Hunter's self-protective armor surfaced. "Something wrong?"

"No." She wrapped her arms around her waist, clasped her elbows.

"Don't you want me at Claire's party?"

She whirled toward him. "Of course I do." She glanced at the swings. "But…well, you're leaving town in a few months, right?"

He patted Tramp's head. "Yep. Good old Hyde Point will be history for me again."

"You hate this town."

I did. "Let's just say it has bad memories."

"I don't blame you." She waited. "You know, the girls…they were badly hurt when Johnny just left."

"Johnny's your ex-husband." He couldn't believe the jealousy that streaked through him at the mention of the guy's name.

"Yeah. He just took off one day, and we never saw him again. Claire cried for weeks. Meli was a brat for months."

"What 'bout you?"

She faced him. "Me?"

"Did you cry? Were you mad?"

"No, it was a relief. I just felt bad for the girls."

"I see. And you're worried about exactly what now?" But, God help him, he knew.

"It's just that…I'm afraid Claire's getting attached to you, Hunter."

He stuck his hands in his pockets. "Nah, it's just Tramp here she likes."

Darcy shook her head. "No, it's you." Then after a

long silence, she added, "We've got to admit what's going on here."

Hunter just stared at her.

"Both my girls like you, Hunter."

How about you? Do you like me? "Something wrong with that?"

"It's not good to get close to somebody who's going to be out of your life soon."

"No, I reckon it's not." It *wasn't*.

"I don't want anybody to get hurt."

"I don't want that either."

She faced him. "So we agree on this?"

Suddenly he wondered if they were still talking about Claire and Meli. "Yeah. I'll make sure the O'Malley women don't get too attached to me." He picked up Tramp's leash. "Thanks for the heads-up on this."

"You still can come to the party. Claire would be devastated if you didn't."

That was the last thing he wanted. But he would never hurt the child if he could help it. "Okay. After, I'll make myself scarce." Damn, he couldn't control the raggedness of his own voice.

Her eyes were liquid with some emotion. He tried to see if she really meant what she said or if she was hiding other feelings—maybe that he wasn't good enough to be around her girls.

He couldn't find any hidden agenda in those green depths. In fact, she seemed upset. But old patterns died hard and, as he walked away, his heart hurt. Bad.

Well, rejection did that to a guy.

THE SUN SHONE DOWN on Claire's eleventh birthday with benevolent warmth. In the backyard of the carriage house, which sprawled invitingly into deep woods,

Darcy surveyed the scene. Jade, Taylor, her husband, Nick, and their baby, Paige and Ian and their twins, sat under a tree. The older kids were playing some game in a circle off to the side, Tramp standing nearby to watch.

Darcy had looked forward to this party for weeks, but today her heart was heavy. It was because of Hunter, who kept to himself, wearing a black, silky-looking shirt, black jeans and a black scowl on his face. He'd been excruciatingly polite to her since he'd arrived with an excited Braden and a demure Tramp. She knew she was probably the cause of Hunter's somber mood.

All week she wondered if she'd done the right thing by warning him about Claire's attachment to him. He'd been reserved the few times she'd seen him dropping Braden off, and downright distant at this week's game and practices. The last thing she'd wanted was to hurt him, to make him feel bad, but she had to protect her kids, didn't she? They all needed to stay detached from Hunter Sloan.

Then why'd you wear your hair down, Darce?

She touched the long locks that hung in waves to her waist. Why, indeed?

Drawn to him, she crossed the lawn. As Hunter sipped a can of soda, he watched her approach. She stopped by the tree he leaned against. "Having a good time?"

Up close, his dark eyes were wary. His yard-wide shoulders tensed. "Yeah, sure."

"I'm glad you could come."

Looking away, he mumbled, "Uh-huh."

"Hunter, we need to talk about what I said the other night. I didn't mean—"

"Darcy?"

Swiveling around, Darcy found David behind her. Dressed casually in expensive golf wear—he'd come directly from the course—he held a wrapped gift in one hand. With his other, he drew Darcy away from Hunter and kissed her cheek. Then he looked inquiringly at Hunter.

"Um, David Carrington, Hunter Sloan."

"Nice to meet you." As Hunter reached out to shake David's hand, Darcy noticed the aluminum can was crumpled in his other hand. Her gaze flew to his eyes, but they were hooded and unreadable. He pushed away from the tree. "I'm gonna check on the kids."

After he left, David slid his arm around her waist. "He looks familiar."

"Maybe you remember him from Rascal's." *You know, David, the night you were at the bar and you made that crack about being bad...*

"Since when did you start hanging around with bartenders?"

She whirled on him. "What's wrong with bartenders?"

He held up a palm. "Nothing." He studied her. "Is something going on, Darcy?"

"No." She took the present. "I'll put this on the table for you. I've got to go in and get the rest of the food ready."

"Need some help?" Jade had come up behind her.

"Sure."

Ian called out, "Hey, Carrington, come over here. I want to ask you something."

Smiling weakly at David, she headed to the house with Jade. Once inside, Darcy took out hot dogs while Jade garnished the salads. When she finished, Jade leaned against the counter and folded her arms across her chest. Big turquoise earrings dangled from her ears as she shook her head. "What's wrong with Hunky Hunter?"

"Don't call him that," Darcy snapped.

Jade was quiet.

Darcy knew she'd just given her friend ammunition to tease her.

Lightly, Jade touched Darcy's arm. "What's wrong, Darce?"

At her solicitous tone, Darcy was appalled to find her eyes tearing. She blurted out, "I think I insulted him after the game the other night."

"What did you say?" When Darcy told her, Jade said, "Yep, you insulted him, all right."

"I didn't mean to."

"Darcy, with his past, and his sensitivity to Hyde Point, he was bound to be hurt by what you said."

"How do you know about all that?"

"We've worked together a couple of nights at Rascal's."

Jealousy, hot and potent, snaked inside Darcy.

Staring at Darcy's expression, Jade shook her head. "No, nothing's happened between us yet, but if I don't snag him, somebody else will. He's a great guy, inside as well as out."

"He's leaving in a few months, Jade. I can't afford a Hunter Sloan in my life."

"Well, then, best get over whatever put that look on your face." She glanced up as David walked through the door. "I'll take these out," she said, picking up the salads.

David crossed to her. From behind, he circled her waist with his arms. "Can I see you tonight?"

"I can't go out, David. It's Claire's birthday."

"Get a sitter. I miss you. You've been busy lately." He nuzzled her neck and she shivered—but not from pleasure. She remembered what Hunter had felt like up close, how virile and unique his scent was. David smelled like expensive cologne. She drew away, horrified that she was actually comparing the man who held her with the man she wished was holding her. "I need to get this food out. Help me carry the meat."

When the hot dogs were cooked and the rest of the food set out, everybody gathered around the serving table. Just as Ian and Paige approached it, one of the babies began to cry. Ian shook his head. "Never fails. As soon as we start to eat."

"I'll get him," Paige offered.

"No, you need sustenance. You were up with them in the night." He kissed her nose and headed toward his kids.

When Ian reached the stroller, the other baby began to cry. A beleaguered Paige turned, but Hunter, last in line, called out, "I'll get her. Go ahead and eat, Paige." He crossed to the carriage and scooped out the child.

Ian smiled gratefully. "Hey, thanks, buddy."

"No problem." He cuddled the baby close to his chest, just like Darcy had taught him. Then he began to walk her.

Darcy closed her eyes to block out the sight of the two handsome men with the two tiny babies, chatting under the tree. But she could still see Hunter's big hands soothe the child's back.

An hour later, the babies were fast asleep again, and Claire was the center of attention as she opened her gifts. "Oh, Jewel," Claire announced excitedly. "This is great."

Darcy looked down at the eye shadows, lip gloss and brushes. "Ja-ade!"

"Come on, Darce. Let your kid live a little." *Even if you won't,* her friend's look said.

"Can I use it, Mama?" Claire asked.

"On special occasions. Not for school, though."

Smiling broadly, Claire reached for the next package. It was a beautiful set of books—*Anne of Green Gables*—from Paige. "You got me my own copies!"

"Well, sweetie, you like to read them so much at my house."

Three gifts later—David's was an expensive stuffed dog, Taylor's a set of perfumes and CDs from Sara—Claire picked up the last package. She read the card and glanced up at Hunter. Next to him, Braden was kicking a phantom soccer ball, not paying attention to the gifts. But Claire only had eyes for Hunter, anyway. "It says from Braden, Coach and Tramp."

Everybody laughed as she ripped off the pink paper. Darcy watched over her daughter's shoulder as Claire drew out a delicate silver charm bracelet from inside a box. The little girl's mouth dropped. Dangling from one of the hooks was a soccer-ball charm. "Oh, Coach, this is so beautiful."

He smiled down at Claire, and Darcy realized in that instant how much Hunter had come to care for her older daughter. The awareness made her want to weep.

Claire turned the charm over. "Oh!"

Darcy put her hand on Claire's shoulder. "What does it say, honey?"

"Coach's helper." A huge grin, worthy of Christmas morning, claimed Claire's lips. Darcy was shocked by it. How long had it been since she'd seen such pleasure on her little girl's face?

That grin stayed there, too, through Darcy's gift of a monster of a boom box that Claire had begged for. Still, her daughter's gaze kept going to the charm bracelet gracing her left wrist.

Darcy was glad when Paige suggested, as planned, that everybody retreat to her house for a swim. Excitedly, the kids, who wore their suits underneath their clothes, grabbed their stuff and headed across the street.

Braden darted ahead with the gang. Hunter called out, "I'll get your backpack and be right there." He went into the house.

David grabbed her hand. "I have to go. I've got a meeting at the club I can't miss."

"It was nice of you to come." In truth, Darcy felt only relief that he was leaving. It turned to chagrin when he took her into his arms, pulled her close and gave her a full-on-the mouth kiss. Then he drew back. "I'll call you later."

She watched him walk around the side of the house, a mass of emotion roiling inside her. Closing her eyes, she brought her hand to her mouth. This was unconscionable. Letting one man kiss her when—

"He's what you want, isn't he?"

She spun around. Hunter.

"Excuse me?"

His eyes were hard as he walked toward her, holding Braden's backpack. "Carrington. He's what you want. For yourself. For your girls."

"I..."

Hunter came up flush with her. "Hey, it's cool, Darce. He's respectable. He makes a lot of money. He's what you should have in your life."

Too bad he doesn't make your pulse spin. Like it's doing right now.

"He's not going anywhere, Hunter," she whispered meaningfully.

"That, too."

"No," she said. "That's most of it."

"Yeah, sure."

"You don't believe me."

"'Course I believe you." He shifted the pack from one hand to the other. "Why wouldn't I?"

"You seem…sad…today."

He shrugged his shoulders. "Naw. Not me."

Darcy recognized bravado when she saw it. "Hunter, please know I'm just trying to protect my girls." *Myself.*

"I know you're trying to protect your girls." He swallowed hard. "From me."

"I hurt you. I can tell."

"Look, I gotta go." His voice was raw.

She grabbed his arm. The muscles of his bare skin pulsed beneath her fingers. She glanced up. His eyes flared. His lips parted. With a blinding slice of desire, she wanted those lips on her. Everywhere.

"Let me go, Miss Darcy," he said resignedly.

Because of his tone, tears welled in her eyes.

He stilled, then raised his hand, capturing a renegade tear in his fingertips. "What's this all about?"

Her gaze locked with his, she shook her head.

He drew in a heavy breath. "I'm gonna get out of here, darlin', before we both do or say something we'll regret."

Turning on his heel, he strode around the side of the house. Stunned, Darcy stood still, feeling as if she'd just lost something very rare and very precious.

Go after him. Maybe he'll stay. Or maybe you could

*leave. There are a lot of options. At least get to know
him better.*

"No."

Go, Darcy.

"No!"

Then you're an idiot.

"Better that than bum gum."

*Oh, yeah. A bum picks out a perfect gift for your
kid...holds Suzy like she was spun glass...holds you
when you let down with him like you do with nobody
else.*

Oh, God.

She darted around the house. On the front lawn by
the driveway, she saw that Hunter had gotten to the road
and was waiting for a car to go by.

"Hunter," she called out. He stopped as he was
about to cross. "Hunter, wait." She was running now.

Slowly, he turned around, surprise replacing the sadness on his face. She stopped a few feet away from him.
Saw his dark eyes widen and his eyebrows arch.

"I—"

A car distracted her. A big white Cadillac pulled into
her driveway. When it stopped, the door opened, and
her mother and stepfather got out. Marian circled the
car and crossed to Darcy. "Hello, dear." She kissed her
cheek. "I hope we're not too late for the party. We
came back early from our cruise just for it."

Darcy stared at her mother.

Marian turned to Hunter. "And who is this?"

Shaking herself, Darcy said, "Mom, this is Hunter
Sloan. He coaches Meli's soccer team."

Hunter's eyes narrowed on Darcy. She hadn't said he
was her friend. "Mom, he's my—"

But Marian's stiffened shoulders and gaping mouth

silenced her. "H-Hunter Sloan, who grew up in Hyde Point?"

"Yes, ma'am."

"I thought you moved away."

At Marian's tone, Hunter frowned, but said nothing. Marian looked to Darcy.

"Yes," Darcy explained. "He moved away, but he came back this summer. Mom, what is it? How do you know Hunter?"

Her mother's lips thinned and her face hardened. "I know this man because when he was sixteen, he stole my car."

CHAPTER EIGHT

"FIRST, TELL ME exactly how you know him." Marian sat in her breakfast nook, sipping Earl Grey tea. Smartly dressed in chic cruise wear, she scowled over the rim of the china cup. Jeremy had gone upstairs—to give mother and daughter some privacy, Darcy suspected—so they were alone in her mother's colonial mansion.

Cringing at Marian's disapproving tone, Darcy tried to steel herself against it. "His son, Braden, signed up at TenderTime just as you left for the cruise. Shortly after that, Hunter took the job coaching Meli's soccer team."

Her mother sniffed. "I'm surprised the town let him back within the city limits."

Darcy's heart bumped in her chest. An image of the police chief's face when she was fifteen flashed before her. She and her current loser boyfriend had been climbing into a window of the school—which she'd broken—with "intent to do mischief," the cops had said. Darcy and whatever-his-name-was had planned to shellac the blackboard in her Latin teacher's room. The woman had embarrassed Darcy the day before for flirting with the guys in the class.

Since it wasn't the first time the cop had hauled her in, he said, *You're a menace to this town. They shouldn't let you within the city limits…*

"What exactly did Hunter do, Mom? You said he stole your car?"

"More precisely, your father's car."

Marian almost never spoke about Sean Shannon, so Darcy was doubly interested.

"You were too little to remember, but Sean was at Zeke's café, his usual Friday-night haunt." Again Marian sniffed. "He parked his vintage 1950 convertible right on the street and left the keys in it."

"That was stupid."

"Your father was not a rocket scientist."

Darcy didn't say anything. She'd always wondered about the man who'd run off when she was three, but of course, Marian wouldn't talk about him. She was embarrassed by her first marriage, by her past, really.

Just like you, Darcy, baby.

"In any case, Hunter Sloan came along and took the car for a spin around town." Marian shook her head. "Your father called it a joyride."

Darcy cocked her head.

"The police pulled Sloan over for speeding before he could return the car, he said. As usual, Sean wanted to let the matter go." She straightened. "After I discovered all the previous things the boy had done, I insisted we press charges."

"What happened?"

"Sloan went to Industry School for Boys just outside of Rochester for the rest of his freshman year."

"He was only in ninth grade?"

"Bad genes manifest themselves early."

Darcy shivered in the air-conditioning. "You don't mean that, Mother. Please, as a proprietor of a daycare, tell me you don't mean that."

"Of course I mean it. Hunter's father was a drunk.

It's no wonder Amelia left town right after Hunter was born.''

Darcy's stomach lurched. Poor Hunter.

"Only Hannah Mitchum managed to make something of herself, and that was because she had Larry's parents to take her in.''

"Take her in?''

Thoughtfully, Marian sipped her tea. "Yes, her senior year, she lived with the Mitchums. Then she and Larry married as soon as they graduated.''

And left Hunter alone with a drunken father. All the women in his life had abandoned him. *Even you.*

"So you see why I'm upset that he's back in town. That he has any connection with you at all.''

The thing was, Darcy could see. If she hadn't known Hunter, she'd have worried, too. "Yes, Mother, I can see your point. But Hunter's changed. He's a great father to Braden.''

Marian's eyes sharpened. "And this Braden? He wouldn't happen to be one of those troubled children you're so anxious to help.''

"He's been diagnosed with ADHD. Hunter's terrific with his son, and the girls love him.''

Marian stiffened. "Surely you're not letting the girls associate with him, not outside of this soccer thing.''

She stifled the urge to fidget. "We've all gotten to know him.''

Her mother's look deteriorated from surprise to horror. "Not you, too.''

"He's a nice man now, Mom.''

"Be that as it may, nobody in town can possibly accept him back. At some point, he alienated every important family in Hyde Point. When he was little, he stole Olivia Casewell's bike. He vandalized the Cutter-

Sealeys' car in junior high. He shoplifted at Rockwell's. And the Hydes—well, you get the picture. He'll never live down his reputation here.''

The town…the school…my family… They just wrote me off. Especially Hannah. I got in some pretty big trouble and embarrassed her around town. Apparently I still do.

Marian's narrowed gaze focused on Darcy. ''Reputations are important, as you well know. I wouldn't want him to besmirch yours.''

This time, Darcy beat back a snort. How convenient memory was. ''I'm afraid I managed to do that all on my own when I was young, Mother. Or have you forgotten?''

''But you've changed, dear,'' Marian said passionately. ''You're not the girl you were then.'' Marian spoke with such distaste, it silenced Darcy.

Then it angered her. Though she was glad she was no longer that confused, scared little girl she'd been when she was a teenager in Hyde Point, she hadn't been all bad.

I miss the old Darcy, Jade had said at Nora and Dan's cottage. *She was fun and interesting.*

A knock at the back door forestalled her retort. After a moment, Marian got up to answer it. As if Darcy had conjured her, Jade stood at the entryway in a stunning Hawaiian strapless bathing suit with a long saronglike skirt tied at her hips. Marian's mouth gaped.

''I'm sorry to bother you, Marian, but I need to see Darcy.'' Her friend's wit was usually more caustic than Jay Leno's and often directed at Marian, so at Jade's sober tone, Darcy threw back her chair.

''What's wrong, Jade?'' Darcy asked, crossing to the door.

''You're needed at Paige's.''

Her heart thrummed in her chest. ''Is someone hurt? Meli again, or Claire?''

Jade glanced at Marian. ''They're okay, except Meli got in a little tiff with Braden. You have to come with me.''

FORCEFULLY, HUNTER HELD his son on his lap with one arm and clamped the ice pack to the kid's temple with the other. Braden struggled to get down, but he'd worked himself into such a state, Hunter was afraid to let him go. Across the pool area, Paige sat with a sour-looking Meli.

''Wanna *go!*'' Braden yelled for the tenth time.

Hunter knew the feeling. Whenever he'd gotten in trouble, he'd run. But there'd been no one to help *him* deal with what he'd done; maybe if he'd had an adult to navigate the muddy waters of childhood, he wouldn't have drowned as a teen.

''You're not going anywhere until this is settled. Now, mind me, Champ.''

As if he finally got the message, his son deflated into his arms, then burrowed close into Hunter's chest, causing it to expand with emotion. God, the kid *needed* him!

Holding Braden close, the ice wedged between them, Hunter's gaze flew to the pool gate as Darcy bolted through it, her mother right behind her. Darcy's red hair flew behind her like a crimson cape. He regretted that their kids had caused the worry that claimed her delicate features. She crossed directly to Meli. Hunter couldn't hear what she said, but she knelt down and inspected Meli's knee, which Paige had cleaned up. Then Darcy checked Meli's eye, covered by an ice pack like Braden's. Finally Darcy stood.

She looked over to where he sat with his son. Out of habit, Hunter braced himself for the blame he'd see on her face. The Sloan men were causing trouble again.

Shockingly, blame wasn't there. Just the same concern she showed Meli. And something else. Determination? He didn't understand it. He thought after her conversation with her mother, she'd be disgusted with him for sure.

She reached out her hand. "Come with me, Mel."

At the brook-no-argument tone, Meli stood. Darcy said something to Paige, who gestured to the house's sliding glass doors. Darcy spoke to her mother; Marian straightened, made a comment, then glared across the pool with the indictment Hunter had expected from Darcy. Finally, Marian stalked out.

The O'Malleys crossed to them. Up close, Darcy looked even more set on something. "I'd like to take the kids inside and get to the bottom of this."

"Fine by me."

"Don't wanna go." This from Braden.

Meli echoed the sentiment. "Me, either."

"Tough!" Both Darcy and Hunter spoke simultaneously. Their unison response drew a small smile from her and a reluctant one from him.

When they were settled around Paige's kitchen table, Darcy looked to Hunter. "What happened, guys?" he asked.

Meli stared mutinously at him, then directed her Intimidator gaze at Darcy. Braden started to rock in his chair.

After a long silence, Darcy said, "We'll sit here till we know, right, Hunter?"

"I reckon."

Meli sighed heavily.

Braden kicked the table.

Finally, Meli said, "It was my turn on the diving board."

"Was not."

"Was too."

"He cut in front of me," Meli whined.

"She pushed me out of the way."

Darcy's sigh was pure exasperation. "You *fought* over who'd go first on the diving board?"

Meli raised her chin. "He fell."

"She pushed me."

"He jumped on top of me." She stuck out her tongue at Braden. "He thinks he can do anything 'cause everybody says he's such a good soccer player."

Ah, so that was it.

Hunter shook his head. "Okay, we got the picture."

"Do you think that's the right way to solve conflicts, Meli?" Darcy's tone gentled, but was still firm. "What have we talked about for a situation like this?"

Of course, Meli wouldn't answer. So Hunter tried.

"Us, too, Brade. What did we say was the right thing to do when you got mad at somebody?"

No answer.

"Answer me, young man."

Both Darcy's eyes and Meli's widened at Hunter's tone and the rise in his voice.

Braden stilled, then sat up straight. "Get away from 'em."

Hunter looked at Meli. Immediately, she said, "Mama says to try to talk it out."

Nodding, Hunter caught Darcy's gaze over their heads. The approval in those green eyes warmed him more than a Florida breeze.

"Well, that's a start." Hunter looked at his son. "Apologize to Meli for hitting her."

"And you apologize to Braden for hitting him, Melanie Anne."

The adults waited. Finally small "I'm sorrys" came from their kids' mouths. Hunter stood. "We'll get your things."

"We leavin'?"

"You bet. We don't want to spoil Miss Claire's party any more than we already have."

Braden's face fell. Guilt was good.

Meli's eyes teared.

Darcy said, "Go on home, Mel. I'll be right along."

The tears vanished. "I have to leave, too? But Claire's party isn't over."

"It is for you."

She grumbled, but Darcy's look quelled it.

"Gotta go to the bathroom," Braden said after Meli left.

Darcy pointed to the right. "It's through there."

Head hanging, Braden trudged down the hallway.

They were alone.

Hunter jammed his hands in his pockets. Darcy wrapped her arms around her waist. They just stared at each other.

"Good job, Mom," he finally said.

"You too, Dad." She watched him. "We need to talk, Hunter."

"I figured."

"Not now. How about tomorrow? Could Ada and Bart watch Braden for a while?"

"They're taking Braden to church, then to do some fishing. I'm gonna work at Quiet Waters in the morning."

''Can I come out?''

''Yeah, I guess.''

She looked deeply into his eyes. They heard Braden coming back down the hall. She reached out and squeezed his arm. ''We're friends, Hunter,'' she said simply. ''No matter what the kids do. Or what I said the other night.''

He wondered where that came from. And why. Had her discussion with her mother gone down a different path?

But Braden reached his side, and Darcy said goodbye and left before he could figure it out.

As DARCY REACHED the hill that led up to Quiet Waters, she caught sight of Serenity House looming about a hundred yards to the left of the turnoff. The sun caught its gleaming black shutters, and for a minute she was back in that house with Jade and Paige, Taylor and Anabelle, Charly and Nora. As she made the drive up the hill, she wondered if the residents of Serenity House still spent Sunday mornings together.

She could just picture Nora, all dressed prim and proper, insisting they go to church.

Taylor and Anabelle and Charly had been cooperative. ''I like going to church,'' Taylor would say.

''It's not bad,'' Anabelle would agree.

Charly would have gone on her own.

Paige didn't much care; she just did what Nora asked.

It was one of the few times Jade and Darcy had stuck together.

''Go change out of those jeans,'' Nora would say to Jade.

''Why?''

"They're disrespectful to wear to church. And Darcy, the skirt's too short. You change, too."

Sometimes it took three tries to get Jade and Darcy presentable, but Nora never wavered. Then she had to deal with church etiquette. Though it wasn't funny at the time, Darcy smiled at the memory.

Hunter's motorcycle was parked in front of Quiet Waters when she reached the newly tarred driveway. For a minute, Darcy let herself appreciate the beauty of the site. Overlooking the valley, the structure had recently been framed in and the outer shell finished. She could hear birds chirping in the trees that rimmed the perimeter. The pond out back wasn't visible, but Nora had gushed about its beauty and the picturesque setting.

Picking up a bag from the seat, Darcy got out of the car and followed the sound of banging. It took her through the front entrance to one of the suites in the back. The smell of fresh-cut lumber was pleasant.

As was the sight that greeted her.

She'd never seen Hunter in shorts, not even at soccer practice. Today, though, he wore cutoff denims with work boots. And nothing else. Mesmerized, she watched his muscles bulge and ripple as he braced the Sheetrock with one hand and nailed it in with the other. Her blood began to heat as his sweat-slickened skin gleamed in the sun streaming though the windows. More than anything, she wanted to run her hands across that smooth, sleek back.

He turned and saw her. "Hey," he said, dropping the hammer. "I didn't think you'd be here this early."

"I was up, and the kids went to church with my mother."

"Ah."

He reached for a gray T-shirt lying on the floor. As

he raised his arms to drag it over his head, she saw inviting swirls of dark hair strategically placed all over his chest.

He took a water bottle out of a duffel bag and drank. She watched his throat work convulsively. Oh, God, she wanted to kiss that throat. Lick it. Lick him. All over.

"Darce? Where'd you go?"

Geez, what was she doing?

Being human, Darce.

"Sorry. I was just thinking…"

He didn't pursue it. "Let's go outside and talk."

She held up the bag she carried. "I brought you coffee. And a doughnut."

His features relaxed. "Really?" he said, as if no one had ever done him favors. The notion knocked her even more off balance.

"Show me around?"

"Sure." He took the coffee from her and sipped it as he motioned to the room they were in. "This is a typical suite."

She wandered through it. "Nice private bathrooms. Whoever thought of that was smart. Jade and I argued nonstop about using the bathroom on our floor."

Hunter smiled.

"Oh and look!" She grinned at the closet space. "Are you doing this woodwork?"

"Uh-huh."

Lovingly she ran her hand over the wood. "This is beautiful craftsmanship. I'm impressed." She studied the shelves and cupboards inside. "Dan really thought of everything, giving the guys their own private space."

As they made their way to the kitchen, he asked, "Was it hard living in Serenity House?"

She praised the layout of the counter and appliances,

then faced him. "Not after I got there. It was my mother sending me there that really threw me." She nodded to a stack of oak boards and touched those for the feel and texture of the wood. "This for the cabinets?"

His gaze riveted on the gesture. He shifted uncomfortably. "Yep." When she said no more he asked, "How long were you in there?"

"Seven months. It was supposed to be two, then four. My mother had just married Jeremy, and I think she was afraid I'd cause trouble between them."

"I'm sorry."

"It's one reason I always put my daughters' welfare first." She added pointedly, "Over what I want."

The ease in his stance disappeared, to be replaced by coiled tension. She was sorry to have caused it.

"Let's go outside. You can tell me why you came."

Darcy had dressed casually—sleeveless plaid blouse with old jeans—so she dropped onto the slope that curved down to the pond and overlooked the valley. Hunter sank onto the grass beside her. The warm September sun dappled the grass and glistened off the water.

Finally she looked at him. "I wanted to talk about two things. First, I'm sorry about Meli and Braden. She's jealous, I think, of his prowess in soccer."

"I figured that out."

"She's also jealous that you're his father."

Hunter's expression was genuinely puzzled.

"I heard her and Claire talking. About you and Braden, and how lucky your son is to have you as a dad."

He rolled his eyes and sipped his coffee.

"He is, you know."

"What?"

"Lucky to have you as a father. You handled yesterday perfectly."

"Yeah, well, you wouldn't say that if you could have seen the tantrum he threw when I told him he had to stay in his room this afternoon, and three more afternoons this week."

"Meli balked at being grounded, too. She's really mad to have missed a pool party."

"The joys of raising children."

"In any case, I think Mel's as infatuated with you as Claire is."

His jaw tightened. "I see. And that isn't good, is it?"

"I know it bothers you, what I said about staying away from them." When he didn't respond, she added, "We need to talk about this. I can't bear for there to be misunderstandings between us."

"I guess it bothers me."

"I meant it honestly, Hunter. There was no hidden agenda, like you seem to think."

"Maybe not before. But now, with what your mama told you about me..." He stared at her, his expression bleak. "You know about Industry, don't you?"

"I'm sorry. It must have been horrible for you to have been sent there."

"Actually, it wasn't that bad. At least I was away from my father's fists for a year."

"Oh, God."

"And it's where I learned to play soccer. We had this great counselor named Bill who was a phys ed teacher. He taught us the game. For me, it built self-confidence. Until I got back to Hyde Point." He scanned the horizon. "You know, in my real life, in Florida, I never feel this bad about myself. About who I am. I've got friends, a job I like. Believe it or not, I'm sought after as a carpenter.''

She glanced back to the house. "After what I've seen, I believe it.''

"Hyde Point drags me down bad, Darce. Everybody makes me feel so worthless.'' He thumped on his chest. "In here, when I'm away from this town, I know it's not true. But bein' back..." He zeroed in on her. "How could you stand to come back?"

"I had no choice. I couldn't support the kids on my waitress job. And my mother's mellowed. She wanted me home. Johnny and I had moved around so much, the girls needed a stable environment.'' She hesitated. "It's why I plan to stay in Hyde Point, at least until they're grown.''

"That's mighty admirable. Maybe it's easier for you. You can't have been as bad as me, anyway.''

"Don't bet on it.''

"You didn't steal a car, did you?''

"No.'' She shook her head. "I can't believe the co-incidence. It was my father's car.''

"Just my luck.''

"Were you really going to return it?''

"Sure. Your father was right as rain. It was just a joyride.''

Silence.

Finally Darcy confessed, "I did get picked up for shoplifting several times.''

"No shit?''

"No shit. And I broke into the school twice. I did a lot of illegal things, Hunter. My mother just got me out of most of it.''

"She must hate me.'' He surveyed the valley again. "Everybody here does.'' He raked a hand through his hair. "God, I can't wait to get out of this place. Even if I didn't have to give Braden back, I wouldn't stay in Hyde Point and subject him to the town's prejudice against the Sloans."

"I feel just the opposite. I've begun to build a life here for the girls. A good life."

"So Hyde Point is your heaven, and my hell."

"I wouldn't exactly say that. Though she's changed, my mother can be narrow-minded about people. She went on and on about the women I invited to Claire's party."

"The women?"

"Women from the group home."

"Excuse me?"

"All of them—Taylor, Paige, Jade and Charly—were residents of Serenity House."

He started to laugh. It was a rich, beautiful sound, low and deep, rumbling through his chest. Darcy was mesmerized by it.

"I can't believe it. Paige is a successful doctor. Taylor's a sweetheart. Charly's so conservative. Now, Jade, I can believe *she* did time in Serenity House."

Darcy swallowed back her jealousy. "Jade likes you."

"I like her, too."

Picking at the grass, Darcy didn't look at him. "Have you, you know, thought about taking her out?"

Hunter didn't say anything. She glanced at him. He was staring out over the valley, sipping his coffee. She couldn't see the expression in his eyes.

"Hunter, I asked if you'd thought about—"

"I heard you." When he faced her, she wished he hadn't. His eyes glittered with sexual intensity. She'd seen it enough in her life to recognize it.

Problem was, she'd never responded like this to it before. Her heart began to beat fast in her chest. Her breasts tingled and she knew if she looked down...oh, God, could he tell?

Still she couldn't tear her gaze away.

"Best you not go there, Miss Darcy."

"There?"

"To who I been thinking about seein'." His accent thickened, and his gaze dropped to her lips. "About kissin'." His eyes focused lower. "About touchin'." The last word was a raspy whisper and flavored with pure southern honey.

She swallowed hard. Leaned closer, not willingly, but her body wasn't listening to her mind.

He tossed the cup away without unlocking his gaze from hers. His hands gripped her arms to hold her back. He said, "You don't want to do this, Darce."

"No, I don't." Closer.

"Why did you come here today?"

Closer still. She could feel his breath on her cheek. "To make sure you knew what I meant about the girls. That I'm just trying to protect them from getting hurt. It's not that I don't think you're good enough for them." She raised her hand to his face. "Please, believe me." She cupped his jaw in her palm.

"Don't do that, darlin'."

She smoothed her fingers up and down his scratchy cheek, closed her eyes to savor the feel of him, to breathe in his scent.

"Darcy. Please. I'm only human, I can't..." She tilted forward; he held on to her harder, but she kept inching toward him.

Finally he got out, "Oh, hell," and his mouth closed over hers so fast that Darcy's mind blanked.

All she could do was feel: his lips smooth and firm, claiming hers; his taste so male, so Hunter; his strong fingers biting into her bare flesh. All the while, he took her mouth, prodded open her lips, then began to explore her with his tongue. She whimpered and felt herself go moist. She inched closer—as close as she could get.

It was all he needed.

The pressure on her shoulders eased her down to the grass. Its coolness, and Hunter's nearness, made her shiver. Her body stretched out to accommodate him. His big solid frame immediately sought every nook and cranny of hers. He was heavy as he covered her. She welcomed his weight.

Their mouths continued to mate. Her hands were everywhere—his back, the muscles in his arms that bunched under her fingers, his firm butt.

He angled their bodies, grasped her leg and dragged it up and over so he could settle between her thighs. Darcy lost it when they came into intimate contact. She moaned, clutched at him, devoured his mouth. His hand claimed her breast, grasped her firmly, kneaded. She moaned louder, the sound echoing in the morning silence.

Still the kiss went on. And on. And on.

It was Hunter who drew back. His handsome face was flushed with arousal, and his eyes gleamed like live coals, making her want more of him. Frantic, she reached to drag him back.

"Darcy, darlin', wait."

"...don't want to wait." Her words were slurred by her lips on his neck.

He drew in a breath. "You know where this is goin'. I won't do it when it isn't what you really want."

She didn't listen. Her leg clamped tighter to him.

"God, don't do that."

Her lower body pushed into his and she pressed against him.

"I won't take you just because you can't think straight."

"I can't think at all. I don't want to think at all."

He said meaningfully, "That's what I'm afraid of, darlin'."

The incoherence started to clear. She closed her eyes.

He drew back farther, then eased down next to her and stretched out on the grass. He tugged her close, fitting their bodies together again. His hand, this time, was gentle on her back.

His heart pounded beneath her ear. She was stunned that he'd pulled back given his own wild response. She'd felt him hard against her.

After a long while, she whispered into his chest, "You're right. I didn't come here for this. I came here to let you know I'm your friend, no matter what others think. To make sure you understood I was only out to keep Claire and Meli from getting hurt. When you leave. Like you said you have to." She drew in a breath. "I need to protect myself, too. I don't want to get hurt when you leave."

"I know. I don't want that, either."

"I'm sorry... This *was* a mistake," she whispered, "If we ever...and then you left... The old Darcy wouldn't have cared. She could screw you and let you go. But who I am now, and with you, I can't...I couldn't..."

He kissed her head. "I know. Me neither. I couldn't be casual about this." He sighed heavily. "All around, this ain't a very good idea, sweetheart."

"It sure feels pretty damn good," she mumbled.

He chuckled. She smiled. They just stayed there together for a few moments. Then he eased her over. Bracing his arms on either side of her, he said, "You are so precious, do you know that?"

She smiled.

"And I won't hurt you. I promise."

"I want to be your friend, Hunter, while you're here. We can be friends and make it work. Maybe if we don't see too much of each other, are careful about the girls…"

He brushed her cheek with his knuckles. "Think so?"

"I want to think so. Can we give it a shot?"

"I guess. I wanna say something first, though."

"What?"

He leaned over and kissed the swell of a breast. She hadn't realized her blouse had come open. "I wanted you—want you—more than I ever wanted anything in my life."

"Hunter—"

His fingers on her lips stopped her words. "No, don't say anything. It's important to me that you know that. We're gonna be friends until I go. That's all. And we'll be careful about the girls."

She looked up into his eyes. "Okay."

He gave a deep sigh. Bent his head. Brushed his lips with hers. "Come on, let's get up before we stop listening to common sense."

He stood and held out his hand and drew her up.

As she rose, the voice inside her head surfaced.

You two are freakin' nuts, you know that? If you think for one minute this is going to work…you're both crazy as loons.

CHAPTER NINE

ARMED WITH a satchel full of books, articles and even a videotape and audiocassette, Hunter walked into Paige Kendrick's office for the first time without Darcy.

We can be friends and make it work. Maybe if we don't see too much of each other...

He had to get used to doing these things alone, making these decisions by himself—and he might as well start now. When he got to the door and found it open, he raised his hand to knock. He paused, though, at what he saw. The two respected doctors of Hyde Point were in a big-time clinch. Hunter was amused—and jealous as hell. He'd been trying all week to forget how right Darcy had felt in his arms, all soft womanly flesh and curves that could make a man swallow his tongue.

You don't want this, darlin'.

Man, he sure as hell had.

Watching the sexy little scene before him made Hunter long for Darcy even worse. The two lovers parted before he could cough or knock or alert them to his presence. When Ian pulled away and saw Hunter, no chagrin claimed his face. Nor was Paige embarrassed. Mischievously Ian circled his arm around his wife and drew her close. "Hi, Sloan. She's all yours. I'm done with her." Then he added with a wink at Paige, "For now."

He strode out; Paige smiled as she sat behind her desk. "Sorry, we get carried away sometimes."

I know the feeling.

For some reason, Hunter wasn't embarrassed either. He wondered if it was because he knew Paige had been in Serenity House with Darcy and wasn't some lofty doctor born with a silver spoon in her mouth.

"So," Paige said when he dropped into a chair, "have you had a chance to look at the Web sites I recommended?"

"Yes, ma'am." And they'd upset him so much, he'd run into the night, right into his sister Hannah, who'd looked at him as if he was Jack the Ripper.

Hunter reached into his backpack and drew out a notebook. While he'd been studying up about ADHD, he'd run across an article in the *Journal of Psychotherapy* that outlined coping strategies for adults with the condition. Things like making lists and planning the best order to get things done, working in a quiet area, doing one thing at a time and creating routines, were among them. Ironically, he'd inherently known to do all four for most of his adult life. This one—write things down in a notebook and keep it with you to record your thoughts—was new.

"I, um, read all the articles and took notes. I wanted to keep my thoughts straight on this." He looked at her. Oh, hell. He might as well tell her. "Paige, after reading all that stuff, I was thinking maybe I've got ADHD, too."

Bracing her arms on the desk, she leaned over. "Tell me, Hunter."

So he poured out the whole seedy story of his childhood. When he finished, he held up the notebook. "I'm doing this now to be better organized."

"You're very wise, to see this condition and manage it all on your own. I admire you."

Everybody here makes me feel worthless.

Hmm. Maybe not everybody.

"Anyway," he continued, "like you said, there're two camps—one favoring medication, one going at it through diet, behavior modification and therapy."

"Right."

He drew in a breath. "Way I figure it, we should do the diet and behavior stuff no matter what. It shouldn't be too hard—" he read his notes "—to balance the fats and oils Braden needs to stay focused, make sure he gets enough calming carbohydrates and concentration-enhancing proteins." He looked up and shrugged. "It's gonna be staying away from sugar that'll be hard to do. The boy has a sweet tooth to beat the band."

"Well, sugar in moderation will be okay."

"I already got Ada looking into alternatives to making cookies and stuff without simple sugars."

"Our nutritionist at the center here could help."

"Great." He glanced back down at this notes. "I think I understand my end in this behavior stuff. Like, this week, Braden was punished for his fight with Meli. But he took it pretty well, did what I told him, and so I spent some extra time with him doing what he likes."

"You're a good father, Hunter."

He sighed heavily. "Problem is, much of this literature—" he held up some articles he'd run off Darcy's computer "—says food adjustment and working on his behavior alone isn't enough. Most kids need medication for any of that to be effective."

"It's called a multimodal approach."

"I'm worried about him going on the medication."

"Because of the side effects?"

"Yep." Weight loss, insomnia, headaches and a sense of sadness were nothing to fool around with.

"Well, we don't know how many he'll experience. And the dosage will certainly affect that. We'd start with a low dose. See what happens."

Hunter leaned back in his chair. "Bottom line is I think we don't have much choice, Paige. I gotta give Braden back to his mother in a bit." He could hardly get the words out. "She won't keep up the diet thing or the behavior stuff, though I'll beg her to. And I suspect she won't continue any counseling we get him."

"But she might keep up the medicine."

"If I pay for it. Hell, maybe I could even buy it and have it delivered to her every month."

"You'd be willing to do that?"

His eyebrows rose. "I'd do anything for my boy."

Paige cocked her head. "Can I ask you something?"

"Sure."

"Why don't you try to keep Braden?"

A lump formed in his throat. "She'd never let me."

"Would you, if you could?"

"Are you kiddin'? Of course I would." He thought for a minute. "I wouldn't stay here and let the town trounce him, though. I'd go back to Florida. I could make a life for him there."

"Sounds like a possibility to me."

"I don't think so, but—God—I wish it was."

"Maybe you should talk to Braden's mother about it."

Insecurity, his constant shadow in this town, snaked inside him. "Braden probably wouldn't want to stay with me. He misses his mother."

Paige gave him a knowing smile. "From what I witnessed at Claire's party, and from how you talk, I have a feeling he might want to stay with you more than you think.''

He just stared at her.

She glanced down. ''In any case, we should try the meds.''

''Whoa, that's my opinion. I want yours.''

She drew a sheet out of Braden's folder and handed it to him. ''I always make my own recommendation before I talk to parents. Then we can compare our thoughts.''

Hunter's hands shook as he reached for the paper. It was like taking a test in school. Would his thoughts square with hers? Geez, he'd barely graduated from Hyde Point High. This woman was an M.D. What the hell did he know?

Slowly he read her recommendation. When he was done, he looked up. Paige was smiling.

''You would have made a good doctor, Hunter. And you obviously know your son. I'd do exactly what you suggest.''

ALL WEEK, Darcy had been drawn to the little boy like a lodestone. Despite Braden's altercation with Meli, Darcy wanted to spend time with him. Since she worked in each of the rooms a bit every day anyway—usually with individual kids—her special interest in Hunter's son wasn't too noticeable.

And Braden had responded. She'd taken him onto the Net to interactive soccer Web sites that the boy had relished. She'd read him picture books of dogs and found out that he could decipher some words. Like his dad, he was full of hidden talents.

You know, in my real life in Florida, I've got friends…a job I like…I'm a sought-after carpenter.

Her heart still felt as if a fist were squeezing it when she thought about what she was giving up with Hunter. The kisses and caresses had stayed with her all week, and she'd dreamed about him every single night.

In those dreams, she and Hunter didn't stop the way they had at Quiet Waters. They played out the whole X-rated scene in living color.

"Darce?" Porter was standing in the doorway. She was filling in for one of the aides, who was sick. "Becky wants you in the 4/5 room."

Rising, Darcy followed Porter out and down the hall. "What's going on?"

"Braden and Tommy Pielher are going at it. To be fair, Tommy's been picking on Braden all morning."

They reached the room. Becky was holding Tommy back, and Braden was sitting in a chair at a table. The two boys were glaring at each other—and yelling.

"Am not."

"Are too. You ain't even smart enough to go to school tomorrow."

Uh-oh. Darcy should have foreseen this. She entered the fray. "What's going on, guys?"

"He says I'm dumb."

"He is dumb. He ain't going to school like the rest of us."

Braden looked up at her with Hunter's eyes.

Even if I didn't have to give Braden back, I wouldn't stay in Hyde Point and subject him to the town's prejudice against the Sloans.

She stood next to Braden and placed her hand on his shoulder. He didn't flinch as he usually did. "Not everybody's going to kindergarten tomorrow, Tommy. But more importantly, it's not nice to call somebody dumb. Braden is just as smart as you. I wonder why you want to be mean to him."

"I beat him at dodgeball," Braden explained simply.

"Who cares about stupid games?" Tommy was undersized, and not athletically inclined. "My dad says jocks are stupid." Tommy's dad was probably a small man, too. With a Napoleon complex.

"Sports are good for you. *My* dad says so."

She'd have to remember to tell Hunter how Braden quoted him. Meanwhile, she could help his son. "I don't want to see a repeat of this. I'll speak to both your parents about it when they pick you up."

Braden's eyes widened. Then she saw something in them that made her almost ill. A resignation, an of-course-I'm-in-trouble-again look. One she'd seen in Hunter's eyes as recently as last Sunday.

"Come with me a minute, Braden," she said. "I want to separate you guys for a while." She held out her hand. He looked at her warily, then eyed her hand. He stood but made no other move. She was about to drop her arm, when he shyly placed his little hand in hers. They walked out of the 4/5 room and down the hall.

When they reached her office, she led Braden to the couch. "Sit down, Sport. Want some juice?"

"'Kay." He sat. Knobby little knees showed beneath navy shorts and a T-shirt with a soccer ball on it. He had brand-new Nikes on his feet.

After Darcy had brought his juice, she settled down next to him, in close proximity but not touching. "Do you feel bad about not going to kindergarten with the other kids?"

"School's stupid," he said.

"Well, I'm sorry you feel that way, because you're

going to a kind of school starting tomorrow, too. I know your dad explained this to you.''

''Here, right?'' There was a hint of panic in his voice.

''Yes. Once September comes, we have a special room, with a special teacher. It's the PreK room, where kids who aren't ready for the public school go for two hours, four days a week.''

''I'm not ready.'' He said the words so defeatedly, she moved closer, took a risk and picked up his hand.

Briefly, she remembered holding Hunter's hand in the gazebo.

Maybe I could have made something of myself, if somebody had helped me control this.

''Well, for one thing you just turned five a few months ago. Jackie Conway has been five since February, and he's not going to regular school either. He'll be in your class. Some kids take a longer time to be ready than others.''

''That place…where my mom sent me…they said I was too bad to go to school.''

You couldn't have been as bad as me, Hunter had said.

Braden was just like his father.

''No, no, honey. You're not bad. You just need a little more time, and a little different structure than other kids.''

His look was disbelieving. ''Hank says I'm bad, too.''

''Hank is your mother's husband?''

Braden's eyes widened. ''He's not my father. My dad's…you know, here.''

Ah, she'd have to remember to tell Hunter about this reaction, too.

"I know Hunter's your dad. But Hank, your stepfather, says you're bad?"

"Yeah. I don't like him."

I don't either.

"You're not bad, you're—"

"What're we gonna do in that new room?"

She let it go. "Well, every week we have show-and-tell. The first month, you get to bring in your most precious object."

Braden watched her. "Can it be alive?"

"Like what?"

"Tramp. I wanna bring in Tramp."

Kids had asked for that before. "Sure, as long as your dad comes with Tramp, you can bring him in."

"He'll come."

Smiling, she reached over and ruffled his hair. Though he ducked his head, he was smiling, too.

"You're a good kid, Braden Sloan. I like you a lot."

"No foolin'?"

"No foolin'." When he said no more, she stood. "You ready to go back to your room now?"

He nodded.

Again, she held out her hand. He looked at it. Then, instead of taking it, he moved in closer and wrapped his arms around her waist.

And hugged her.

Her heart swelled. She bent down and returned the hug.

He mumbled, "I like you, too, Miss Darcy," drew back and scampered out of the room.

Stunned by his display of affection—he was as cautious as Tramp—she followed him into the hall, feeling a cold prick of guilt.

We'll be careful about the kids...

Braden had gotten too close to her.

Like father, like son, the little voice said.

Though she tried to regret Braden's feelings for her because of the potential problems they could cause, she couldn't wish that the little boy didn't care about her.

Any more than she could wish his father didn't.

HUNTER EXITED the hardware store in a hurry. He'd picked up several samples of kitchen-cabinet handles for Nathan Hyde to consider and was headed over to the Winslow place. Right out front, he bumped into Claire O'Malley.

Her books spilled onto the sidewalk and she startled. "Oh."

"Hey, Miss Claire." Hunter bent down. "I'll get your stuff." He scooped up everything and handed it all to her, catching sight of the charm bracelet around her little wrist. "Have a nice day at school?"

Her eyes were sad. They became the color of fall leaves when she was down in the dumps. Her mother's eyes turned even greener when she was sad…or aroused.

"School was okay."

He tipped her chin. "You doin' all right, honey?"

She nodded.

We'll be careful about the kids…

Still. "You gotta be somewhere?"

"I have to go to TenderTime."

Along Main Street, lining the sidewalks, were benches under the trees. "Come sit with me a minute."

They sat. A pink headband held back her hair, drawing attention to her face.

"Is something wrong? Don't you like school?"

Tears welled in her eyes.

He pulled out a handkerchief and handed it to her. "Who's making you cry, Miss Claire? If it's some boy tugging on your pigtails, I'll come over and—"

She giggled, which was what he'd hoped for. Too soon she sobered. "It's not a boy."

"What is it?"

Her eyes still moist, she stared up at him. "I miss seeing you and Tramp."

"You see us at the soccer games and practices."

"Not after, though. I don't get to play with Tramp in the playground 'cause we don't go for ice cream or pizza like we used to."

Hunter scrambled for an excuse. "Now that school's started, everybody's got to get home to get to bed early."

Her look was so adult, so disbelieving, it shamed him. "Don't you like us anymore, Coach?"

Shit! What did he do with this now? "Of course I like you, darlin'. Don't ever think that I don't. It's just that—"

"Claire?"

Claire's head snapped up, as did Hunter's. Oh, great, just great. This was all he needed.

"What are you doing sitting out here with…with him?" Marian Mason's words were delivered in just the tone all his teachers had used.

"Miss Claire and I bumped into each other on her way to the daycare. She was telling me about school."

Marian snatched Claire from the bench and drew her close to her side as if she was saving the little girl from oncoming traffic. He felt his heart being ripped right out of his chest. "You stay away from my granddaughter."

"Grandma, what's—"

"Do you hear me?"

Hunter stood. "Claire and me, Meli and me, Darcy and me are friends, Mrs. Mason." He looked down into Claire's wide, frightened eyes and decided not to pursue this further. It would only hurt her. "I'll see you at the next game, Miss Claire." And he walked away.

Mechanically he found his truck, got in and started the engine. "Don't feel it, Sloan. It's your own fault for getting close to her. To her mama." He put the car in gear and drove away.

"You'll be gone soon." Which meant of course, that he'd be giving Braden back. Something he couldn't bear to think about.

Can I ask you something?

Sure.

Why don't you try to keep Braden?

"Oh, yeah, that'll be the ever-lovin' day." Marian Mason's utter contempt brought that little fantasy to a screeching halt.

He was in a vile mood when he reached the Winslow place, but he tried to contain it because Nathan's Mercedes was parked in the driveway. The front door was open, so he could just walk in. Trekking through the living spaces to the kitchen, Hunter expected to find Nathan there. But it was empty. He looked out the window. From here, he could see the wing off to the right and, through a window, he saw a figure. He slipped out the French doors and headed to the large, circular turret. That door was ajar, too, so he went inside.

"Hey," Hunter said simply.

Hands stuffed into the pockets of expensive slacks, Nathan had been staring out the window; he turned. "Hi, Hunter."

Hunter looked around. The plaster was cracked, the

floorboards slivered, and the circular staircase leading upstairs was rickety. "Aren't you renovating this room, Nathan?"

"Yeah, but I'm going to wait until after the congressional election in November. I want to do it all by myself."

"How come?"

Nathan shrugged. "I feel an affinity with this room. Like I should do it myself." He gave a self-effacing grin. "You probably think I'm nuts."

"No, I feel that way about places, too." Quiet Waters, for one. Hunter had felt an immediate connection with it.

Suddenly, he saw Darcy outside the boys' home on the grass all rumpled from his hands and mouth. He beat back the image.

"Well, let's go to the kitchen. Did you bring the hardware?"

"Yep."

They made their way to the main part of the house. Hunter had just spread out the samples, when a cell phone rang.

"Sorry," Nathan said. "I have to take this. I'm expecting a call from my daughter, Kaeley."

"Go ahead." Hunter crossed to the other side of the room to check out the oak that had been delivered. Trying not to eavesdrop, he gave Nathan his back.

"Nathan Hyde... What? Who is this? How did you get this..." A pause. "Damn it!"

Hunter circled around. Nathan's face was flushed and he gripped the phone. "Problem?"

The other man looked up. He took in a breath. "Maybe. I've been getting crank phone calls at my offices here and in Washington. Telling me not to—" He halted as if he'd said too much. "I've never gotten one on my private line before."

"Have you reported it to the police?"

"Dan knows."

Hunter smiled. "Well, then, you're in good hands."

Nathan nodded and studied the cabinet hardware, but Hunter could tell he was disturbed. "So what do you think timewise on these things?" Nathan asked.

"Now that the wood is cut, and we've got the design, I'll start putting them together. It should take a few weeks."

"How long you planning to be in Hyde Point, Hunter?"

"As short a time as possible," he said, thinking of Marian Mason.

"Pardon me?"

"Sorry. Something happened." He drew in a breath and folded his arms across his chest. "People in Hyde Point got long memories, you know that? They don't forget anything."

Nathan glanced at the turret room. "That's what Anabelle Crane always said."

"Darcy's friend?"

"Mmm. She used to work for me. She was a girl then and had just gotten out of—" He stopped abruptly.

"—Serenity House," Hunter finished. At Nathan's surprise, he said, "Darcy told me."

"It's no secret." He leaned against the counter. "I think it's amazing how all those women made something of themselves despite their dysfunctional beginnings."

"Yeah."

Nathan studied him. "You, too, Sloan."

"What?"

"No offense, but word gets around. You were pretty wild in high school, I hear. Seems to me, you turned your life around, too."

"Not hardly."

Nathan nodded to the cabinets. "You have a real talent in woodworking. But your kid's a true testament to your success, don't you think?"

"I'd do anything for my kid, but I can't take credit for him." At Nathan's questioning look, he said, "I only got him temporarily. It's a long story, but I gotta give him back to his mother in a bit."

"Goddamn. You going to be able to do that?"

"Sometimes we have no choice, Hyde."

Nathan's face shadowed. "Yeah, I know. I almost lost my kid once. I don't know how you survive that."

Hunter straightened. Like the last time, he and Nathan Hyde seemed to be getting into personal territory that two strangers had no right sharing. He wondered why they talked about these things. They couldn't be more different. "Well, I'll survive. I always do."

Nathan's phone rang again. He stared at Hunter a moment then flipped it open. "Hey, it's about time, sweetheart, I was worried about you."

Nathan's daughter.

Hunter turned away, wondering what Braden would be like in ten years. Would he ever call Hunter in the middle of the day like this? Would Braden even remember spending these months with him?

I don't know how you survive that, Nathan had said.

You're a good father, Paige had told him...

Damn it all.

He saw Claire's face.

Hunter didn't want to feel all these attachments—to Braden, to the O'Malley women. He'd purposely lived his life without them. But Hyde Point was crowding him again, and he didn't know what to do about it.

"DARCY?" Marian's words carried through Tender-Time's office. "Darcy Anne, where are you?"

"I'm in the filing room." Darcy was not anxious to hear what had brought that strident tone to her mother's voice. The day had been too emotional, the week too much of a roller coaster, starting with Hunter kissing her.

Just the thought made her warm.

And so sad she could barely stand it.

So do something about it.

Bracing herself, she came out of the filing room and found Marian huffing and puffing at the door. She held a white-faced Claire by the hand.

"What happened?" Darcy asked, alarmed.

"I found Claire sitting on a bench out in front of the hardware store talking to Hunter Sloan."

Claire let go of Marian's hand and ran to Darcy. She buried her face in Darcy's chest. "I don't understand, Mama. Why's Grandma so mad?"

But Darcy understood only too well.

Hyde Point drags me down so bad...

No wonder he felt he had to leave town.

To leave her.

Gently she drew Claire back and peered down at her. When had her little girl grown so tall? They were only a head apart in height. "Grandma doesn't like Mr. Sloan because of things that he did when he was young. I don't want to go into it because it's private for him. I—"

"I'll go into it. The girls should know—"

"Mother, don't say another word." She addressed

Claire. "Remember how we talked about it not being nice to hold grudges and how everybody makes mistakes?"

Claire shook her head.

"Mr. Sloan made mistakes when he was young." She glanced over Claire's head at Marian. "So did I, honey. Everybody does, some more than others."

Claire pivoted but stuck close to Darcy. "Why do you hold a grudge, Grandma?"

Marian sputtered, but didn't get anything coherent out.

"Claire, go down to see if Porter needs any help with the babies, would you? I want to talk to Grandma alone."

Nodding obediently, Claire headed to the door, but she hugged Marian on the way out. "Mr. Sloan's a nice man, Grandma," she said and left.

Darcy closed the door behind her, then faced her mother. "That's what this is all about, isn't it, Mom?"

"What?"

"Why you seem to hate Hunter so much. It has something to do with me."

"I don't know what you mean."

"I think there's some connection here. Does he remind you of how bad I was?"

"No. Those Serenity House women do, though. Really, Darcy, inviting their children to Claire's party. Employing the current residents at TenderTime. I have to tell you, Jeremy and I don't like this at all. Up until this we've been satisfied with your performance at TenderTime..."

"Don't change the subject. Why do you object to my associating with the Serenity House girls?"

"Because...because..."

"Because you don't want to remember what I was like."

Her mother's face crumpled. She walked over to the couch and sank onto the cushions. Darcy crossed to her and knelt in front of her.

"That's it, isn't it?"

"Maybe some of it. I hate remembering those years. I felt so powerless. And...guilty for putting you in that place."

Ah, something Darcy never knew.

"Well, at least I had Serenity House. It helped me, Mom. Nora helped me a lot."

"In a way I couldn't." She sighed. "I hated that, you know."

"No, I never knew that." Marian said nothing. "But it was good for me, nonetheless. It's too bad Hunter Sloan never had a place like that to go to."

"He went to Industry, instead. Where he belonged."

At least I was away from my father's fists for a year...it's where I learned to play soccer...it built self-confidence.

"And that helped him." At Marian's skeptical expression, Darcy asked, "Look, do you think I've changed since then?"

"Of course."

"Then why can't you accept that Hunter's changed? He's a wonderful man, a good father, a great coach."

All the softening in Marian's face disappeared. "Oh my God, Darcy, don't tell me...you aren't..." Her mother grasped her by the shoulders, almost unbalancing her. "Don't tell me you have *feelings* for this man. Have you forgotten all those *bums* you attracted when you were young? Please, dear, tell me you don't have feelings for him."

God, I can't wait to get out of this place.

This isn't a good idea.

I'm trying to protect myself, too. I don't want to get hurt when you leave...

What was the sense in telling her mother that she had myriad feelings for the town's former bad boy? It would only upset Marian more and for what? They had this thing between them under control. Besides, he was leaving...

"No, Mom, I don't have feelings for him like you mean. He's a good man, but there's nothing between us."

Marian expelled a breath. "Thank God."

Darcy had to stand to relieve the pressure in her chest. She turned so her mother couldn't see her face.

She felt a little like Judas Iscariot, and didn't like the comparison at all.

WHEN HUNTER CAME to pick up Braden at five, he went first to Darcy's office. He felt bruised and battered by the day...talking with Paige about Braden's treatment...Claire's distress over not seeing him...Marian's stinging contempt, and even the conversation with Nathan Hyde. All had drained him. He needed to see her.

Darcy watched as he came to the door. As she stared at him across the room, her pale face and bleak eyes told him she was as raw as he was.

"Hi." Her voice was sandpapery.

"Hey."

"Bad day?"

"You don't wanna know." He couldn't take his eyes off her stricken face. "You too?"

She shook her head. "It's been a horrendous *week.*"

"Since Sunday."

She nodded. "Braden had an altercation you need to know about."

"Tell me."

"Come inside."

"No, best I stay here." Far away from her.

She told him about the school incident. "I think he's okay. But, Hunter, I'm afraid what we feared is coming true. He...he likes me, just as Claire likes you."

"Why wouldn't he? The Sloan men..." He closed his eyes. "Never mind." He took in a breath. "I guess you know about your mother finding me and Claire sitting outside."

Darcy nodded.

"Before Marian came, Claire cried, Darce. She says she misses me."

"Why wouldn't she... The O'Malley women..."

His hands curled to touch her, just once.

"I gotta go."

"All right."

"You gonna be okay?"

She nodded.

He turned, then heard her call out.

"Hunter? What about you? Are you all right?"

He didn't face her. He couldn't. He was afraid of what he'd say or do. "I'm fine, Miss Darcy. Just fine."

Almost overcome by his feelings of loss, he left the office and walked out onto the street, feeling more alone than he'd ever felt in his life.

CHAPTER TEN

CHUCK E. CHEESE'S was a cacophony of sounds and a kaleidoscope of colors. As a woman who spent most of her time with kids, Darcy could appreciate the sheer genius of the place. Encompassing hundreds of square feet, a series of rooms provided various entertainments for children of all ages: singing mannequins, stage shows, little rides, video and bowling games for older kids. The most popular attraction was the ball crawl— a netlike cage filled with primary-colored spheres the size of baseballs and the consistency of whiffle balls.

Today, Meli's soccer team had planned a party at the place because, three-quarters of the way through the season, they were undefeated. All the parents had come with their little ones. While Meli and Claire jumped around in the ball crawl, Darcy sat off to the side— trying not to scour the place for Hunter. Last she saw of him, he was watching an Elvis-type dog sing its heart out. He'd been trying to explain to Braden who the King was.

"Hey there, woman. What you up to?"

Darcy turned. "Jade, hi."

"Having a good time?" Dressed in skintight white spandex and a cropped zebra-print top, Jade looked sexy as hell with her blond hair curled around her face and down her back.

Apparently, Hunter thought Jade was sexy, too.

Darcy recalled her friend coming to see her early in the week...

"I want to know straight out. Are you interested in Hunter Sloan?"

"Yes, but it's not going anywhere. We're staying away from each other."

"Why?"

"A thousand reasons."

Jade had scanned the daycare office. "Marian the Librarian's orchestrating your love life, isn't she?"

"What do you want, Jade?" Darcy snapped.

"I'm going to ask Hunter out. We've worked together several nights. He's met Jewel, and she adores him. I like him a lot. I just didn't want to trespass."

"Can't trespass on what isn't mine."

But she'd wished he was hers. Badly...

"Darce, I asked if you were having fun?" Jade was saying now.

"Oh, yeah, sure." She cocked her head. "What are you doing here?"

"Jewel begged to come. Apparently she heard about the soccer team's outing from Claire and Meli. Mrs. Stanwyck and I decided to have lunch here with her so she wouldn't be left out."

"Jade, dear, introduce me to your friend."

Darcy pivoted to find a trim and fit older woman in white spandex, like Jade, matched with a long pink top. Her hair was the color of snow and her eyes were a clear sharp blue.

"Lila Stanwyck, Darcy O'Malley." Jade's eyes twinkled. "Her surname used to be Shannon, Mrs. S. She was in one of your English classes."

Mrs. Stanwyck's face lighted. "Ah, now I recognize you. Didn't you have lovely long red hair?"

"She still does. She just scrapes it off her face like Cinderella's stepmother these days." Jade eyed Darcy's conservative navy pants and knit white top. "And she knew how to dress, then."

Mrs. Stanwyck chuckled. "You used to sneak a *Cosmopolitan* to read in class." Mrs. Stanwyck smiled. "Once or twice you left it behind. My husband and I found the articles...interesting."

Darcy laughed. She sobered when Hunter appeared in the doorway of the room and approached them.

"Hello, ladies."

The women returned his greeting.

Mrs. Stanwyck shook her head. "And this one. I had him, too, though he was rarely in class."

Damn, not another ghost from his past. Poor Hunter. No wonder he wanted to leave Hyde Point. Darcy was about to change the subject to protect him from the teacher's onslaught about his behavior, when Hunter smiled broadly at the older woman. "But when I was there, I was good for you, wasn't I, Mrs. S.?"

"Yes. I even got you to read *Madame Bovary*."

"That the one about the woman who tried to be something she wasn't? Wanted to live up to all society's standards?"

"Yes. Though I never thought of Emma like that. I always believed she was afraid to be herself."

Hunter captured Darcy's gaze. "Yeah, she probably was. She changed in order to make something of herself, then after she married that boring lawyer, she was miserable tryin' to live up to the new image she'd created."

"Emma's husband was a doctor, dear," Lila Stanwyck said.

Hunter gave Darcy a meaningful look, then turned away. "I gotta go find Braden," he finally said.

Mrs. Stanwyck put her arm through Hunter's. "I'll go with you, Hunter." As they walked away, Darcy heard her say, "We can talk more about your interesting views on Emma Bovary."

Jade grinned as she watched them go. "Who would have thought? The town bad boy and one of the toughest English teachers in the school."

Staring at his broad back, Darcy felt the sadness rise in her throat. It had been two weeks since the meeting at Quiet Waters, but if she closed her eyes she could still feel his muscles bunch under her hands, still smell him. So she took her frustration out on the woman she now considered her friend. "You didn't waste any time, did you, Jade?" she asked nastily.

"Why should I? You said he wasn't off limits."

"Is he as good in the sack as he looks?"

"I'll never tell."

Darcy was appalled to find moisture prickling behind her eyes. "I have to go." She started away.

"Darce, wait." Jade grabbed her arm.

"Let me go."

"God, woman. It's as plain as the nose on your face that you want him."

"Stop it. Just stop it!" She yanked away and strode to the ladies' room.

Inside, she found a stall and sank down on the toilet. Burying her face in her hands, she told herself it didn't matter if Hunter was sleeping with Jade.

But it did.

You're pathetic, you know that?

For once, Darcy wholeheartedly agreed with her alter ego.

THE WEEK FROM HELL—the second one in a row—was almost over. Thank God, Hunter thought as he watched the kids on the small carousel at the far end of Chuck E. Cheese's. Being around Darcy was as painful as medieval torture. He didn't know how much more he could take.

The worst was seeing her with Carrington. He'd bumped into them on Thursday when he was picking up Braden for lunch. Hunter had taken the afternoon off to spend with the boy and met the slick lawyer and Darcy coming out of TenderTime...

"Hi, Hunter," she'd said nervously.

He tried to close down, tried to block out the vision they'd made: Carrington in a suit that probably cost a week of Hunter's salary, Darcy slim and sleek in a navy dress with red trim. They were a perfect match.

"Miz Darcy." He glanced at the other man. "Carrington. Nice to see you again." Now there was a lie.

"Sloan, is it?" Carrington asked, moving closer to Darcy. He slipped his arm around her waist and his fingers pressed into the indentation at her middle. Hunter knew how supple she was there.

At the intimate gesture, Darcy stiffened. Almost as much as Hunter did.

Carrington added, "Nice to see you, too." He looked down at Darcy. "Come on, honey, we have reservations at the club for twelve-thirty." He'd spirited Darcy away.

Honey. Hunter had stood on the sidewalk watching them leave. Knife-sharp jealousy had twisted inside him. He'd been depressed all day thinking about how Carrington had the right to touch her, to call her pet names...

"Hey, handsome, how you doing?"

Hunter smiled at Jade, who'd come up to him. "Great, gorgeous. Where's that little treasure of yours?"

"She and Mrs. Stanwyck are in the dress-up room. Now, that lady's a gem, let me tell you."

"Yeah." Hunter was shocked that one of his teachers would take a shine to him. "Where's Darcy?"

"I don't know. She got mad at me and took off."

Alarm shot through him. "Where'd she go? Is she all right?"

Jade shook her head. "You two are a pair. Why don't you just admit how you feel and do something about it?"

"I told you I don't wanna talk about this, Jade."

"Fine." She surveyed the scene. "Uh-oh, look over there."

Hunter tracked her gaze, wondering if he should go find Darcy. But the choice was taken from him as he saw Darcy's daughter and his son square off over a soccer pinball game. Even from a distance, he could sense trouble brewing. He hurried toward them, and bumped right into Darcy.

He grabbed her arms. "You okay?" She wasn't. Her face was white, her eyes liquid. Had she been crying?

"No."

"It's *my* turn," came Braden's strident voice.

"Is not." Meli.

"Oh, Lord," Darcy said, "Not again." Together they closed the distance to the kids. "What's going on *now*, guys?" It was obvious that Darcy had reached her limit today by the strain in her voice.

Braden looked up at her. The kid had *longing* in his eyes. And fear that this woman, too, might turn on him. *Welcome to the club, little guy.*

"She cut on line, Miss Darcy."

"I did not. You're just causing trouble again."

Something about Meli's tone. Hunter's head cocked. Darcy said, "Meli, we went through—"

"Don't take his side, Mama. He's a troublemaker."

"Melanie Anne."

The little girl raised her chin, and Hunter's gut clenched.

"He is, Mama. Grandma says he's bad, just like his daddy."

It was as if the world froze. Hunter could no longer hear the pings of the games, couldn't smell the buttery popcorn and spicy pizza. Everything focused on the little girl he'd come to care about. He hadn't realized a seven-year-old could have that kind of power over him. He came to when his son sidled into him.

"...Meli. That was a nasty and hurtful thing to say." Darcy's voice was horrified.

Tears formed in Meli's eyes. She moved as if to run away.

"No, you're not going anywhere." Forcefully Darcy held Meli back. "Turn around and apologize to Hunter and Braden right now."

Immediately Meli did. "I...I'm sorry. I didn't mean it. Honest."

But Braden wasn't listening to her apology, heartfelt though it was. He'd turned and was looking up. Oh, God, how could Hunter withstand his own son's contempt?

"Is that true? Were you bad?"

Darcy said, "Braden, listen, Meli didn't mean—"

Hunter held up his hand for her to stop. He squatted down to eye level with his son. "Yeah, Champ, I was bad when I was young."

Big dark eyes widened. "Like me? You were bad like *me?*"

He heard Darcy moan, and Meli began to cry.

"You're not bad, Braden."

"Did you get in trouble like me? When you were little?"

"More than you, son. A lot more."

"No foolin'?" It was then that Hunter caught the tone of Braden's voice. It wasn't condemning at all, though he couldn't identify what it was.

"No foolin', Brade."

A smile split Braden's face. "Cool!"

Hunter chuckled. He couldn't believe it.

Nor could he believe it when Braden threw himself into Hunter's arms and, in front of everybody, hugged him tightly.

"THE CLUB LOOKS GREAT, doesn't it?" David took Darcy by the hand as they entered the front door. Hyde Point Country Club's Fall Fling was well underway when they arrived. The place was already packed with the town's elite celebrating the coming of autumn.

"Hmm. Yes."

"I wish we could have gotten here earlier."

"I'm sorry, David. I had things to do this afternoon and couldn't get out of the house any sooner." Truth be told, Darcy dreaded being here. All she wanted was to stay home and lick her wounds. She had no idea how she was ever going to get through tonight. The only saving grace was there wasn't a shot in hell of bumping into Hunter at the club.

After today, she wasn't sure how much more she could take.

"Aren't the grazing stations a good idea?" David

asked as they melded with the crowd gathered in the Donald Ross Room. "Our committee thought of them instead of a sit-down dinner."

"They're great." Who *cares,* she thought, that there are twenty food and drink stations spread inside and on the grounds of the place? She wouldn't be able to eat anything anyway.

But a scotch sure would taste good. Maybe a double. Or a triple.

"Is your mother here yet?"

"I know she left the house early. She and Jeremy were meeting some of their friends."

David scanned the crowd. "There's Nathan. Let's go talk to him. I want to ask him something about the campaign. I'm helping out, you know."

"No, I didn't know that. Is Nathan a good congressman?" she asked, thinking of Anabelle.

"The best. He's a shoo-in for reelection."

Wending their way through the crowd, they found Nathan and his fiancée, Barbara, talking with a man whose back was to them. A charcoal pin-striped suit stretched across his broad shoulders. Shoulders that were—

"Nathan, good to see you." David shook Nathan's hand and kissed Barbara on the cheek. "Barbara, you look gorgeous, as usual."

Nathan smiled. "You remember Hunter, don't you, David? Darcy?"

Oh, hell. Goddamn son of a bitch.

It was worse when he turned around. Only two years of quelling her honest reactions kept Darcy from drooling. With the suit, he wore a snowy-white shirt that showed off his dark coloring. A demure tie with a perfect Windsor knot graced his powerful neck muscles.

He'd even gotten a haircut somewhere between Chuck E. Cheese's and the Fall Fling.

David stiffened. "Yes, of course. Sloan, good to see you again." With a lot less warmth, David shook hands with Hunter.

Hunter didn't seem to notice. Instead, his eyes lingered on Darcy's beaded top. The garment was strapless, but she wore a shawl over it. Satiny black pants and strappy sandals completed the outfit. Hunter finally found his voice. "Nice to see you, David. Darcy, you're lookin' mighty nice tonight."

"Hunter's the one who looks like a million bucks," someone said from behind her.

Darcy turned to see Jade carrying two drinks.

"Here's your scotch, handsome. Neat."

Hunter dragged his eyes away from Darcy and made room for Jade.

"Jade, have you met Carrington?" Nathan, always the politician, asked.

David's eyes practically popped out of their sockets when he turned his full gaze on Jade. Over tailored white tuxedo pants, she wore a sheer knee-length coat of delicate ivory lace. It had one satin button holding it closed; underneath was a flesh-colored tank top, which looked like bare skin at first glance. "I don't believe I've had the pleasure," David whispered.

Hunter glanced from Jade to David. From David to Jade. Then he caught Darcy's gaze. He winked at her. The band of the emotion constricting her heart loosened. There was not a whit of jealousy in his reaction.

Thank God.

"Can I get you a drink?" Nathan asked Darcy.

David recovered some and said, "I'll get it."

"Come and sit at our table, Darce." This from Jade.

"Your table?"

"Yeah, we're guests of Paige and Ian." She looked at Nathan. "You got somewhere to sit, Congressman?"

"We have to mingle, but we'd be glad to join you after I get my last vote-for-me round in."

Jade looked him up and down. "You got my vote, sugar."

Nathan laughed. Barbara didn't. Stiffly, she grabbed Nathan's arm and pulled him away.

"What did I say?" Jade asked.

Hunter took her arm. "Nothin', sweetheart. You just have to exist to make other women jealous."

Darcy swallowed hard. The band was back, looping around her heart again.

"You coming, Darce?" Jade asked.

"No, I'll be along in a minute. I'm going to, um, help David…get my drink."

Hunter scowled at her. Did he even realize what he'd done? He called some other woman sweetheart in front of her, made a sexy comment about her.

The night went downhill from there.

Trying to delay facing Hunter, Darcy told David, once she found him, that she was hungry, so they visited the shrimp bar. Next, she needed another drink. Finally, she had to go to the ladies' room. When she returned, David was seated with Paige, Ian, Jade, Hunter, Nathan and Barbara.

She had no choice but to join them.

Yeah, thinking you don't have a choice seems to be your mantra lately, Darce.

Shut up! she told her inner voice. She couldn't deal with that tonight.

Because you know I'm right. You're running out of

time, girl. Jade's going to snag him. Or somebody else.
He looks like the Hunk-of-the-Month in that suit.

She made her way to the table. Unfortunately the only empty seat was right across from Hunter and Jade.

"Wow, Darce, you look fantastic." Paige eyed her clothes.

"Thanks." She took in Paige's pink and red jumpsuit. "You, too."

Ian reached over and smoothed a hand down her back. "Hmm. My favorite outfit."

They made chitchat about the coming election, about the Winslow place, about the imminent adoption of Ian and Paige's twins. When the band struck up, people began to dance.

Ian pushed back his chair. "Let's get out there so I can hold you."

"Get a room, you guys," Jade said saucily.

Ian grinned. "Do they rent them here?"

Jade stood, too, and pulled Hunter to the floor. Finally, Nathan and Barbara joined in.

Darcy and David watched the other couples dance. Only when a slow song came on did the two of them take the floor. Meanwhile, it was pure agony watching Hunter move. Weren't men supposed to look like frogs in blenders when they danced fast? Why did he have to have the grace of a Baryshnikov and the sexiness of Sting?

She was grateful when he returned to the table with Jade.

"Hey, Counselor, how about a dance with me?" Jade asked when a particularly erotic slow tune ensued.

David flushed.

"Oh, come on, Darcy can spare you a minute."

David let Jade lead him to the floor.

Darcy and Hunter were left alone.

"You cut a pretty mean rug out there." Darcy tried to sound cool.

"Your boyfriend doesn't dance much, does he?"

"Just slow songs."

Boring.

"I don't suppose you want to twirl around the floor with me."

The old Darcy popped out before Darcy could quell her. "I want to twirl around the floor with you more than I want to take my next breath."

His smile was intimate and sexy.

She glanced out at the other couples and caught sight of her mother and Jeremy. Marian was shooting disapproving looks at her for just sitting alone with Hunter.

He tracked her gaze to the Masons. When he looked back to her, his eyes turned hard and glittered with anger. He threw back his chair. "Never mind, Darcy. I wouldn't want to embarrass you." Standing, he stalked away.

That was it. Enough was enough. She rose and bolted in the opposite direction. At the door to the back grounds, she bumped into Nora Whitman. She and Dan were coming in from outside.

"Darcy, dear, how are you?"

"Just peachy, Nora," she said and took off.

Nora found her on the other side of the pro shop, in back of the building where no one could see her. Nora placed her hands on Darcy's shoulders. "Sweetie, what's wrong?"

Darcy shook her head. "What isn't?"

"Tell me." Nora circled her around.

And suddenly it was too much. The wanting and not having. The craving and the denial. Watching Hunter dance with another woman was intolerable. Knowing she'd offended him cut her to the quick.

Darcy burst into tears.

Nora gathered her close and soothed down her hair. "Shh, it's okay. Whatever it is, it'll be okay."

"No, no, it won't," she gulped.

She'd just begun to calm down, when she heard a deep male voice say, "I'll take it from here, Nora."

WHEN DARCY TURNED to face him, Hunter saw the tears in her eyes and cursed his earlier angry reaction. As soon as Nora left, he drew Darcy to him, beating back the thought that he could only hold her because they were hidden from Hyde Point Country Club patrons by the building.

What the hell had he been thinking, anyway, to come here tonight?

Still, he cradled her to his chest.

"I'm sorry," she mumbled into his shirt. Her hands grasped the lapels of the only suit he owned.

"Shh. It's okay." It wasn't. "I know you don't want your mother to see you with me."

She shook her head. "It was a knee-jerk reaction because of what she did with Claire the other day. I was worried she might embarrass you here."

Was that true? Or was Darcy worried Marian might embarrass *her?* Knee-jerk reactions were, after all, the most telling kind because they showed how you really felt before you could censor your response.

And what the hell did it matter anyway?

"God, I hate this town," he said forcefully.

She burrowed into him. The shawl slipped, revealing luscious skin that was luminescent in the light from the halogen lamp above the pro-shop entrance. He grazed her shoulder with his lips. She shivered. Then she laid her cheek on his chest. Drawing up her shawl, he snuggled her in and rested his chin on the top of her head.

"I'm sorry about Meli and Braden today, too. I'll talk to my mother about that, I promise."

"No need, Darce. It just underscores the fact that this place isn't for me or Braden. God, when I think of what he'd be subjected to if we stayed here."

"Stayed here?"

"Just conjecture. If I ever got to keep Braden, I couldn't stay here with him."

"I wish you could keep him."

"I do, too." They were silent. It was cooler now at night, but the scents of summer still lingered in the air. He breathed them—and her—in.

Darcy said, "I saw Braden's reaction to Meli's comment today."

Hunter chuckled. "I'm not sure that it's a good thing to have a kid think his dad's cool because he was bad. Each time I try to discipline him from now on, he'll probably throw that in my face."

"No, he won't. Braden respects you. I told you about the incident with Tommy the other day. He was so proud of you."

"Maybe."

"Besides, you're not bad."

Slowly, he slid his hand down her back to her bottom. The satiny pants made him think of expensive sheets and being on them with her. He pressed her against him. "I sure as hell feel mighty bad right now, Miz Darcy."

His wry comment didn't make her laugh, as he'd intended. Instead, she drew back and peered up at him. Lashes, still spiky and wet, shaded eyes filled with conflict. Shamelessly she pressed herself even closer, making him moan. "I can't stand it anymore, Hunter. I want you."

His response was violent. His whole body jerked into hers and for one terrifying second, he was afraid he'd go off right there.

"Darcy, darlin', you're killin' me."

Then she snuggled into his chest. The tenderness of the gesture confused him even more than her admission. With complete lack of sophistication, she said again, "I want you so much."

His willpower deserted him. "Then let's do it."

"*What?*"

"Let's do it. One time. Get it out of our systems."

"Now?"

He shook his head, though he was more than ready. "No, not now." He thought a minute. "Tomorrow's Sunday. Can you get away in the afternoon?"

"Yes. Mom and Jeremy are taking the girls to a harvest festival in Watkins Glen."

"Meet me at the Boxwood Inn. It's on this side of Elmwood. I bid on a carpentry job for new cabins, so I was just out there. The place is a half hour from here, and pretty remote. Nobody we know will see us." He pushed away the unsettling knowledge that he had to hide his relationship with her.

"I hate sneaking around."

"Me, too. I couldn't do it for long, it'd hurt too much. But I gotta have you, Darce. Once." He drew her closer. "I'm dyin' here."

"Me, too," she repeated.

"The whole afternoon, darlin'," he whispered in her ear.

She looked up at him.

"I want you the whole afternoon. If it's gonna be just this once, we're gonna make it last."

She trembled violently. In the glow of the overhead lamp, he could see her eyes glitter. They'd be green as hell now. He edged away. "I gotta go, or I won't be able to control myself." He started to back up.

Giving him Eve's grin, she said, "Hunter?"

"Yeah?"

"You won't have to control yourself tomorrow. When we're together." She drew close. He could smell her perfume, see the goose bumps on her shoulders.

He moaned again. How was he gonna make it through the next twelve hours?

CHAPTER ELEVEN

GRIPPING THE PICNIC-BASKET handle, Darcy stood at the door to cabin number six but didn't knock. While she thought about what she was doing, she let the breeze pick up her hair and swirl it around her face. Somehow, she knew that when she entered this little log structure, her life would never be the same again.

I want you for the whole afternoon. If it's gonna be just this once, we're gonna make it last. His voice had been gravelly and his eyes dark with sexual promise.

She shivered. The basket she carried bumped into her leg. It contained food she hoped Hunter would like. And condoms. Again, she knocked.

No answer.

He'd called at 8:00 a.m.

Meet me at cabin six. I feel like I'm gonna jump out of my skin, so I'll be workin' at Quiet Waters for a while. Then he'd added, *Don't be late, darlin'.*

Two more knocks and the door swung open.

Darcy thought she was prepared for this. But her mouth gaped at the sight before her. He was dressed in jeans, which had a button fly with the top fastener undone. His hair was damp and he had a towel slung around his neck. Droplets of water beaded on his chest, darkening the hair there. His feet were bare.

But it was his eyes that captured her—they glittered with raw desire and made her insides go soft. His gaze raked her outfit—the green jumpsuit she'd worn that night with Jade at Rascal's. He said nothing, but his mouth hardened into a grim line as he reached out and drew her inside. Though he was gentle, there was a restrained violence about him.

She tumbled through the entryway, and he shut the wooden door forcefully.

"Did you take a show—" Her words were cut off by his lips.

No gentle seduction, no coaxing. He took her mouth like a man possessed, a marauder out to conquer. The door was hard at her back. His muscular frame dwarfed her as he pressed her into it; then, still silent, his hands wedged between the wood and her back groped for the zipper of her jumpsuit.

Her fingers found the fly of his pants, which bulged arousingly. The jumpsuit slid to her waist.

"Oh. God…you're…" His words were ragged and unfinished.

Fumbling badly, she undid his jeans and slid her hands inside. "Hunter," she said against his shoulder when she found no underwear. She cupped him boldly and he swore.

Sensations rushed through her—his mouth closing over a nipple clad in black lace, his teeth scraping sensuously. His soapy scent filled her head.

The jumpsuit slithered down her legs. He followed it and knelt before her. Teeth on the tender skin of her stomach traced the lacy black band of the thong. Her head began to spin and buzz when his face nuzzled her intimately, but she thought she heard him swear again and mumble, "…killin' me."

Nails dug into his shoulders. Scraped. "Up," she begged.

It was a long time before he roughly tore the thong off and stood. Then her bra was gone. She pushed at his jeans. Naked skin met naked skin. Again, the door, hard at her back. His body pulsed everywhere.

''Darce.'' Tiny bites on her shoulder. Strong workman's fingers gripped her hips.

She wrapped her legs around him.

He jerked toward her. ''Son of a bitch. Condoms.''

''The b-basket.''

When he was ready, he lifted her legs back up and plunged into her. The world dimmed. Then burst with color. She pushed to get closer. He thrust, pounded.

''God…Hunter.''

''Darlin'…''

''Oh, oh, oh…''

He groaned.

The entire universe exploded around her like hot, bright fireworks illuminating a dark sky.

She might have screamed.

He moaned long and loud.

Harsh breathing…

It seemed to last forever, but later Darcy would realize this first time had taken all of about four minutes.

''THERE?''

''Oh, man, yeah.'' His muscles relaxed as the heel of her hand ground into a spot on his back.

She kissed his spine.

''Where did you get the scar on your leg?'' he mumbled into the pillow.

''Shh. I'm concentrating here. I'll tell you later.'' Her hands went to his butt, kneaded there.

''Geez, Darcy, I…oh, man, what are you…ahh.''

''Relax, babe. Enjoy it.''

"Not with your hands there. You're in dangerous—"

She kissed him.

His groan was gruff.

As she worked her way down his body, her unbound hair trailed behind her like wet silk. It was almost as stimulating as her delectable massage, which aroused first, then soothed, then aroused again.

His thigh muscles bunched. Then let down. Her tongue licked behind his knees. He never knew a foot massage could make his toes curl and his heart thump.

"The other side," she whispered sexily in his ear as she eased him over.

And giggled.

"Proud of your handiwork, woman?" he growled, reaching for her.

Fast, she grabbed his hands and brought them over his head. Wrapping his fingers around the spindles of the four-poster, she said, "Don't let go."

"I wouldn't think of it." All kinds of fantasies ran through his brain.

She made every single one look tame.

Her hands went everywhere except for the one spot he wanted them most. "Darce, you'd better—"

"Shh, I—" But he didn't hear the rest as her mouth closed over him.

"THIS IS *SO* NAUGHTY."

"Mmm. Spread your legs a little more."

A blush crept up from her waist to her forehead. "Hunter…"

"Shh. I want to see every inch of you."

Not that he hadn't already. Up close and personal. But this was sexy. She spread her legs wider.

"Watch me. No, don't look down. In the mirror."

Her eyes were glittering like emeralds as she held his gaze in the wide glass mirror of the armoire at the side of the bed. His knuckles grazed her auburn curls and she startled. With an arm around her waist, he kept her locked to him, loving how sensitized she was to his touch.

"Tell me about the scar."

She recited the story, and he shook his head when she finished. "Sitting here like this with you " he kissed her temple "—I can almost believe it."

Turning, she kissed his jaw. "What about you? Where did this scar come from."

He brushed his knuckles against her again then stopped. She whimpered. He'd learned something from her earlier *massage*. "Believe it or not, a similar incident. A girl…another guy…in a bar when I was seventeen…" He bit her shoulder. "Now, turn back around. No more talk about the past. I gotta concentrate here." His hand ground against her. She jerked forward.

He smiled.

"Proud of yourself?" she asked.

"I'm proud of you. You came four times already in—" he glanced at the grandfather clock in the corner "—just two hours."

She reached behind her back to fondle him. "It's because of this big boy."

He laughed. "Oh, yeah." Grabbing the hair that would haunt his days and nights forever, he let its lemony scent envelop him as he fisted his hands in it. Lightly, he brushed her nipples with a heavy lock.

"Ahh."

Her stomach.

"Ohh."

Her navel.

He abandoned her hair and, this time, when his hand went lower, he used his fingers.

"Hmm," he whispered afterward. "Knock that number up to five."

THE HARD PASSION, the naughty teasing, even the fun was gone by five o'clock.

He was inside her for the last time. On top, in the age-old position, he peered down into her eyes with sadness in his. "I'll never forget this, Darcy."

She raised shaky hands to his face and brushed the stubble that had burned the tender skin of her thighs. "Me neither."

Take the risk, Darce.

"I've never felt this way during sex, Hunter."

He closed his eyes. "Don't tell me that, darlin'."

The resignation in his voice brought moisture to her eyes. Damn, she vowed she wouldn't cry, would be grateful just for one day with him.

It wasn't enough.

Tell him.

She hesitated.

Please.

"This isn't enough, Hunter." Her voice was a throaty whisper. "I'm sorry, I know we said it would have to be. But it isn't."

He braced his arms on the firm mattress.

She felt him pulse inside her, telling her that at any time, the passion would flare. "What do you want, Darcy?" he asked harshly.

"You." She thrust forward and he sucked in a breath. "This. Not just for today."

"We agreed it'd be just once."

"I know." God, could he have done what he did to her today and not feel the same?

Ask him.

"Don't you..." Her throat clogged. "Don't you feel the same way?"

"Aw, shit, that's it..." He thrust wildly inside her.

They came simultaneously in a cataclysmic climax.

Afterward, he rolled off her, breathing as if he'd run the New York Marathon; she turned her back to him so he wouldn't see the tears. It was a while before he pulled her spoonlike against him and banded an arm around her waist. The other crisscrossed her chest.

"I feel the same," he said simply. Then, "What do you want to do about it?"

"Can we see each other until you leave?"

She felt his sigh. "Like this?"

Secretly, he meant.

Ashamed of her request, she only nodded. She had no right to ask him to hide their relationship. But she *did* have reasons. "I wouldn't ask you to hide our relationship if it wasn't for the girls and Braden. They'll get false hopes if we date openly."

"I know," he said. "But, Darcy, I'm not sure I can sneak around. Do you know how that would feel?"

She turned and buried her face into his chest. "Awful. But I can't let you go, Hunter. Please, just for a little while..."

He gripped her tight. She could tell he was struggling. Finally he said, "All right." Again a pause. "Now that it's fall, the cabins are available by the week." He waited a moment. "How long should I get it for?"

"When is Shelly's baby due?"

"Less than a month."

"When will you leave here?"

"Shortly after."

She snuggled into him, drew in the scent of his arm. "Until then."

Again, he tensed. "Damn it. We should have known this wouldn't work like we planned." A very long pause. "All right. Until I leave."

"Hunter, I—"

"No!" His voice was harsh. "Don't say anything. I understand all the reasons. So do you. I just hope we're not making a whale of a mistake."

"Me, too," she said simply.

CHAPTER TWELVE

"COME *ON*, BOY." Braden rested his hand on Tramp's head and bent over to speak quietly in the animal's ear.

The dog no longer shimmied away from the boy, but Tramp hadn't yet warmed up to Braden the way he had to Claire. Those O'Malley women were stealing everybody's heart, and if Hunter was any indication, there wasn't a thing they could do about it.

"Pu-lease, Tramp. It's my *class*." Dressed in pants and a nice shirt Ada had ironed for this special day, Braden gestured to the ten kids gathered in the PreK room. Brightly lit, drenched in vivid primary colors, smelling slightly of finger paint and peppermint, the large airy space had desks to one side and several stations around the room for learning and for play. Braden loved the class. Since being on the medication, he'd been able to sit still and cooperate more. Only the food alterations had been hard for him, but even that was improving.

When Tramp didn't move, Braden looked to Hunter for help. He did that a lot. Sometimes it almost brought tears to Hunter's eyes. He stepped forward to coax the dog, when suddenly Tramp rose willingly and accompanied Braden to the middle of the room.

Leaning back against the wall, Hunter watched his son approach Josh Jacobs, a soccer buddy who'd unexpectedly joined the PreK class at TenderTime. Another break. Must be his lucky week.

"Hello, Mr. Sloan."

Speaking of luck...

Hunter pivoted.

And there she was.

His insides turned to mush at the sight of Darcy O'Malley. She wore a prim beige suit today, but in his mind, he saw her in a lacy black thong, her skin soft and creamy in the light from the inn's lamps. As she took the last few steps toward him on high heels, he pictured her barefoot, kneeling in front of him. He could practically smell the flowery scent from her hair. His voice was gruff when he said, "Mornin', Miz Darcy."

Her eyes sparkled, and she gave him a private smile that said, *I remember.*

There were kids around, a teacher and aides, as well as parents who'd come for show-and-tell, but he couldn't resist flirting with her. "You look rested today. Have a nice weekend?"

"Mmm." She stopped a decent space away from him but her voice—a sexy purr, really—reached out and curled inside him; he reacted as if she'd stroked his naked back. "Yesterday was particularly renewing."

"Ahh. That's good to hear."

She sobered. "How are *you?*"

"I'm right fine."

When she'd left him yesterday, he'd been angry, and she'd known it. He'd cursed himself for agreeing to see her on the sly. Nonetheless, he'd gone to the proprietor of the inn and rented the cabin for the month of October. He'd been frustrated at first, but after the best night's sleep he'd had in months, and having learned a long time ago that resentment did no good, he woke up glad she was in his life, even if it was only temporary. And determined not to spoil the time they *did* have.

Besides, she was right not to flaunt their relationship. He was leaving soon. They didn't want their kids to get the wrong idea. Also, she needed to keep her life here intact. He didn't know, though, what he'd do if that meant she'd be dating Carrington while she was sleeping with Hunter. The thought of the other guy touching her made Hunter want to die.

"Can I see you after this?" he asked, nodding to the kids.

"Sure."

He was distracted by the teacher, Becky, saying, "If the parents would like to take a seat, we'll begin."

With a smile for Darcy, he found a chair. "Hunter, hello," the woman next to him said. It was Julie Jacobs, his assistant soccer coach.

"Hey, Julie."

She reached out and squeezed his arm. "I knew your son was in this class. Josh talks about him all the time."

"Braden, too, about Josh."

All the kids sat in a circle, each holding their precious objects. The things they brought in ranged from trophies, to stamp collections, to action figures, as well as some pets. Each child got a few minutes to explain why his belonging was precious. One little tyke held up a fishing pole, and talked about the first time his grandpa took him fishing and he, the boy, tossed the pole in the river and yelled, "Here, fishy, fishy."

Everybody laughed.

Braden was next to last. "This is Tramp," Braden said proudly and petted the dog's head. "He's mighty shy, 'cause he was 'bused." Braden smiled over at Hunter, who nodded for him to continue. "But he's gettin' better. Learnin' people like him. That people'll take care of him. That nobody's gonna hurt him."

Hunter caught Darcy's gaze. She smiled. He smiled back. Life was damn well looking up these days.

To top it off, before Hunter left the PreK room, Braden hugged Tramp. Then, spontaneously, he hugged Hunter, too. "Thanks for bringin' him."

"You're welcome, son."

Hunter waited for Darcy outside the room and down the hall, holding the dog's leash, unbalanced by Braden's spontaneous affection. She joined him and reached out to pet Tramp; the dog leaned into her touch.

"He likes you."

Darcy looked up. Her hair was in a braid but a few tendrils had escaped to frame her face. She seemed contented and happy. "The dog?"

"All the Sloan males."

"That's nice to hear." She studied him. "I thought you were angry."

"Not anymore." He shrugged. "I get over things fast."

"Hunter, I—"

"No, don't say anything. 'Cept maybe yes."

"To what?"

"I want to…see you again. Soon."

Her eyes widened, dilated a bit. "When?"

"How soon can you get away?"

"I usually do errands on Wednesday afternoons."

"Hell, darlin', that's near to forty-eight hours."

"I think we'll survive."

"Barely." His eyes dropped to her breasts. He remembered how heavy they were in his hands. "I'd better go. I'm gonna embarrass myself." He turned to leave.

She touched his arm. ''Hunter?''

He pivoted, but felt a tug on the leash.

Then he heard a growl.

When he looked down, Tramp had tensed and bared his teeth. When he looked up, he saw Marian Mason coming toward them.

THE BRIGHT OCTOBER sunshine beat down on Darcy's head as she walked along the street holding Braden's hand. The PreK class was studying pumpkins. Today, they'd been to Milligan's Pumpkin Farm to see how pumpkins were grown, and now, after lunch, were on their way to Hannah's Place for homemade pumpkin pie and cider. It hadn't been easy getting Hunter to let Braden go...

''I don't want him at the diner,'' Hunter had said, handing back the unsigned permission slip.

''I understand. But how will you explain it to Braden? The kids are really excited by the outing.''

''I'll find a way. All I know is that I won't have him feeling like he's not good enough. What if she's mean to him? Or, worse, if she's nice to the other kids, and snubs Braden. I can't stand thinking about her pretending there's nothing between them.''

In the end, Braden had thrown such a tantrum—rare these days—about not being able to attend, that Hunter had relented. Darcy promised to stick close to him and compensate for anything his sister did—or didn't—do.

Hannah met all the kids at the door dressed in a pumpkin costume, complete with a sprout of green coming out of her hair.

''Cool,'' Braden had said when he saw her.

She reached out to give him a pumpkin coloring book, but stopped suddenly. The smile on her face died.

Darcy moved in close and put her arm around Braden. Sensing the other woman's reaction, Braden moved toward Darcy, too. Oh, God, Hunter had been right. What's more, it brought home once again just how awful things were in this town for him. No wonder he was leaving.

"Hannah," Darcy said forcefully.

Her chiding tone seemed to shake Hannah out of her daze. She smiled, albeit weakly. "Hello. How are you today?"

Braden relaxed. He accepted the coloring book. "I'm right fine." He glanced around, said, "Gonna go see Josh," and took off.

Hannah stared after him. Ready to do battle, Darcy squared her shoulders. Before she could say anything, Hannah whispered, "He looks just like Hunter."

"Yes, he does."

Hannah glanced at the pies, sitting on the counter. Their fresh-baked aroma filled the diner. "Hunter used to love pumpkin pie."

That ambushed Darcy. "Really? I got the impression nobody ever baked for him."

Hannah reddened. "He was—"

"Oh, stop it, Hannah. I've heard it all about how *bad* Hunter was. Well, a lot of us were. That was then and this is now." She nodded to where Braden accepted a glass of cider from the waitress. "You've got a terrific nephew there, who, by the way, isn't going to be in town much longer. If I were you, I'd seize the opportunity to get to know him." At Hannah's pallor, Darcy reached out and squeezed her arm. "Life's too short. And Braden's a great kid. Give him a chance." *Like nobody ever gave your brother.*

She left Hannah standing in the doorway and circulated, keeping an eye on Braden. Much later, when Hannah approached the boy, Darcy made a beeline for him. She'd watch over Braden for as long as he was here, despite her mother's concerns...

Really, Darcy Anne, what is this with you and the Sloans? I'm always finding you with the boy, or worse, his father. Her mother had looked tired yesterday at the daycare.

Don't worry, Mom, they're not staying in town much longer.

Thank God.

Darcy could barely entertain the thought, let alone be grateful for it.

Braden was sitting on a stool at the counter. Hannah came up behind it. "Would you like some more cider, Braden?" she asked, studying the little boy.

"Yes, ma'am."

Hannah seemed awkward as she poured the drink. But she didn't leave. Instead she smiled. "Are you having a good time?"

"Uh-huh."

"Was the pumpkin farm fun?"

"Yep. My daddy says he'll help me decorate the pumpkin they gave us. We don't do this stuff in Florida."

"Pumpkins are fun to decorate."

Cocking his head, Braden asked innocently, "You got any kids?"

Hannah cleared her throat. "Yes. Two. They're a lot bigger than you, but they used to love to decorate pumpkins, too." She glanced at Darcy, guilt bright in her eyes. Braden had cousins he'd never met.

"What're their names?" Braden asked.

"My older boy's Bart, the younger one is Bryce."

"Bart's my grandpa's name!"

Hannah's eyes widened.

Darcy was about to intervene, when she heard, "Hey, Champ, how ya doin'?"

Braden turned. He looked up at Hunter. "Doin' just great." He slid off the stool and nodded to a display of painted pumpkins. "Wanna look at the pumpkins over there?"

For a moment, Hunter just stared at his sister. "Yeah, sure."

Taking Hunter's hand, Braden dragged him away.

Hannah said, "He's a good father, isn't he?"

"Yes, he is." When Hannah didn't respond, Darcy continued. "And he'd be a good brother if you'd give him half a chance." Again, Darcy squeezed her arm. "Think about it. You don't have much time left." As she walked toward Hunter and Braden, Darcy's own words hit home. She didn't have much time left with Hunter, either.

On Wednesday in the cabin at the Boxwood Inn, the old Darcy surfaced and wouldn't be quelled. As far as Hunter was concerned, she could have top billing permanently. Ever since Darcy had confided in him that there were remnants inside her of the girl she used to be, Hunter looked forward to the old Darcy's appearance. Sitting across from him, dressed in his shirt, sipping a glass of champagne he'd brought to spoil her, Darcy's eyes sparkled emerald green. In her other hand she held a copy of *Cosmopolitan* magazine.

"You have to take this test."

He sipped his own bubbly and popped a strawberry in his mouth. "I have to, huh? What do I get for it?"

Pure sexual delight flushed her face. "You already got it, buster."

He had. She'd barely gotten inside the room when she began to tear at his clothes, and he at hers. The lovemaking had been fast and intense.

"I'm not done with you yet, woman."

She shivered. "Oh, good. This first." She read from the magazine. "Write down your name and mine."

He picked up a pen and jotted their names on Boxwood Inn stationery, then handed it over to her.

"Ah, perfect. My name's bigger than yours." She toyed with her hair, which was draped over her shoulders like a fiery cape. "It means you worship the ground I walk on."

Well, that was true.

"And if the letters are angular—" they were "—then you're revved up sexually." She gave him an admonishing look. "That can't be true after what we just did."

"Don't bet the farm on that, darlin'."

She giggled. "Next question—what color do you picture me in most of the time."

"I picture you *naked* most of the time."

"Hun-ter. Play."

Thoughtfully he sipped his drink. "All right. Green. 'Cause of your eyes."

"Really? This says you're interested in romance."

I am. And, he was beginning to think, a lot more.

They went through the rest of the questions. "Last one. Unwrap this piece of chocolate and eat it."

He peeled the wrapper off a truffle and popped the candy in his mouth. It was bittersweet and rich. Taking the foil paper, he crushed it up then smoothed it out.

She read the test. "If he rolls the paper up in a ball, it means he only wants sex. If he smushes it then

smooths it, he wants to make things perfect for you.''
She grinned.

He didn't smile. He wished like hell he could make
things perfect, but he knew he could never do that for
her.

Carrington could.

''Hunter?''

''Hmm?''

''What's wrong?''

''Nothing. Are there any more questions?''

She got up and circled the table. Snuggling onto his
lap, she curled into him. His denim brushed her bare
legs. ''Are you okay?''

''I'm great.'' He fed her a piece of candy, and was
mesmerized watching her teeth close on the rich chocolate. He vowed nothing would spoil this time with her.
''Read me something else fun.''

''All right.'' She picked up the magazine again.
''How about 'Four Things He's Afraid to Tell You.'''

''That sounds dangerous.''

''Number one. He has a stash of porn.''

He nuzzled her neck, tasted the lotion she must have
used that morning. ''I'm throwin' mine all out. I'll just
relive what you did on that bed.''

''Number two. He wants more oral sex.''

''Well,'' he drawled jokingly, ''I wouldn't complain
if you'd step it up in that area.''

She whispered in his ear, ''My pleasure.''

He laughed.

''Number three. He worries about the size of his
penis.''

''I worry about pleasuring you.''

About being good enough for you.

''You do, Hunter. Pleasure me. Make me happy.''

He kissed her. She tasted like champagne and straw-berries and chocolate.

"Number four. He wishes you weren't more suc-cessful than he is." She sobered. "I'm not more suc-cessful than you, Hunter."

"You are, darlin', but I love your success. I want you to be everything you can be."

Again he thought of Carrington, the successful attor-ney, who could court her openly.

"Hunter? You look sad."

To distract her, he said, "I am," and glanced at the clock. "I have to go soon."

She studied him to see if there was hidden meaning to his words, then slid off his lap to her knees. "Then we better get started on number two."

As she knelt up in front of him, he closed his eyes. He felt her unzip his jeans. When her mouth closed over him, he didn't think at all.

CHAPTER THIRTEEN

THE GROUNDS of the Hyde family estate, where the Hydes had lived for generations, sparkled in the warm sun of Columbus Day. Rolling acres of grass were as green as a golf course. Indian summer had come to town, with its warm breezes and hot sunshine, making the sixty-five-degree day pleasant. It was a perfect setting for Nathan's preelection party for specially chosen guests.

"Mama, will Coach be here?" Claire asked as they crossed from the parking area to the front lawn. Claire held her hand, while Meli ran ahead. Claire had confided in Darcy that she was worried she wouldn't get to see Hunter now that the last soccer game was over. Hunter had done wonders for the little girl's self-confidence but, despite their best efforts, she'd gotten too attached to him.

Join the club.

"Yes, honey. Coach will be here."

"I still don't understand that one," David, on her left, commented.

"Why don't you like Coach, Mr. Carrington?" Claire asked. Her tone was more belligerent than Darcy had ever heard it. Even her ponytails were bobbing.

David had the grace to redden. "It's not that, Claire. It's just that he and Congressman Hyde have so little in common. Sloan's pretty rough around the edges."

Darcy stiffened. "Claire, why don't you catch up to Meli."

When Claire was safely away, she turned on David. "Don't you ever again express that kind of prejudice in front of my children."

"What's *with* you today?" As he spoke, David threw up his hands, then slapped them down on his tailored casual pants. "You've been sniping at me since I stopped by to pick you up."

He was right. She'd been surprised, and not happy, when he'd shown up at her door...

David, what are you doing here?

Didn't your mother tell you? She asked me to fetch you and the girls since Jeremy isn't feeling well and they won't be going to Nathan's today...

"I'm sorry. I don't mean to be a shrew. But I won't listen to you put down Hunter."

The little voice inside her practically choked on that lie. *You are* not *sorry. You shouldn't be here with him, Darce, and you know it.*

It seemed David was on a roll. "And I don't understand your concern for Sloan. If I didn't know better, I'd think there was something going on between you and him."

When she didn't respond, but stared guiltily at him, David's brown eyes were stormy and his fists curled. Drawing her to the cover of a copse of trees, he pulled her close. "There isn't, is there? Anything between you two?"

She stared up at him. Could she make a future with this man? Hunter was leaving in a few weeks. Even so, was David ever going to be right for her after she'd been with Hunter?

No way, girl.

"Look, David, I think we need to talk. I'm not sure—"

He yanked her into his arms and kissed her—the way he had that night she'd gone dancing with Jade at Rascal's. She was so startled by his aggressiveness, she was momentarily unbalanced and grabbed his arms; he must have mistaken her reaction for interest. His hands slid from her back to her bottom and caressed her.

Oh God.

She tried to pull away; he held fast. Then she felt something sidle in between them. A nose. A wet nose. And a plump body. She heard a growl.

"What the hell?" David let her go and she drew back fast.

She wanted to weep when she saw what had interrupted them.

Tramp.

Whirling, she found Hunter standing about twenty feet away, an utterly stunned look on his face. Braden stood beside him for a moment, then he raced toward the trees.

"Hey, Miss Darcy." The boy eyed David suspiciously.

"Hi, Braden." She bent down to pet Tramp. He nuzzled into her. "Hi, boy."

Dear God, what was she going to do? What could she say to Hunter?

He approached them. She straightened and smoothed down the pretty, sage-colored sweater and pants she'd bought yesterday because he'd said he pictured her in green.

His face was like a blank canvas when he reached them. Even his eyes were a cold, flat black. But she noticed his hand was shaking when he reached down and picked up Tramp's leash. "Sorry to interrupt. But Tramp here got away."

David moved in and rested his hand on the small of her back. "No harm done."

Turning on his heel, Hunter said, "Let's go, Brade," and strode away. Braden, looking confused, followed.

Darcy faced David. "You and I need to talk."

"I don't think this is the time or the place." He started to walk away.

She grabbed his shirt. "Now, David."

He sighed, as if he knew what was coming. "All right."

"Our relationship isn't what you think it is, David."

"No?"

"No. I'm not interested in you the way you seem to be in me."

He glanced after Hunter. "This wouldn't have anything to do with Sloan, would it?"

Tell him yes, end all this secrecy.

"It has to do with you and me. I don't feel the same about us as you do. It's not fair to mislead you that our relationship is going anywhere."

"I see." He reached out and brushed back her hair, which she'd left down. For Hunter. "Are you sure?"

"I'm sorry. I'm sure."

He looked up at the sky. "I've been expecting this, given your behavior lately. But I was hoping for more."

Again, she apologized.

He gave her a resigned smile. "I'll take you home, anyway, since you rode with me."

"You're a nice guy, you know that? But you don't need to watch out for me. There are a lot of people we can catch a ride with."

Nodding, he said, ''Well, if you ever change your mind...''

She smiled. ''Somebody else will have scooped you up by then.''

She watched him make his way to the party, and the panic returned. She had to talk to Hunter.

When she arrived at the back of the house, she saw that there were easily a hundred people on the grounds. Where was Hunter?

Catching sight of Paige, Ian, Jade and Charly sitting at a table, she crossed to them.

''Hi, Darce.'' Paige smiled at her. ''Where've you been?''

''I was delayed.'' She glanced around.

''Looking for somebody?''

''Oh, um, have you seen the girls?''

Coward. You can't even tell your friends.

''They're over there.'' With her long red fingernails, Jade motioned to the left. ''Nathan's set up a children's play area complete with clowns and face painting. The handsome congressman thought of everything.'' Eyeing Darcy thoughtfully, Jade stood. ''Come on, Red. I'll walk with you there. I want to check on Jewel. Claire's watching her.''

Darcy allowed herself to be led away.

''What's wrong?'' Jade asked when they were a safe distance from the group.

Darcy shook her head. ''I've really blown it.''

Jade pulled her down onto the bench of an empty picnic table. ''Tell me.''

''It's Hunter.''

''Surprise, surprise.''

''I'm involved with him.''

''That's the best news I've had in a long time.''

"Something just happened."

"What?"

She told Jade about David's unexpected and unwanted kiss and Hunter witnessing it.

"Damn it, Darce. What's *wrong* with you? You can't hurt Hunter like this."

"We decided to keep our relationship a secret. He's leaving town soon, we're worried about Claire and Braden getting too attached to us, and we didn't want to..." She trailed off, sick of the sorry story herself.

"So you're going to continue to date David?"

"No, I just told him I didn't want to see him again."

"Does Hunter know there's nothing between you?"

"No. I have to find him. To tell him."

Jade stood. "Then go. I'll keep an eye on the kids."

THE MEN—Dan, Nathan, Ian and Hunter—were seated on a flagstone patio that jutted off the mansion where Nathan lived. Hunter was having trouble concentrating on the conversation; he had to keep his mind blank or he was going to lose it right here in front of Hyde Point's elite. Not that he cared.

It was time to get out of Dodge.

Dan Whitman spoke to him. Dressed in jeans and a western shirt, Dan looked a lot younger than fifty-five today. Marriage had been good for him. "So when will the work be done on the Winslow place?"

Not soon enough. How long could he sleep with Darcy and then watch Carrington kiss her, touch her intimately? "I'll be done by the end of this week."

"That little guy of yours is certainly a character, Hunter." Also dressed in jeans, probably designer, Nathan lazed back into a lawn chair, sipping a beer. He looked pretty relaxed considering that the election was only a few weeks away. "Does Braden know how to read? He was looking at some of Kaeley's books I put in the kids' area, and I swear he knew the words."

"Darcy says... Yeah, I think he's getting the hang of it."

"I remember when Kaeley began to read."

Hunter tuned out as Nathan talked about his daughter. Instead he plotted how soon he could get Braden weaned from the daycare. At least he wouldn't have to worry about leaving his grandparents.

Think about that. Not her...with him...

Bart had come downstairs last night when Hunter had gotten home from Rascal's. "I want to talk to you, son."

"Did Braden do something?" He felt older than dirt and couldn't imagine dealing with the kid's misbehavior right then.

"Other than entertaining us all evening, you mean?"

Hunter smiled at the old man. "He's right fond of you."

"We love him, Hunter."

"The medicine's working. He's been better, hasn't he?"

"Yeah, but Hunter, there's more to it than that. Braden likes being with me and Ma. He needs his family around him."

Hunter could barely get the words out, but it wouldn't do, letting his grandparents get too attached. "He'll be going back to Shelly in a couple of weeks, Pa."

"I hate to see him go."

This time, Hunter couldn't respond.

"As a matter of fact, me and Ma been talking. We have trouble with the cold weather here in the winter."

"Yeah, I do, too."

"And you say Shelly lives two hundred miles from you?"

"Yeah."

"Well, we been thinking about spending the winter in the Keys. Then coming back here, where Hannah is, in the spring."

Hunter had felt a flood of feeling for his grandpa. "No kiddin'?"

"No kidding."

"Pa, that's great. You can live with me. We'll get a bigger place, get Braden to come as often as we can."

"That gonna be enough for you, son?"

"Do I have a choice?"

He was snatched from the pleasant thought when Nathan tried to draw him into the conversation. "So, Hunter, when do you think you'll be leaving Hyde Point?"

Dan shifted in his chair. "I wish you wouldn't go."

"What?"

"I wish you'd stay in Hyde Point. Work with us at Quiet Waters."

"As a handyman, you mean?"

"I think there are a lot of possibilities."

Hunter started to respond, then—from the corner of his eye—he saw Darcy approaching them. With her was Nora Whitman. Shit, how could he get out of here? Before he could try, Dan's cell phone rang.

Dan frowned. "I asked not to be contacted unless it was an emergency." His expression was worried as he flicked the phone on. "Whitman here."

Something made Hunter stay, even though Darcy had reached them.

Dan's healthy complexion paled. "*What?*... When?... Did you talk to my cousin? No, of course not. I'll call him. You sure the report didn't say anything else?'' When he clicked off, his gaze focused on Nora for a second, then swung over to Nathan.

"That was my office. Anabelle Crane has been shot in an undercover sting out in Seattle."

THE LIBRARY OF NATHAN'S house was stunning. Darcy had never seen it before, but today she was unable to fully appreciate its lofty ceilings, wall-to-wall bookshelves and heavy mahogany furniture. She was worried about Anabelle.

Nora was across the room with Dan. Slowly she soothed his arm. He sat in a stuffed chair staring at his cell phone. "Why doesn't Herb return my call?" he asked.

"He probably didn't get your message yet, dear."

Nathan pivoted from where he'd been staring out a huge double window. Barbara sat near him in an exquisite wing chair. "Did the report on your computer say when the shooting occurred?" Nathan asked.

Nora had told Darcy that Dan kept tabs on Anabelle by getting the police reports from Seattle through the computer in his office. He said he felt better knowing she was safe when no incident involving her came through. His cousin Herb, Anabelle's boss, had allowed the access, and teased Dan about being too protective of his little chick.

Who'd been shot. Dear God, poor Anabelle.

"The report came in about an hour ago. With the time difference, the shooting would have occurred about noon."

Nathan's face was ashen. "In broad daylight. God." He ran a hand through his hair. "Isn't there somebody else you can call?"

"No. We just have to wait."

Barbara grasped his arm. "Nathan, dear, be pat—"

"Try your cousin's cell again, will you?"

Wearily Dan shook his head, just as Charly, Paige and Jade entered the library. Nora stood and crossed to them.

"Hunter said Anabelle's been shot?" This from Jade whose usually mischievous face was full of worry.

"Yes. We don't know the details."

"Is she…" Charly's eyes were watery. "Is she alive?"

"The report just said an officer was down. Come on in." Nora ushered the women over to Darcy, who was off to the side standing by a chair. They all hugged.

And waited.

For what seemed like an eternity until Dan's cell phone rang. "Whitman… How is she, Herb?"

Everyone held their collective breath.

"Thank God." He covered the mouthpiece. "She's alive. Herb said she should be out of surgery any time now. He didn't want to call until he knew more. He forgot about my surveillance of the Seattle calls." Dan went back to the phone. "Yeah, Herb, I'm here. What happened?"

Dan listened. Darcy saw Nathan stuff his hands in his pockets. He was as brittle as a board.

"What? Oh, yeah, go ahead and talk to him."

Dan muted the phone. "The doctor just came out of surgery into the waiting area. Herb's getting the information now."

"What happened?" Nathan asked.

"She got shot when she was undercover as a waitress in a restaurant frequented by drug dealers she was investigating."

"Drug dealers! Je—"

Again, Barb touched his arm. "Nathan, let him talk."

"A guy came on to her, and she fended him off. He pulled out a pistol and shot her. He wasn't even one of the people they were after."

"Son of a bitch." Nathan's vehemence seemed to startle everyone.

Dan was back on the phone. "Yeah, Herb. Oh, geez, that's terrific. Just a sec." He told the group, "She's fine. The bullet went right through her shoulder. She'll be out of commission a while, but she'll recover fully."

Everybody began to talk at once.

Everybody but Nathan. Without a word, he strode out of the room. Looking confused, Barbara followed him.

Nora crossed to Darcy. "That's good news, isn't it?"

"Yes."

Jade was crying. Paige wiped her eyes. Charly looked dazed.

Darcy said, "I have to find Hunter."

HUNTER AND MELI went looking for Claire once he realized she'd left the children's area. They followed a trail into a wooded area that led to a clearing.

Claire was sitting on the ground, her back against a rock. Tramp was cuddled up to her, his head in her lap. She was petting his head.

She didn't see Hunter and Meli as they came up behind her.

"I don't want you to go, boy." Claire's sweet voice was threaded with tears.

The dog whimpered and licked her face.

"You don't want to go either, do you?"

Tramp emitted a soft woof that surprised Hunter, so seldom did the dog make any noise.

Then his ears stood up and he rose to all fours. He'd sensed Hunter and Meli.

"Hey, Miss Claire, what are you and Tramp doing out here by yourselves?"

As Hunter approached her—Meli stayed back—Claire swiped at her cheeks.

He squatted down in front of her. "Why are you crying, honey?"

She stared at him.

"Did Tramp here say something to hurt your feelings?"

Claire smiled.

"Can I sit?"

"Uh-huh."

"Come on, Mel, you too." Hunter eased down facing Claire, his back braced against another boulder.

Meli joined them but sat close to Claire. Tramp went to Hunter, nudged his hand, got a few pats and then returned to Claire, sidling back in close to both girls.

"He likes you two."

Claire scratched the dog's head.

"We like him, too," Meli said.

He watched Claire struggle. "We like you too, Coach."

"Aw, honey, that's about the nicest thing anybody's ever said to me."

"I like Braden," Meli said heatedly. "I act like I don't sometimes...but I do. I just get mad when he's better at stuff than me." She raised honest eyes to Hunter. "But I do like him, Coach."

"I wish..." Claire began.

He steeled himself for what he suspected was coming. "What do you wish, Claire?"

"That you didn't have to go away. That you and Braden could stay in Hyde Point with us."

"Me, too." Meli's voice was more demure than he'd ever heard it.

I wish that, too. Man, where did that come from? No way did he want to live in this godforsaken town.

"You're not going to stay here, are you?" Claire asked.

"No, Claire. I gotta give Braden back to his mama soon."

"How come?" Meli wanted to know.

Good question.

"Because it's the right place for him. How would you two feel if somebody took you away from your mama for good?"

"Like my daddy?" This from Claire.

"Yeah."

"He doesn't want us," Meli said. "Me or Claire."

"Oh, don't say—"

"We know," Claire added. "We heard him tell Mama we were too much responsibility." She peered up at Hunter. "Is Braden too much responsibility for you?"

"N—"

"'Cuz if he is, I could help you take care of him. I didn't help Mama enough with Meli. Maybe Daddy would have stayed if I'd—"

"Oh, Claire, you couldn't be more wrong. I told you that daddies don't leave because of nice little girls like you two. They leave because…"

Because they're assholes.

"Because of their own issues. His leaving isn't your fault. Either of you."

The girls spoke simultaneously.

"Honest?"

"You sure?"

"I'm sure."

Claire stood suddenly and disrupted Tramp. Before Hunter realized what she was going to do, she threw herself into his arms. "Don't go away. Please."

In a moment, Meli joined her, and hugged Hunter, too.

His eyes clouded. "Girls, I don't have a choice."

Her face buried in his chest, Claire asked, "Will you ever come back?"

"I don't know."

She cried into his sweater. When tough little Meli's tears began, he almost lost it.

But he struggled to find a way to help them. Mostly, he just held on to them, stroked their hair, much as they petted Tramp. When they quieted, he said, "Listen, do you do e-mail?"

"We know how," Claire said. "From school."

"Well, before I leave, we'll set it up so the three of us can be e-mail buddies. We can talk to each other a lot online."

As compromises went, it was paltry. But he didn't know what else to say. "It's not enough, but it's the best I can do right now."

Claire pulled back and said, "Okay."

Meli nodded.

Their easy acceptance broke his heart. Right now, he'd like to wring Johnny O'Malley's neck.

With one last hug, they stood, and clasping hands, headed down the trail.

"Go with them, boy," he said to Tramp. He thought the dog might be able to comfort them.

Miraculously, Tramp complied.

Hunter was still sitting there fifteen minutes later berating himself for being irresponsible about letting Claire and Meli get too attached to him, when Darcy came down the path.

She reached him and stood before him, looking prettier than ever in her new outfit. "Claire said you were here."

"How's Anabelle?"

"Fine. The bullet went through her shoulder. She'll be laid up a while, but the injury is not life threatening." She stared at him. "How are *you*?"

As good as can be expected after having my heart ripped out—twice—today.

"What do you want, Darcy?"

"I want to talk to you."

HER HEART POUNDING like a thousand drums, Darcy folded her arms across her chest and faced him squarely. "I told David I wasn't going to see him anymore." Her voice was full of emotion. She didn't care. She just wanted to take away the hurt she'd caused Hunter.

He stood and dusted off the seat of his jeans. Sticking his hands in his pockets, he nailed her with an accusatory gaze. "He didn't look like he got the message right."

"It hurt you to see him…"

"What? To see him kiss you? Touch you intimately?" She stepped back at the vehemence of his tone. "Yeah, darlin', it hurt."

Make this better, Darce.

She crossed to him and reached out to touch his arm but he shook her off. "Hunter, he ambushed me. I didn't want to come with him today—my mother arranged it. And he caught me off guard when he kissed me. I didn't want it."

He jammed a hand through his hair. "I don't even know why I'm makin' such a fuss. You're gonna be sleeping with somebody else the rest of your life after I leave."

"Don't say that."

He turned his back on her. "It's true."

It doesn't have to be.

Emotion engulfed her. "Hunter, please. I don't know what else to say. I should have broken it off with David as soon as you and I made love. I'm sorry."

His shoulders slumped. He sighed heavily.

She came up behind him. This time he didn't flinch, didn't shrink away when she got close. Moving to face him, she took his hand in hers. "I can't stand the thought of another man touching me." She kissed his fingers, held his palm to her cheek. "I only want your hands on me."

"You've got your whole life ahead of you. You'll find somebody else."

"Don't talk about that. I just want you to know how I feel right now."

He drew her close, tunneled his fingers through her hair. His scent—woodsy, sexy—surrounded her.

"Please don't be mad," she said.

"I'm not." He drew in a deep breath, his chest rising and falling with it. After a while he said, "I want to be with you."

"I want that, too."

"For longer than a few hours."

She drew back to look at him.

"Josh Jacobs invited Braden for a sleepover Friday

night. Then Saturday they're going to a Red Wings game in Rochester.''

She stared into dark eyes shining with need. "I'll find somebody to take the girls."

"What about your mother? She'll know you're gone."

Tell Marian to go jump in the—

"I'll worry about that later." Darcy moved in close again. "I want to be with you, too, Hunter. All day. All night."

"There isn't much time left," he whispered achingly.

"I know."

Once again the reality of his leaving, the reality of never seeing him again, never touching him again, hit home. Darcy wasn't sure she could survive it. Moving in closer, she held on even tighter.

CHAPTER FOURTEEN

VANILLA CANDLES SCENTED the air.

A low-burning fire spit and crackled, warming the room.

The small stereo in the corner crooned some soft Harry Connick Jr. As Hunter ran his hand over Darcy's skin, he felt her shiver beneath his fingertips. Her hair was like silk gliding down her back. Irresistible...he buried his face in it.

A moan escaped her as his scraped knuckles traced the scar on her leg, flirted with the back of her knees.

"Move a little apart here, darlin'." She shifted. "That's right."

She raised her head to look at him. "Hunter..."

Gently he eased her down into the soft pillows. "Shh."

Moans. Groans. A long, sexual litany of them. "Hunter, oh, God, yes, right there..."

Nosing her hair aside, he bit the back of her neck gently, tasted the skin there. "Ah, love."

Her breathing escalated. So did his. But he didn't let her peak. It was important to draw out the lovemaking, to savor it.

He knew their times together like this were numbered.

DARKNESS ENVELOPED the room when Darcy awoke, broken only by the dying fire. Chilled, she moved in close to Hunter. His body gave off furnace-like heat. In his sleep, he turned to his side and let her nestle in.

"Mmm." His arms circled her.

She snuggled in and wedged a knee between his legs. She buried her face in his wide chest, breathed in. He smelled like soap and sex.

Stroking his shoulder blade, where his tattoo was, scraping long, painted fingernails on his skin, she rubbed him with her knee. He swelled against her. More sleepy moans. Lowering her head, she licked a nipple. It became taut.

"Darlin'…what are you doin' to me?"

"Loving you."

"IT'S TOO COLD to ride a motorcycle."

"Hush up. I brought you a jacket, and you got those sexy little leather pants to keep you warm." He nodded to her overnight bag. "Did they belong to the old Darcy?"

"Yep." She struggled into a matching vest, which would have been indecent if she hadn't had a black Spandex top beneath it, though it did dip low in the front. He tossed her the pants, and she sat on the bed to slip into them. "I couldn't bear to throw them away."

"Thank the Lord." He drew a black T-shirt over his head, then put on a black checked shirt and tucked it in. With his beltless black jeans, he looked sexy as hell. A real James Dean.

He sat, too, to put on his boots, and watched her finish dressing. "Not sure I want to share you with all those cowboys, though."

She gave him a Jezebel grin. "You said you wanted to dance with me."

"I do." He stood. "Come on, before I change my mind and drag you back to that mattress."

In minutes they were at his motorcycle. The sky was dotted with a thousand stars that twinkled and winked at them. He handed her a helmet. "Here, stuff all those curly locks underneath. I wouldn't want to harm a single hair."

She placed the helmet over her head. He grinned and kissed her nose.

Darcy shivered as they mounted the motorcycle. She reveled in the feel of Hunter's hard body against hers. In the old days, she'd spent hours on various Harleys and Kawasakis with boys.

With bums.

When she'd been bum gum.

Hunter isn't a bum, you jerk.

Of course he wasn't. Though he *was* doing a pretty good imitation of the bad boy he used to be. The cycle sped up, rounded a corner fast and leaned to the side. The cold air slapped her face. It was fun; she felt free. Young. Unrestrained. She hadn't realized how much she'd missed those feelings.

The notion returned at the bar. They walked into Long John's at midnight like gang moll and mob boss, cowboy and saloon girl, Hells Angels biker and his squeeze. Hunter snaked his arm around her and drew her close. They'd locked up the helmets and their jackets in a duffel on the bike, so her leather vest and pants slid beneath his hands. "There's a stool at the bar, doll. Let's go."

Doll. Oh, God.

He took the seat himself. Pulling her to stand between

his legs, he braced his feet on the bottom rung of the stool next to him, effectively trapping her. ''I like you right here.''

She shivered, she couldn't help it. He ran his knuckles down the deep vee of her top, playing the possessive role to the hilt.

''What'll ya have, lover boy?'' the bartender asked.

''A beer.'' He named a popular brand.

''What about you, little lady?''

''She'll drink from mine.''

Darcy smiled and lowered her eyes.

He reached up and cupped her face, drawing her close so that he could kiss her. Hard. His hands never left her until the beer arrived. Locking his gaze with hers, he sipped from the bottle then held it out to her. She drank, the icy liquid going down smoothly. He took the bottle back. Before he brought it to his lips, he let the bottom of it graze the exposed skin of her chest. She shivered violently with the cold against her heated skin. ''Hunter,'' she gasped.

He scowled. ''I told you to call me boss.''

She bit back a grin. ''Yes, Boss.''

''That's better. If you're a good girl, I'll dance with you.''

''Yes, Boss.''

They shared the beer. His knees caged her legs, kept tightening and bringing her closer. All the while his hand played with her hair. ''I want this on me, later.''

''Anything you say.''

He leaned over and whispered exactly what he planned to do to her, in graphic detail, making her blush. He laughed when he saw her redden. The long, low lusty sound rumbled out, turning more than a few female heads.

Scowling, she draped her arms over his shoulders and moved in. "The ladies like you."

He kissed her nose. "Then you'd better be good." He scanned the room. "They're not bad-lookin' chicks."

She remembered how to pout.

"Hush." Leaning over, he brushed her lips with the pad of his thumb. "I only got eyes for you, darlin'."

Once the band started, he was even more outrageous on the dance floor. A master at line dancing, he twirled her expertly, yanked her to him, two-stepped with her. He instructed her in the electric slide and teased her when she couldn't get the moves. He covered the floor with her in a fast swing.

She was breathing hard when they returned to the stool.

"Sit," he told her and eased her down onto it.

He ordered another beer. The bartender winked at her.

Hunter moved indecently close and growled in her ear, "Better watch it, doll. Flirtin' will make me get rough later."

"Yes, Boss." But her look was sassy and earned her another full-mouthed kiss.

At three, when the bar closed, they climbed onto the bike and sped back to the Boxwood. Feeling mellow and settled for the first time in her recent memory, Darcy held on to him and pretended they were young and carefree.

Once the door of their room closed behind them, he leaned against it. When he said, "All right, doll, now strip for the boss," she realized the game wasn't over.

As Hunter left the Boxwood's restaurant at ten the next morning, with hot coffee and flaky croissants in a bag, he smiled to himself. What had gotten into them last night? He couldn't believe some of the things he'd pulled. Chuckling, he remembered her drinking his beer and obeying his orders at the bar like the best of bad girls. Then when they'd gotten back to the inn, she'd practically blown his head off his shoulders with the sex.

As he made his way to the room, his mood was dulled only by one thought. How was he ever going to let this fascinating, wonderful woman go?

You got no choice, buddy.

Just like he had no choice with Braden.

Don't think about either now.

He didn't. Instead, he woke her with tender kisses. She was rumpled and sleepy as he propped up the pillows and passed her the coffee.

With those green eyes slumberous over the rim of the cup, she said, "You pack a powerful punch there, *Boss,* when you're being a bad boy."

"Yeah?" He lazed at the foot of the bed, leaning against a post, sipping his own hot brew. "I had a lot of practice." He eyed the covers, which were slipping to dangerous territory. "You were mighty convincing yourself."

She laughed, the sound low and sexy in the intimacy of the room they shared.

"Hungry?" He nodded to the bag. "I got croissants. We could eat them outside. There's a picnic table down by the river."

"All right."

Bundled in a soft pink sweat suit, her face devoid of makeup, her hair uncombed, she was the antithesis of who she'd been last night. They sat at the table and stared at the river. It rumbled past them, lapping and swishing in the sun. He'd brought his leather jacket and draped it around her shoulders, but the sunshine made the day warm, so she shrugged it off.

He put butter on a croissant for her and held it to her mouth. She tore off a piece of bread with gleaming white teeth.

"Happy?" he asked. He didn't need her response. How she felt was mirrored in those emerald eyes. It struck him, then, in the warm fall morning, that they were good for each other. Somewhere along the line, she'd given him this—the confidence in his ability as a man to establish a relationship and be *good* for somebody.

"What are you thinking?" she asked.

Putting down the roll, he straddled the bench and faced her. "That I'm good for you."

Her eyes widened. "Oh, Hunter, yes, you are."

He toyed with her hair.

"And I'm good for you," she told him.

"No doubt about it." Something made him ask, "So, what are we going to do about it?"

She opened her mouth to speak, when Hunter heard, "Darcy? Is that you?"

Hunter stiffened. *Please, don't let anything happen to ruin this.*

"Taylor? Nick? What are you doing here?"

Hunter didn't look at Darcy's friends. Instead, he studied *her,* afraid she was going to turn back into prim Miss Darcy, not knowing how he'd handle it if she did.

He heard Taylor say, "It's my birthday, or at least the day we picked for my birthday at Serenity House. Nick and I always come to the Boxwood this time of year."

"Happy Birthday."

There was an awkward silence. He waited for her to acknowledge him, like she wasn't ashamed of being with him.

She didn't.

Sighing resignedly, he swung his leg over the bench and faced the couple. His heart heavy, he held out his hand. "Hey. Hunter Sloan. We met at Claire's party."

The other man shook his hand. "Yeah, I remember. Nick Morelli, and Taylor."

Her expression bleak, Darcy looked from him to the Morellis.

Hunter said, "I, um, bid some work at the inn. You know I'm a carpenter. We're here..."

His voice trailed off as he felt an arm curl through his, a breast grazed his chest—Darcy leaning into him right here in broad daylight. "We're in cabin four, Taylor. Hunter and I. Maybe we can get together later."

He didn't hear Taylor's response, for the pounding of his heart. He only hoped he'd said goodbye when the Morellis left.

Darcy crawled onto his lap. She cuddled up to him and said, "What? Did you think I was gonna play the carpenter and the lady?" When he didn't answer, she kissed his cheek. "I really like biker boss and his girl better."

Closing his eyes, he whispered into her hair, "Don't tease."

She cradled his head. "Hunter."

Waiting a minute, trying to get some control, he finally drew back. "I didn't know..." He halted. "I had no idea...how much it would mean to me to have you openly acknowledge your relationship with me."

"It hurt that I didn't before."

"We agreed…for the kids, because I'm leaving…I just didn't know…"

Darcy's heart ached for him. Though they both kept saying it was the right thing to do, she guessed she'd known from the start that keeping their relationship hidden had kicked into all his insecurities. Faced now with the real evidence of how much that secrecy had hurt him, she longed to erase the pain. So she listened to her inner voice and said the only thing she could think of. "I love you, Hunter."

He froze.

"And I'm done letting people think differently."

Still he didn't move.

She waited. She kissed his head. "Did you hear me? I love you."

He shuddered against her. She just held him.

Finally he drew back. His eyes were wet when he looked at her. "Then come to Florida with me."

She hadn't expected that. And old fears tried to sneak into her heart, tried to retract the spontaneous decision she'd made out here in the sunshine. But she battled them back. She *was* done with all that. Suddenly everything became clear. "All right."

"All right? Just like that?"

Slowly, surely, she nodded.

"Darce…"

"The girls will love it. We'll get Braden as often as we can—"

He grabbed her neck and pulled her toward him. "Hush, just for a minute." When he was composed, he drew back and looked her square in the eyes. "I love you, too, darlin'."

"Oh, thank God."

You're damn right, Darce. You should thank the holy Lord. Maybe, just maybe, you didn't blow it this time.

THEY MADE LOVE AGAIN, sealing their commitment.

But before they could leave the Boxwood Inn, they received two calls on their respective cell phones.

The first was on Hunter's. While he and Darcy had been playing bikers at the bar last night, Shelly Michaels had given birth to a baby boy.

The second was for Darcy. While she and Hunter had been making love at 3:00 a.m., Jeremy Mason had been taken by ambulance to the hospital with chest pains.

CHAPTER FIFTEEN

DARCY RUSHED into the ICU waiting room and found her mother sitting in the corner sipping a cup of coffee. Marian's always perfect hair was disheveled, and her sweater and slacks were wrinkled. As Darcy approached, Marian looked up; tears formed in her eyes. Dumbfounded by the display of emotion—she couldn't ever remember seeing her mother cry—Darcy was further surprised when Marian put the cup down, stood and hugged her. Her mother felt slight in her arms.

"Oh, Mom, he isn't—"

Marian held on, then pulled back. "No, no, he's resting. I came out here to wait for you." She wiped her eyes. "I was just so afraid."

"I'll bet. Here, sit down. Tell me what happened."

They sat. Amidst the bustle of hospital routine—phones ringing and the occasional pages for doctors—Marian sighed deeply. "There are a few things I haven't told you, dear. Jeremy's been having chest pains off and on for the last few weeks. We've been to see Dr. Conway, and they did some tests. His condition was diagnosed as angina. No one was too worried. Then last week, the day of Nathan's preelection bash, the pains returned. They were more severe. James Conway sent us to a cardiologist and he decided to do an angiogram." Her eyes teared again. "The cardiologist didn't seem to think it serious. They were even going to wait till Monday to do the test.''

"Mom, I'm so sorry." She took Marian's hand. "How bad was it this time? Did he have a heart attack?"

"They don't think so, at least the blood work so far doesn't indicate that. They're sticking with a diagnosis of severe angina for now. But they're going to do the angiogram today. If it shows blockage, but not severe enough to warrant surgery, then they'll do an angioplasty immediately." She squeezed Darcy's hand. "That's where they balloon the artery and insert a stent."

"Yes, I know."

"Everyone here says it's a minor procedure. If all goes well, he can go home tomorrow."

"Thank God." She smiled at her mother. "So that's not too bad then. They wouldn't be telling you it wasn't serious, they wouldn't be letting him go home so soon, if his condition was life threatening."

"No." She eyed Darcy's sweat suit. "Dear, where were you? When I called down to the carriage house, you weren't there. I was so frightened..."

"I'm sorry I wasn't there for you."

Marian reddened. "I figured you were at David's, since the girls went with that Kendrick woman to Six Flags. I didn't really want to call his house in the middle of the night, so I waited until this morning."

Be careful, Darcy. Stick to your guns.

Darcy's heart sped up.

"David wasn't home. I thought perhaps you went out to breakfast. Finally, I remembered your cell phone."

Darcy didn't say anything.

"But you were with David, right?"

For a second, Darcy's whole future flashed in front of her. She felt as if she were on a precipice. Hunter's words about what it had meant to him to be able to openly acknowledge their relationship came to her.

But was this the right time to tell her mother?

Will the time ever be right?

As if she sensed something, Marian started to talk fast. "Darcy Anne, I want to tell you something else. Given Jeremy's health over the past several weeks, we've had papers drawn up."

"Papers? Like a will?"

"No, we already have that. Papers about the daycare."

They're going to sell TenderTime, was her first thought. Though losing what she'd worked so hard for hurt, she felt instant relief. She was going to Florida with Hunter, and this would make it much easier.

"Mother, if you're selling the daycare, it's fine with me. I understand."

"Selling it? Why would we sell it? We're turning it over legally to you. You know we've been easing ourselves out of it for months. This just hurried our decision along. We want to rest, to travel." She patted Darcy's hand. "David was so thrilled when we told him. He said he'd love being a part of the business, and helping you. I feel so comfortable giving TenderTime to you with David to help out."

Tell her, Darcy.

"Mother, David and I aren't—"

Marian cut her off as if she wasn't speaking. "I'd be wary of your running it without his help, dear."

Stand up to her, Darcy. Now.

"I'm sorry, then my taking over TenderTime isn't going to happen. David and I aren't seeing each other anymore."

"No?" Marian studied Darcy. "Where were you last night?"

Darcy didn't answer right away.

Marian stood. "Never mind, don't answer that. I want you to think about all I've just said. And consider the children's welfare. Owning TenderTime will secure their future for you. You can be sure you'll always be able to support them and pay for college. If that's not enough to convince you, I want you to think about all you've worked so hard to achieve since you came back to Hyde Point. You're respectable now. A valued member of the community." Leaning over, she kissed Darcy on the cheek. "I just wouldn't want you to do anything stupid to ruin all that." She straightened. "I'm going in to see Jeremy. Come with me."

HUNTER SAT beside Braden's bed and watched his son sleep with Tramp cuddled beside him. There wouldn't be many more nights like this. Shelly's call had forced him to face facts...

"It was an easy delivery, Hunter. The baby's beautiful. I can't wait for Braden to see his brother."

Hunter had swallowed his grief. "When do you want him back?"

A pause. "Hank says I have to get used to the baby first. Maybe the end of the week?"

"I don't think I can get him down there that soon, Shelly."

She seemed a little relieved.

"And we need to talk before I give him back. There's

a whole regimen of things to do for his ADHD. Plus, I want to see him a lot. Be part of his life. I won't take no for answer.''

''I'll, um, talk to Hank about all that...''

Braden turned over in his sleep. Hunter stood and brushed the boy's hair out of his eyes. Had he ever realized how the kid's hair was the exact texture of his own? He was baby clean tonight, smelling of soap and shampoo from the shower Hunter had had to wrestle him into. Leaning over, he kissed Braden's forehead. ''I love you, Champ.''

He was just coming down the steps, thinking it might not be too bad if he could have Braden on weekends, vacations and summers—and trying not to admit that he was kidding himself big time—when the doorbell rang.

It had to be Darcy. She'd called from the hospital during the day. The last time, she asked if she could come over. He wondered how Marian had taken the news of her leaving town with him.

Throwing open the door, he smiled. She was still dressed in her pink sweat suit. ''Hey.'' Gently, he drew her inside and hugged her close. Maybe, just maybe, if he had her and the girls, he could handle having his son part-time. ''You okay, darlin'?'' he asked when she held on tight.

''Now I am.'' She burrowed into him, seemed to absorb him, then drew back. ''I need to talk to you.''

''Sure.'' He nodded to the right. ''In there. Bart and Ada are upstairs watching TV in their bedroom.''

She gripped his hand as they made their way into the family room. After they sat, she asked, ''How did Braden take the news about Shelly's baby?''

"I didn't tell him. He was wired when he got back. He'd had a lot of junk to eat and couldn't settle down. So I decided to wait till tomorrow." He rolled his eyes. "It was the easy way out, anyway. When he celebrates going back to his mama, I need to be together about it all."

Her hand came up and smoothed his jaw. "I don't think he's going to celebrate. You should be prepared for that."

"What do you mean?"

"He's going to want to stay with you."

"No." He couldn't let himself think that. "How's Jeremy?" he asked, changing the subject.

"Resting. Did I tell you they put in two stents?"

"Yeah. How's your mother?"

"Shaken. I brought her home and got her settled, then came over here."

"I'm sorry. At least Jeremy's not in any danger now."

They sat on the couch, close, and he toyed with her hair, which she'd braided back off her face. "What did she say about you being with me last night?"

"I didn't tell her outright, Hunter. I did make it clear I wasn't with David, though."

He didn't like that, but hell, he could understand that Darcy might not want to broach the volatile subject during a crisis. "It's okay, darlin'. It probably wasn't the right time to tell her about us."

"That's not why I didn't tell her. I found out some things that you and I need to discuss."

"What?"

"Even before today, my mother and Jeremy had drawn up papers to turn TenderTime over to me."

"Turn it over?"

"Yes, they want to get out of the business so they can rest and travel. They're giving me legal ownership. David's drawing up all the papers. They were just waiting until all the terms had been set before they signed the documents."

"What terms?"

She flushed. "I don't know, exactly."

"Well, it doesn't matter, I guess. You're not gonna be here to accept their offer." He smiled sadly. "I'm sorry, love. I know that place means a lot to you."

She stared at him.

"Darce?"

Briefly, she looked away.

An insidious thought occurred to him. "What is it, Darcy?"

"Can we talk about this?"

"Talk about what?"

"About going to Florida."

"What's there to talk about?"

"My mother's plans put everything in a new light."

"How?"

"Hunter, it's been my dream since I came back to own that business, to run it the way *I* want to. Think of all I could do for kids who are like we used to be. And Mother was right. Having the daycare will secure the girls' whole future. I'll never again have to worry about supporting them, about putting them through college."

"I can support them. I can put them through college."

"Can you? With your financial commitments to Braden?" She shook her head. "No, don't answer that. It's a moot point, anyway. I want to be able to take care of my own children myself, not depend on any man to do it. Like I have in the past.''

He felt as if she'd slapped him. ''I didn't realize I was just *any* man.''

''Don't twist my words.'' She took his hands and grasped them tightly. Hers were icy. ''Let's not fight about this.''

He drew in a breath. He needed to stay cool. Overreacting would only make things worse. ''Look, I know you like working. Taking care of yourself. That's fine by me. You can work in Florida, maybe eventually open your own daycare there. After your success in Hyde Point, it shouldn't be too hard.''

''Hunter, it takes money to open a business. Neither of us has that kind of financial base.''

''What exactly are you saying?''

She blew out a breath. ''I don't really know. I just want to examine all the options.''

''There are no options.''

''There's one.''

''What?''

''For you to stay in Hyde Point.''

He thought of Carrington. Of Hannah. Of Marian Mason and her utter distaste for him, and his son. ''When hell freezes over.''

''No, really, it could work. After Jeremy's better, and the threat of all this is past, I'll sit down with Mother. Explain things. She'll come around.''

He didn't want to think what he was thinking. ''You wouldn't be of a mind to accept the daycare under her terms, start running it, then spring me on her when it was too late, would you?''

''No, no, of course not.''

He didn't believe her.

"I wouldn't go for that, Darcy. I'm not letting you be ashamed of me."

"I'm not ashamed of you."

"Well, to use your words, it's a moot point, anyway. You've left out one thing in this little scheme you've cooked up. Braden's got to go back to his mama. She lives two hundred miles from me in Florida. I'm going to ask for joint custody, and I think I'll get it, especially since there were never any legal papers drawn up giving her sole custody when he was born. But I couldn't pull that off if I was two thousand miles away."

"I hadn't thought of that."

Fighting back his natural instinct, which was to run, or to attack, he tried one more time. "So, does that mean you're going to tell your mother everything now?"

She just looked at him.

His gut clenched. "You're not, are you?"

"Hunter, please, so much has happened today. Give me some time to sort it all out."

He stood and stared down at the woman he loved. When would he ever learn? He couldn't *really* trust anybody. It drove him to say, "I want an answer tonight. Tell me you're coming with me. Now. Or I'm going alone."

She stood, too. God, she was little. She was so feisty, sometimes he forgot about her size. "I don't like ultimatums."

"And I don't like being your dirty little secret."

"Don't say that."

"It's true, isn't it?"

"Why are you *doing* this?" she asked.

"Why are you?"

"I just want some time."

"No, you want the daycare and me."

"What if I do? Is that so wrong?"

God, he hadn't wanted to be right. The smidgen of hope that she'd give in, that she'd see things his way, disappeared like mist off the water. "It's not wrong, just impossible. If you don't know that, I'm wasting my time here." He turned and walked out of the room. He reached the staircase before he heard her come out of the family room.

"Hunter, wait."

His back to her he said, "No, darlin'. I'm done waiting." For her to accept him. For anything to go right in this miserable town. As he trudged up the steps— even when he heard the front door close loudly—he kept telling himself that this was for the best.

He went to Braden's room. Opening the door, he stepped inside. Quietly, he crossed to the bed, kicked off his shoes and eased down beside his son and the dog.

It was a long time before he fell asleep.

When he did, he dreamed that Marian, Carrington and Hannah were holding Darcy hostage at Tender-Time. Even in the dream, the fact that Darcy was smiling tore him apart.

BRADEN SAT at the breakfast table calmly spooning Shredded Wheat into his mouth. Would Shelly make sure he had sugarless cereal in the morning?

"Don't forget your vitamin," Hunter said. His voice sounded like sandpaper on steel.

Big dark eyes glanced up at him. "Can I have Wolverine?"

"Huh?"

"The X-man vitamin. I want Wolverine today."

Would Shelly buy vitamins he'd take? Maybe Hunter should supply them and the Ritalin. Maybe then she'd make sure Braden took them.

"Yeah, sure, you can have Wolverine." Hunter shook out the vitamins, found the yellow one, and handed it to his son. Then he watched the boy finish his breakfast, beating back the thought that he wouldn't get to share meals with Braden every day.

"You gonna go to church with Grandma and Grandpa and me?" Braden asked.

"Yeah. But I gotta talk to you first." He glanced at the clock. "I got some good news." He choked on the lie.

"What?"

"Your mother called last night."

The boy started kicking his foot against the table leg. "I had fun at the game yesterday with Josh."

"I know you did, Champ. But about your mom?"

"I caught a ball. Did ya see it?"

"I saw it, son." He leaned over. "Brade, your mom had the new baby."

Braden slid off the chair. "I'm gonna go get my baseball."

Reaching out, Hunter tugged the boy back by his pajamas top. "Braden, wait. Did you hear me?"

His back to Hunter, Braden nodded.

"You got a brother."

Braden stood stock-still.

Hunter looked to heaven, praying to a God who'd

never helped *him* before, to give him guidance for his son. "He's big. And healthy."

Nothing.

Swallowing hard, Hunter tugged the boy back. Braden resisted, but Hunter knew how to do this now. With gentle force, he sat Braden on his lap and circled his arms around the small frame. Would Shelly and Hank coax him into listening when he didn't want to? Or would they yell at him? Would they give him the affection he craved but pretended he didn't?

"Brade, we need to talk about your going back home."

Again, Braden tried to pull away. Hunter held fast.

"Your mama wants you to come back as soon as possible." Not quite true. "We gotta make arrangements."

After a few more attempts to get down, Braden slumped in his arms. Hunter rested his chin on Braden's shoulder. "Listen to me good, son. I'm gonna give you back to your mama, but I'm not giving you up. I'm gonna see you as often as I can. I'll come to Delmont to spend time with you. It's only two hundred miles from where I live. And you can come visit me weekends and vacations. We'll still see each other a lot. I promise."

No response. Out of his depth, emotionally depleted, Hunter scrambled for what to say, what to do.

Then his son took the choice away from him. Braden whirled on his lap and threw his arms around Hunter's neck. "Don't wanna go back."

Hunter's shoulders sagged and he grasped Braden tight. "I don't want you to go either, Champ. But we got no choice."

"Please." He could barely hear the boy. "Don't make me go back to them, Daddy."

Daddy.

The lump in Hunter's throat choked him. He'd been waiting months to hear Braden call him that, hoping against hope that the kid would see him as a real father. Now, when the world had caved in, he got his wish. He said the only thing he knew to say. "I love you, Braden."

"I love you, too."

Hunter closed his eyes to keep back the moisture. It didn't work. Holding on to Braden, he cried for all he was losing. God, how had this happened?

Braden was crying, too. They stayed that way for a while, on the hard, straight-back chair, in his grandpa's kitchen, listening to the clock tick and the refrigerator turn on. Finally, the boy calmed, and Hunter managed to gain some control of himself, then drew back. Braden wiped his face. Hunter wiped his. "Listen, Brade. She's your mama, she needs you back."

"She's got another little boy. You don't have any."

His heart, close to breaking already, splintered into a thousand pieces. "It doesn't work that way."

"Can't I see *her* on weekends and stay with you the rest of the time?"

Oh God, I want that. "Like I said, it doesn't work that way. You belong with your mother." Didn't he?

Huge eyes peered up at him. The were wet, but shining with such love it poleaxed Hunter. "Can't you keep me, Dad? I'll be good. I won't cause trouble like before. I promise."

"I…" He could barely get the words out. "I can't do that, son."

And right before his eyes, Braden changed. Hunter recognized the Sloan tactic immediately.

"Then I don't *wanna* stay here anymore." He jerked off Hunter's lap. "Send me back. Who cares? I hate this crummy town. I hate you."

"Braden, you're just saying that 'cause you're mad. It's okay to be mad. I'm mad, too. But this isn't the way to handle things." Though right now, it felt exactly right to Hunter, too, to rage at what fate had brought them. He'd been teased by the opportunity to be a father to Braden and felt cheated by losing the boy now.

"I don't care." The steady stream of tears coursing down the kid's cheeks belied the statement. "Send me back. S-send me away. Just like she did."

Then Braden tore out of the room. In a few seconds, Hunter heard the door slam upstairs. He sat at the table. Having no idea what to do next, he buried his face in his hands.

WHEN DARCY GOT BACK from doing errands for her mother, Claire and Meli were in her office, sitting in a corner at a little table. She'd arranged for them to come to TenderTime after school all week so that they didn't get in Marian's hair.

"Mama, where's Braden?" Claire asked.

"He didn't come today."

"Again?"

"Yes."

"Why?"

She recalled the note she'd gotten early in the week. *Braden's refusing to come to the daycare. He's upset about leaving. I'll let you know what we're going to do.*

"A lot of reasons."

Meli, who'd been tossing up a baseball and catching it in her glove, stopped. "He mad at you?"

"What?"

"Is Braden mad at you?"

No, his father is. Time to take the bull by the horns. "Come over here to the couch and sit down, girls. I have something to tell you."

Claire's eyes widened. She fingered the bracelet Hunter had given her for her birthday and which she never removed. "What's wrong with Braden?"

"Nothing, honey." When she sat between her girls, she slid her arms around each of their shoulders. Their solid weight leaning into her soothed her. "You knew Braden was only here temporarily until his mother had her baby."

Claire nodded.

Meli reached over and touched Darcy's stomach. "If you had another baby, would you send us away?"

The thought of another child growing inside her, of Hunter's child growing inside her, strained the floodgates holding back the emotion inside her. She'd been keeping herself sane, but just barely. "I'd never send you away, honey. Never."

"Why did Braden's mom?" Meli asked. "And why's Coach letting him go back?"

Were there answers to these obscene questions? "He doesn't have a choice."

On the other side of her, Claire stiffened. "Why not?"

"Well, Braden's always lived with his mother. He has to go back to her." Darcy wondered about that though. Hunter had said there weren't any papers ever drawn up. "In any case, she had the new baby, and now Braden's going back to Florida."

"When?"

"I don't know."

"But why's Braden missing PreK this week?" Claire asked. "He loves it."

"He's upset. He doesn't want to do much of anything."

In the one stilted conversation she'd had with Hunter when he finally accepted her call, he'd said Braden was refusing to take his medicine, wouldn't come out of his room most of the time and had torn apart the family room in one of his temper tantrums.

"Let's go see him, Mama. Maybe we can help." Claire's earnest pleas echoed her own.

Darcy had suggested that to Hunter.

No, he's too attached to y'all already. I'll handle this by myself.

"Mr. Sloan doesn't think that's such a good idea."

"Aren't we ever going to see them again?"

"I don't know, Claire." She could barely tolerate the thought.

Meli, who'd been unusually quiet, slid off the seat. "I'm going outside to the playground."

"Mel, don't you want to talk about this?"

"Nope." She headed for the door.

Claire stayed where she was. When Meli left, Claire buried her face in Darcy's shoulder. "I don't want them to go, Mama."

"I know, honey. I don't either."

"Then can't you make them stay?"

"No. I can't. It's out of our control."

Claire began to cry.

Darcy clasped onto her daughter and fought to hold back her own tears. Then she heard a knock on the open door. Composing herself, she turned to find Hunter standing in the doorway with a death grip on Braden's hand. Darcy and Claire both stood.

"We came to say goodbye," Hunter got out.

Then, before she knew what was happening, Claire bolted across the room, just as Braden yanked away from his father. The boy ran to her and threw himself at her, just as Claire did the same to Hunter.

"Don't wanna go, Miss Darcy," Braden mumbled into her skirt.

"Please don't go, Coach," Claire said against Hunter's chest.

Bending down, Darcy hugged Braden.

Hunter held Claire close.

Over their children's respective heads, the two adults stared at each other.

STANDING BEFORE the mirror in the tiny bathroom in her tiny doll's house, Darcy uncoiled the knot of hair at the back of her neck. She stared blindly at herself in the glass. Instead of seeing her drawn pale face, other images haunted her.

At the daycare last Thursday…

She'd held on tight to Hunter's son. *Oh, Braden, I'm so sorry, I don't want you to go, either. I'm really going to miss you.*

Her daughter had kept a death grip on Hunter. *Coach, please don't go.*

Claire, honey, don't cry. We have to go back to Florida. His voice had been raw and hurting…

Because the memory was so painful, Darcy forced it

away. She shook back her head and pulled at the heavy locks. They fell down her back. But the visions continued...

So, when do you leave? she'd asked when the kids quieted.

On Saturday.

So soon?

The psychologist Paige recommended we talk to thinks it's best just to get out of here.

I see...

Darcy swung her head, and her hair fanned out around her shoulders.

She hadn't let him go that easily, though. She'd gone to Rascal's on Friday where he was putting in his last night of work...

Hunter, please talk to me.

Nothin' to say, Miss Darcy.

I'm staying on this stool until you talk to me...

Watching herself in the mirror, Darcy lifted a heavy lock just as Hunter had, that night, in the back room of Rascal's where he'd taken her...

You're cruel, you know that, to come here. He touched her hair. *With this down. Don't you care what you're doing to me?*

I love you, was all she could think of to say.

Not enough, darlin'...

With her other hand, Darcy reached down to the vanity counter. She picked up the scissors...

She'd practically begged. *There's got to be a compromise.*

There's only one answer to this. Come with me.

Hunter, give me some time. I'll...

He'd lost his temper then. Kicked the wastebasket.

Swore violently. *No! I deserve better than this. Ironically, my time here in Hyde Point showed me that. I'm a good person, a good father, and I deserve a good life, free from prejudice and old grudges...*

Extending a lock of hair, Darcy opened the scissors. Looking into the mirror, she noticed that tears were streaming down her cheeks...

Without me? You deserve a life without me?

I deserve a life without a woman who's going to sell me out for her business. I let it go when you wouldn't dance with me at the club because your mother was watching us. I agreed to seeing you secretly, hiding our relationship for the kids' sake, even though it cut to the bone. I ignored it when you hedged your bets with Carrington even after you and I were sleeping together. But I'm done with that. I deserve better than that.

And he'd walked out...

With the image frozen in her mind, she inserted the lock of hair between the blades of the scissors. He was right. He deserved better. In the week since he'd left, she'd come to realize that. Viciously, she closed the scissors.

Again and again.

Snip. Snip. Snip.

COULD THINGS get any worse? That last night at Rascal's was one of the most gut-wrenching things he'd experienced. Saying goodbye to Bart and Ada, even temporarily, hadn't been easy. Braden had sobbed and clung to them, not believing the older couple was heading for Florida by plane soon.

But the two-day trip from Hyde Point to Delmont had been a nightmare. Braden had been either sullen and withdrawn, or outright crying in his seat on the other side of the Ford. Twice, when they stopped, he'd tried to run away.

But the worst had been when the kid had crawled into bed with Hunter both nights in the motels where they stopped, and silently cuddled into him, hanging on tight. Hunter had held him through the long and dark hours, knowing their time together was ending.

As he pulled up into the gravel driveway of the address Shelly had given him, he wasn't sure he had the strength to do what he had to today. "We're here, Champ."

Mutinous black eyes glared over at him.

"Seems like a nice house."

Actually it was pretty seedy. The outside needed painting, and the flowers along the sidewalk were brown and wilted. The structure itself was small for three kids and two adults.

"Braden, do you have your own room here?"

The boy stared at the house as if it were a torture chamber.

"Son, answer me."

"Yeah."

"Oh, good."

The kid scowled at him.

"Before we go in," Hunter said, "I wanna tell you something."

Braden reached for the door handle. "Nothin' to tell."

Hunter remembered saying those exact words to Darcy. He stayed Braden's hand. "Yeah, there is." Gently, he took his son by the shoulders. "I love you, Brade. I really do. And I'm gonna come and get you soon." He handed the boy a slip of paper. "But here's my cell phone number. Use it whenever you want to talk to me. I'm gonna call you every day for a while, but if you need me…"

"I don't need you."

Ah, the boy was so much like him.

"Well, I need you."

Some of the kid's bravado slipped. "Dad, can't ya—" Tears welled in his eyes.

Hunter pulled Braden to him. "I can't. But I got a surprise for you."

"What?"

He nodded to the back of the seat. "I'm gonna ask your mama if you can keep Tramp, once you get settled in. I'll bring him back in a few days if she says yes."

Braden drew away. Hunter had expected to see joy on his face. It wasn't there. "I'd rather have you."

"I'm sorry. It's the best I can do right now."

Finally, they got out of the truck and walked slowly toward the small, faded yellow house. Florida was hot for the end of October and there wasn't a breeze. Even wearing a T-shirt and shorts, Hunter began to sweat. Braden kept a grip on his hand and held tightly to Tramp's leash.

They climbed rickety steps that led to a porch that needed to be reinforced. Hunter rang the doorbell.

There was some yelling from inside.

Braden said, "It's Hank. We prob'ly woke him up. He sleeps during the day."

The door opened. Shelly stood before them holding a tiny baby. At her skirts was another child—a girl; Braden had said her name was Mary. Both were clean and well kept, though the little girl's clothes were worn.

Shelly's hair was askew and she looked downright exhausted.

But she had a great big grin for her son. "Braden, oh my God." She knelt down and reached for him. Awkwardly, with the baby between them, she hugged the boy. Braden let her, but didn't return the embrace. "I'm so glad you're back, honey. I missed you so much."

"What's his name?" Braden asked, nodding to the baby.

"Henry James Junior." The words came from behind Shelly. Hunter looked up to see that a man had come out of a back room. Dressed in a muscle shirt and wrinkled shorts, he stared stonily at them.

Braden moved closer to Hunter.

"Close the door, Shelly. You're letting out the cool air."

Braden, Hunter and Tramp stepped inside.

Hank said immediately, "What the hell is that?"

Squaring his shoulders, Hunter faced Braden's stepfather. "It's Braden's dog. We were gonna ask—"

"Can't have no dog here," he said gruffly. "I already can't sleep during the day, there's so much goddamn noise."

Braden bristled. "But—"

"Don't sass me, boy."

Braden backed up a step.

Shelly put the baby down in a small crib and returned to Braden. Again, she knelt down and whispered, "Maybe we could get a kitten, honey. They're quiet. You'd like that, wouldn't you?"

Braden turned his face into Hunter's leg.

Hunter said, "I have to talk to you about his medicine and diet."

Hank snorted.

Standing, Shelly faced Hank. "Hush up now, Hank. Why don't you go lie down?"

The man disappeared into a bedroom off to the right. Shelly said, "Want me to show you where you're gonna be sleeping now, Braden?"

"What about my room?"

"Well, we needed a space for Hank Junior, near our bedroom. So we fixed up the back porch for you."

Hunter was sorry he'd asked himself how things could get worse. "Don't seem to me like you got the space here for Braden, Shelly. Or the time. He's gotta take his medicine. He needs a special diet."

"H-how much is the medicine?"

Hunter said, "He's on my insurance. I'm paying for what's not covered. I'll buy it, too. And bring it to you. You just gotta make sure he takes it."

"What does he need to eat?"

Hunter told her about the carbohydrates and proteins and no sugar.

"Well, Hank likes his sweets. But I can keep Braden away from them."

Oh, fine. That'd last about a day.

Hunter shook his head. He scanned the living room. It was clean, but chock-full of baby stuff and toys. Mary sat in a chair, sucking her thumb, vaguing out in front of the TV. For a minute, a picture of Braden doing the same thing instead of kicking soccer balls and romping with Tramp superimposed over the little girl. "I wanted to talk to you about enrolling Braden in sports, too. He needs the outlet, and he's really blossomed—"

"Hank doesn't like sports."

That did it.

Hunter drew in a breath. "Brade, let's go out to the truck and get your things."

Braden gasped at the reality of Hunter leaving him here. With good reason. Grabbing his son's hand, he said to Shelly, "We'll be just a minute."

Nervously Shelly nodded.

Practically dragging Braden along, holding Tramp's leash, Hunter opened the front door and pounded down the porch steps. He strode toward the car, and when Braden struggled to keep up, he scooped the kid into his arms. At the truck, he dragged open the door. "Get in," he ordered the dog.

Obediently Tramp hopped in the back of the Ford.

Then, with more confidence than he'd ever felt about anything in his life, Hunter plopped Braden on the front seat.

"Dad, whatareya—"

"Hush." He snapped the boy in a seat belt and closed the door. Quickly he circled the truck, got in the driver's side and without hooking his own belt, he started the engine and tore out of the driveway.

"Holy cow, Dad, whatareya *doin'?*"

Once he was away from the house, he fastened his own seat belt and smiled over at Braden. "What I shoulda done before, Champ." He hadn't fought for Darcy. But he'd be damned if he wouldn't fight for his son. Shelly had never sought legal custody, so he had as much right to keep his son as she did. After what he'd seen today, he couldn't leave Braden in that house for even a day. And he couldn't risk reasoning with them. Hank Michaels didn't seem like a reasonable man. "I'm gonna try and keep you."

"Honest?"

As Shelly's house disappeared in the rearview mirror, he grinned broadly. "Honest."

Hoots and hollers came from Braden.

Loud barks came from the dog.

And, for the first time since Darcy had rejected him, Hunter felt some hope.

When they stopped at a diner halfway to the Keys, Hunter got Braden a sandwich and some milk. While the kid ate, Hunter took out his cell phone. He dialed the only person he could think of that might be able to help him.

Sorry to see you leave, Sloan. I feel some kind of connection with you. Damned if I know why. But if you ever need anything, call me. I'll tell my secretary you're on the put-through list.

A secretary answered. "Congressman Hyde's office."

"This is Hunter Sloan. I'd like to talk to Nathan."

CHAPTER SIXTEEN

THOUGH SHE'D SEEN her friends a few times in the weeks since Hunter had left, Darcy had avoided any private talks with Paige and Jade and even Charly. They'd had plenty to say about her new haircut, but she refused to be drawn into any significant conversation. However, circumstances forced her to have lunch with them a week after Hunter's departure.

In a totally atypical move, Dan Whitman had flown out to Seattle and coerced Anabelle Crane to come back to Hyde Point to stay with him and Nora while she recuperated from her gunshot wound. Today, Nora had invited all the original Serenity House girls to lunch.

Darcy was afraid to face them because, mostly, they made *her* face things about herself—things she didn't want to deal with. This was especially true of Jade. When Darcy arrived at the Whitmans', the other women were clustered around Anabelle, who lay on the couch in the big sunroom off the kitchen. She appeared tired and in some pain.

"Your hair looks great, Anabelle," Jade said after they'd greeted Darcy. "It's a little blonder than the last time we saw you."

Nora told her, "It's a lovely color."

Anabelle stared at Darcy. "I can't believe what you did to *your* hair, Darce."

Reaching up, Darcy fingered her chin-length locks.

"I like it." Actually, she did like it. Though she'd cut it off in a fit of despair, she'd come to appreciate the shorter style. "I can wash it in the morning, and I just blow it dry." She flipped the ends. "And it's got curl."

"Yep," Jade put in. "It was that easy to get rid of the old Darcy, once and for all."

"*Jade,*" Paige said warningly.

Paige had seemed unusually distracted since Darcy's arrival; she kept glancing at her watch. Darcy wondered if something had happened with her search for her daughter. Last Darcy knew, Paige had registered online with Ian's adoption-matching agency but had found no adoptee who fit the profile.

Charly intervened. "I like Darcy's hair, too. I've been thinking about lightening mine. It's such a mousy brown."

"Go for it," Jade said. "Live a little."

"I'll color it for you." Taylor smiled sadly. "I like to do hair." She touched her own thick, dark locks. "I wonder if I was interested in cosmetology once."

Anabelle studied her like a cop assessing a suspect. "You look tired, Taylor."

"It's this time of year." She threw a glance at Darcy. "Like I told you at the Boxwood, we picked late October for my birthday. But every year when I celebrate it, I feel bad that I really don't know when I was born."

"The Boxwood?" Jade asked. "That cozy little inn outside of Elmwood?"

"Yeah, Nicky and I saw Darcy there with...what did you call him, Hunky Hunter?"

The room got quiet.

"Did I..." Taylor glanced to Darcy. "Did I say something wrong?"

"No," Jade said. "We just didn't know Darcy was sneaking around at the Boxwood with Hunter."

"Shut up, Jade." Darcy meant it. "I'm done being teased about him."

"You're done with pretty much everything, aren't you?" Jade eyed Darcy's dark-green suit critically. "Soon you'll successfully have turned yourself into your mother. When do you sign the papers to take over the daycare?"

At the others' blank looks, Jade said, "Marian's giving Darcy the daycare. At great cost."

"Jade, sweetie," Nora said, "Darcy needs support now. Not criticism."

"What Darcy needs is a good swift kick in the butt."

Darcy drew in a breath. "Jade's right. I sold out." She stared at her friends. "Hunter wanted me to go to Florida with him. I stayed here instead, to run the daycare."

Paige squeezed her hand. "Sometimes it's hard to change the way a man wants you to. Ian and I had a terrible time with that. We still do."

"You like it here, Darcy," Anabelle commented. "Why did he think you'd leave?"

"Because I told him I would. I told him I loved him, and that I'd go to Florida with him." She glanced at the skylights. "But I chickened out. He was so hurt. And I'm really worried about how *he's* handling it, especially since he had to give up Braden, too."

"He didn't give up Braden," Paige said. "He's got his son with him in the Keys." She glanced at her watch. "As a matter of fact, that's why I can't stay for lunch. I've got to leave in a few minutes. Ian's taking me to the airport."

"I don't understand."

"Hunter's suing for custody of Braden. Since there was no legal agreement initially, and since Hunter's name is on the birth certificate, Shelly doesn't have any more legal claim to Braden than Hunter. He asked me as Braden's pediatrician to come to a preliminary hearing to testify to his qualifications as a father."

"What made him decide to sue?"

"Apparently he didn't like the vibes he got when he went to deliver Braden to his mother. Nathan wrote a letter to the courts for him, and it was enough to get a hearing scheduled for tomorrow. Meanwhile, Hunter's keeping Braden."

"Nathan?" Anabelle asked.

"Yeah, Hunter called him for legal advice. Nathan helped him with the initial filing, then got a lawyer friend of his to represent Hunter in Florida." She looked uncomfortable. "Nathan and I are both leaving for Delmont today. He's testifying in the preliminary hearing, too."

Darcy sat openmouthed, staring at the women. "I—"

The doorbell rang. Nora rose to get it.

"That's probably Ian." Paige stood. "Sorry to cut our visit short, but I really want to help Hunter."

"That's okay. Good luck. I hope..." Anabelle's words trailed off as Nora came back into the porch.

Nathan Hyde accompanied her. Usually so calm and sedate, Nora looked furious.

Nathan scanned the room, his eyes resting briefly on Anabelle. "Hello, ladies." He addressed Paige. "I've come to take you to the airport."

"Ian was supposed to pick me up."

"I know. I talked him into letting me drive you instead since we're on the same flight."

Paige folded her arms across her chest. "Why did you talk Ian into letting you do this, Nathan?"

He focused on Anabelle. "Because I want to talk to Anabelle before I leave."

Darcy watched Anabelle. She didn't shrink into the cushions. She didn't even seem upset. Cool as the cop she was, she straightened her shoulders and faced Nathan bravely.

Nora found her voice. "I'm sorry, dear. I didn't know—"

"It's okay, Nora." Anabelle looked at Nathan. "What do you want?"

"Just a bit of time alone with you." When she didn't respond, he added, "Please, Annie. A few minutes."

"Fine." She nodded to Nora.

The rest of them went into the kitchen.

"Dan won't be happy about this." Nora fussed at the counter. "He can't have known what Nathan was planning."

"I'm going to *kill* Ian," Paige muttered.

"What the hell is with all you guys? If Anabelle and Nathan have a history, they need to work it out." Jade rolled her eyes in disgust. "Just because Darcy here's turned into a shrinking violet doesn't mean everybody—"

"Oh, and you deal just great with your past? I don't see you settling your relationship with Lewis Beckman."

Everybody went silent.

Darcy clapped a hand over her mouth. She'd betrayed Jade's confidences about her confusion over Beck. "Jade, I'm sorry. I didn't mean to say that."

"No, you're right. While watching you act like a jerk about Hunter, I decided I've been avoiding this thing with Beck. I'm going to New York for Thanksgiving to do exactly what you say—deal with him.''

"I didn't know that.'' Paige's face reddened.

Jade spared her sister a glance. "I didn't want any grief from you.'' She turned to Darcy. "So I *am* dealing with him. I'm not burying my head in the sand like you are—pretending you're happy as a lark when it's obvious you're miserable.''

Taylor leaned over and grasped Darcy's hand.

Charly moved in close and put an arm around Jade's shoulders. "Stop it, you two,'' Charly said. "You don't need this between you.''

Nathan appeared at the doorway. He looked as if he'd been beaten with a club. "I'm ready to go, Paige.''

Nora said, "Is Anabelle all right?''

"Anabelle's just fine.'' His usually calm voice, which rang out at speeches in town and in Congress, was threaded with frustration. "I can't believe she's the same—'' He shook his head. "Never mind. Let's go.''

With one last glare for Jade, Paige started out of the kitchen. Jade rushed to her. "Don't fly off somewhere mad at me, sis.''

Paige turned around and sighed. "I'm not mad, I'm just worried about you hooking up with a married man. It's obscene. We all always hated that even when we were girls at Serenity House.''

Darcy noticed Nathan's face turned bleak.

"I know what I'm doing,'' Jade said. "Trust me.''

Paige hugged her sister. "Okay, I'll try.''

"And go help Hunter get Braden back.''

Darcy moaned and turned to face the window.

Days before the November election, Nathan was flying to Florida to help Hunter. Paige, the busy doctor, wife and mother, was putting herself out, too.

Everybody was there for him.

Except her.

She thought she couldn't feel any worse until, after lunch, when she got a phone call from Porter, who was sitting with the girls. "Mrs. O'Malley. I'm so sorry..."

Gripping the phone, Darcy asked, "Is someone hurt?"

"No, the girls are all right physically. They're just...upset. I think you need to talk to them."

When Darcy hung up and told her former house sisters why she had to leave, Charly stood. "I'm coming with you."

Darcy raced home, comforted only by the knowledge that the girls weren't physically hurt. They were upset! Well, hell, they'd been upset since Hunter left. In her typical good-girl fashion, Claire had been withdrawn. Meli had been belligerent. At the front door of the carriage house, she found Porter waiting for her.

"Where are they?"

"In their bedroom."

Darcy hurried to the girls' room with Porter and Charly at her heels. Meli and Claire were sitting on the bed. Darcy's mouth dropped. "Oh my God, what did you do?"

Claire stood and looked away.

Meli came to her side. "We cut our hair, Mama, just like you did!"

Porter shook her head. "We were doing art projects in here. When I finished mine, I went to clean up the kitchen. I thought they were old enough to be around scissors. I'm sorry...I..."

"It's not your fault, Porter." Darcy tried to make her voice strong. She crossed to the corner where they'd obviously done the deed. On the floor were skeins of red hair. She bent down and picked up a handful. Oh, God, what was happening to her and her family? And what kind of example was she setting for her daughters?

Charly was sitting with Porter when Darcy came out of the bedroom. The young teenager had been crying. Darcy sat down next to her. "Porter, honey, this isn't your fault. The girls have been upset for days. A friend of theirs left town."

"I should have watched them better." She looked to Charly. "I'm really trying, Charly, to be good, to be responsible. My mother says if I show more responsibility, I can come back home. I *want* to be responsible after all the bad things I've done."

Darcy swallowed hard.

"I let everybody down. Again."

Darcy took Porter's hand. "It's important to be responsible, Porter. But it's not the most important thing. Caring about people, being there for them and loving them, that's important. I couldn't be more pleased about your relationship with the girls."

Later that night, after supper and a bath, and some pretty good trimming, thanks to Taylor, who dropped by after Charly called her to come and fix the girls' butchered hair, the three O'Malleys all snuggled in Darcy's bed. They were watching a sitcom when an ad for a Thanksgiving special came on.

"What are we gonna do for Thanksgiving, Mama?" Meli asked.

Darcy could barely think about the holidays. "I don't know, honey. It's weeks away."

"We'll be here with Grandma and Grandpa just like the last three years." Claire couldn't have sounded more despondent. "It's what we're supposed to do."

Again, Darcy wondered what kind of role model she

was being for her daughters, especially the older one. Would Claire grow up doing everything she was *supposed* to do instead of what she wanted in her heart?

That worry stayed with her through a restless night. Near dawn, she finally gave up and decided to go into work. Luckily Porter was coming early to baby-sit.

At six-thirty, Darcy was heading into TenderTime when she spotted Hannah Mitchum opening the diner. Drawn to Hunter's sister, Darcy walked down a few storefronts.

Hannah faced her in the doorway. "Hi, Darcy. How are you?"

Darcy fidgeted with the belt of the dark slacks she wore with a peach blazer. "I'll survive."

Hannah eyed her carefully. "Want some coffee?"

"Sure. Won't you be busy, though?"

"The crowd starts coming in about seven."

They entered the diner. Hannah got them both coffee and they sat in a booth.

"Did you get to say goodbye to Hunter?" she asked Hannah.

"No."

"Oh, Hannah."

"But I made up for it." The other woman's smile was broad. "I finally did something I should have done years ago."

"What?"

"Made a truce with my brother." She continued to smile. "Did you know Bart and Ada went down to Florida for the winter?"

"No." How many surprises were there going to be about this man?

"Well, it got me to thinking. So did you, that day you came in here with Braden. Life *is* short. I decided

I didn't want to spend Thanksgiving without my family. My whole family.'' She drew in a breath. ''So I called Hunter. He invited us all down for the holidays. He's hoping to have Braden full time, you know.''

''Yes, I know.''

''He's fighting like hell for his son.''

Like I wouldn't fight for him. Darcy was ashamed.

She listened for as long as she could to Hannah's excitement, then excused herself when customers trickled into the diner. Feeling lonelier than she could ever remember, she walked back to the daycare. It was early, but a few workers and kids had arrived. She let herself into her office and fixed coffee, then sat at her desk. As she scanned the office, she remembered when she'd taken the job at TenderTime and all the work she'd done to bring in new aides and teachers, start new programs, upgrade the computer system.

Slowly, she rose and crossed to the couch. She remembered meeting Hunter for the first time here.

I just moved back to Hyde Point and I gotta work. I need care for the boy...mostly he's a handful... Shelly says she can't take care of Braden... If he were mine, I'd find some way to keep him.

Closing her eyes, she thought about Thanksgiving, and how the Sloans would all be together for it. And she'd be here with Marian and Jeremy and the girls—unhappy as hell.

She touched her short hair.

She was no longer the old Darcy. But was she really the new one she created in those two years when she was trying to become responsible?

I want to be responsible especially after all the bad things I've done.

Darcy went back to her desk and sat in her chair for a long time before she heard a knock on her open door.

"Hello, Darcy."

"David."

"Your mother asked me to meet her here."

"Come on in."

He looked handsome and safe in his Brooks Brothers suit and styled hair, carrying a chic briefcase. "You okay?" he asked.

"Uh-huh."

He inspected her briefly. "Your hair looks good."

"Thanks."

"Hello, dear." Marian came up behind David. "Did you tell her, David?" she asked.

"Not yet."

Bustling in excitedly, Marian said, "The papers are ready, Darcy Anne."

"Papers?"

"To sign the daycare over to you. I asked David to meet me here so we could review things."

Darcy stared at David, knowing she could never be happy with a man like him.

She stared at her mother, wondering if she could ever please Marian, searching to remember why it was so important.

And then she heard something she hadn't heard in days, something that made her think maybe she wasn't so hopeless after all. *Come on, Darce. Make me proud.*

PORTENTS, an establishment so sophisticated Hunter was forced to wear the vest, pants and bow tie of a monkey suit to tend the bar, wasn't crowded yet on Friday night. As he wiped up a spill, he scanned the clientele who had come for happy hour.

They were Darcy's kind.

Immediately he banished the thought. Though he was happier than he'd ever been in his life, he missed that woman so much, sometimes he couldn't breathe for it. Nights were the worst. Dreams of them together haunted him, and he woke up often in a sweat.

Concentrate on the good things in your life, Sloan...

"Where ya goin', Dad?" Braden had asked from the bed in the second bedroom of the trailer Bart and Ada had rented close to his bungalow.

"I gotta work, son."

Braden had sat up halfway and hugged him. "Okay. See ya in the mornin'."

Tramp had barked, then they'd both settled down right easy...

The owner of Portents approached the bar. "Good to have you back, Sloan."

"Good to be back, Nelson."

The man smoothed a hand over the long mahogany surface. "Everybody comments on this craftsmanship. I could set you up with a lot of jobs, except I'd probably lose you as the world's greatest bartender, then."

"As a matter of fact, I'd be interested in some jobs." He'd spent the whole morning with Nathan and Paige before they flew back home talking about setting up his own carpentry business. He smiled; he still didn't believe they'd come all this way to testify to his fitness as a father.

Even though it hadn't been necessary.

"Well, I guess I could..." Nelson's voice trailed off. He whistled under his breath. "Wow...who's the looker?"

Hunter glanced up to see a woman had entered the

bar. She was in profile, and for a minute, she reminded him of Darcy. But hell, what didn't?

In the dim light, it looked like the woman had the same hair color, but it was cut short around her face. She wore a pretty, dark-green outfit; it was sophisticated and chic, but not either of Darcy's styles—the prim Miss Darcy or the bad girl. Hunter turned to face the bottles to hide the sick feeling in his gut from just thinking about her.

Can't Miss Darcy and the girls come and live in Florida like Grandma and Grandpa?

No, son, they can't. I'm sorry.

The kid didn't know how sorry. For days, Hunter had been wondering if he'd been too rash and handled things poorly with her. If he'd been more patient, more compromising, would he have lost her?

I just want to examine all the options.

"Hey, it's your lucky day," Nelson said. "She's headed this way." As Hunter pivoted, Nelson pulled out a stool for the woman who approached the bar. "I'll let her sit right here, Hun—" The owner stopped midspeech. "Hey, Sloan, you okay?"

But Hunter didn't answer. What he saw before him robbed him of his ability to speak.

"Hello, Hunter."

He felt his chest constrict. For a minute, he was deathly afraid he was going to cry like Braden on a bad day.

She slid onto the stool.

"Darcy," was all he managed to say.

She smiled. Then she leaned over, rose up and kissed him full on the mouth. Her scent, something sinful, encompassed him. When she reseated herself, she scanned his outfit. "Now, don't you look downright fetching," she said, imitating his southern accent.

"Breathe, buddy," Nelson joked as he started to walk away. "And get the lady a drink."

"I'd like a glass of champagne, if you have it."

Somehow, Hunter managed to uncork and pour the bubbly. When he came back to her, he tried to be cool, but he spilled the drink as he set it before her. She grasped his shaking hand. "I've missed you so much."

"W-what happened to your hair?" was all he could think of to say.

She fingered it. "The old Darcy's gone, Hunter."

"I don't understand."

"I'm not the girl I used to be."

"No?"

"Nope. But I'm not the woman I made myself into these last two years, either. With the knot at the back of her neck."

"W-who are you?" He knew he sounded like an idiot, stuttering and asking dumb questions, but her presence had stripped him of reason.

She lifted her glass as if she was giving a toast. "I'm Darcy Shannon O'Malley. A woman with faults. A woman who makes mistakes." She shook her head. "A woman who's been traveling for hours trying to find the man she loves."

He scowled. He was really losing it. He had no idea what she meant. "Traveling?"

Again, she grinned at his pitiful response. "I decided to show up at the hearing to testify for you along with Paige and Nathan. I wanted to give my input as Braden's daycare worker."

"You did?"

"Yep. Except when I got there, the court people said

the hearing had been canceled.'' She sipped. ''What happened?''

''Shelly caved, right before the hearing got started. She said Hank didn't really want Braden living with them. She said it was obvious he was happy with me, and she'd let me go for primary custody as long as she got to see him.'' He knew he was babbling but couldn't stop himself. ''I felt sorry for her, she does love the kid but she felt that she had no choice.''

''I'm so glad you got him.''

He looked down at her hand covering his, then back up at her.

''I want to tell you what I was going to say to the judge, Hunter.''

''Darcy, you don't have to—''

''I want to. I was going to say that you were the best father I'd ever seen in my years at TenderTime. Kind and considerate with a very troubled boy. Willing to put yourself on the line for him. Knowing when to be stern and discipline him, but always so gentle.'' She was rubbing her fingertips over each of his fingers. Her nails were polished a pretty peach and scraped his skin slightly.

''I don't feel particularly gentle right now, Miz Darcy.''

''Hush. Let me finish. I would have told the court how you always had his best interests at heart. That any boy would be lucky to have such a warm, sensitive, caring man as a father.'' She looked up, and her eyes sparkled like rare jade. ''That you were wonderful with girls, too. How much Claire and Meli love you. I would have said you should have more babies.'' She placed a hand over the middle of her pretty, green outfit.

His eyes widened. ''Darcy, darlin', you're not...''

Somewhere inside him, he relished the thought of her pregnant with his child, but down deep he *didn't* want that to be the reason she'd come to him.

She shook her head. "No, I'm not pregnant. But I'd like to be. I want to have your baby, Hunter."

He remembered a line from an old song about a carpenter and a lady having his baby.

She didn't give him a chance to respond. "Hunter, please forgive me for how I've acted. For not treating you right in Hyde Point. I was confused. I had some growing up to do." She kissed his hand. "You helped me to. You made me see—"

He picked up the glass of champagne and put it to her lips. "Drink," he ordered. "And stop talkin' for a minute."

She closed her eyes. "Sorry, I'm nervous." She drank. "And I'm afraid I won't be able to convince—"

He put the glass to her lips again.

"There's nothin' to be afraid of, darlin'."

Those lips began to tremble. "No?"

He set down the glass and cradled her cheek in his palm. "I love you, Darce. And I want you with me." He looked around. "I don't care where anymore."

Tears sparkled like stars in her eyes. "I'll move here. With the girls. We'll start a new life, the five of us."

He glanced at her stomach. "Six."

She gave him a watery smile.

He said, "We don't have to discuss all that now. I think we should get the kids together and decide as a family where we'll live."

"But, Hunter, you hate Hyde Point."

"No, Darce, not anymore. I got a lot of people I care about there—people who care about me, like Paige and

Nathan. Hannah's there. Bart and Ada would go back with us, I think."

"I—"

"You're not the only one who's grown up. I have, too. I've learned a lot in these last few months. Nobody can make you feel inferior or not good enough unless you let them. I'm about done letting anybody do that to me."

"Oh, Hunter."

"Anyway, we don't need a *place* to feel like we belong, love." He touched her heart. "This is where I belong." He took her hand and put it his chest. "This is where *you* belong. That's enough."

He lifted the glass and drank some champagne then put it to her lips again. She sipped, too.

Reaching out, he touched her hair. It was still thick and heavy. "I like this. It suits you." He leaned over the bar and whispered, "But will you still dress up in those little leather pants for me from time to time, Darce?"

She grinned. "Anything you say, Boss."

His hand curled at her neck and brought her forehead to his. "Ah, darlin', that's all I need to hear."

* * * * *

Please turn the page for an excerpt from
AGAINST THE ODDS—
the next title in Kathryn Shay's
SERENITY HOUSE
trilogy.

CHAPTER ONE

February 1987

HER HEART THUMPING in her chest, Nora Nolan raced up the rickety steps of the Cranes' house with her friend, police officer Dan Whitman. She'd never seen him so upset. He practically ripped off the screen as he yanked it open and pounded on the front door.

"Anabelle, it's Sergeant Whitman."

No response. He swore vilely. The February wind whipped around Nora's face, chilling her.

"This is the *police*," he shouted. "Open the door."

Still no answer.

"That's it." He drew himself up. "Step back, Nora."

"Dan, I—"

Before she could finish, he slammed his body against the door, easily unhinging the dried-out, battered wood. It crashed backward like an old tree toppling in the wind.

Dan stepped inside. "Stay out here, Nora."

She didn't. She followed him into the house. The dim living room was cramped with a couch and a few scattered chairs that were worn and faded. The TV was on, but the screen was snowy and buzzing. The house smelled like burned bacon and mildew.

"Anabelle?" Dan yelled again. His voice vibrated with anger.

They heard a crash upstairs. Dan whirled, catapulted to the staircase and took the steps two at a time. Again, Nora followed. At the end of the long hallway stood a big man, swaying drunkenly on his feet.

He was slapping his hand on a closed door. "Goddamn little shit...let me..." He never got to finish.

Dan was on the guy in seconds, dragging him back, pushing him against the wall and grabbing him by the shirt collar. "You son of a bitch."

"What the hell—"

"If you touched her, I'll kill you." For emphasis, Dan hoisted the guy up against the wall—none too gently—then let him go. He went down like a rag doll. The smell of stale booze rose from him to where Nora stood.

Pivoting, Dan drew in a deep breath. He turned to the door. "Anabelle? Are you in there?"

No response.

"Anabelle, it's Dan Whitman. I got here as soon as I could after you called. Nora's with me. Open the door."

Still, no answer. Dan glanced worriedly at Nora. "Anabelle," he pleaded, gentling his tone. "You can open the door now. We're going to take you out of here for good. To Serenity House. Nora's got a nice room waiting for you."

After what seemed like interminable minutes, Nora heard a small voice ask, "Sergeant Whitman? A-are you sure? Is that you?"

"Yeah, honey, it's me. I promise, no one's going to hurt you again."

The lock snicked open. The door was pulled back.

Nora gasped. Inside the tiny bathroom was Anabelle Crane. The sixteen-year-old's face was obscured by a fall of dark hair. There were hand-size welts on her arms. Her chin dipped to her chest, calling attention to the torn T-shirt. It was ripped down the front as if someone had tried to yank it off her.

Dan stepped forward, as did Anabelle. He enveloped her in his arms and held her close. The girl's thin shoulders shook. "I...I was so scared."

"Shh, it's okay. We're here." He rested his chin on Anabelle's head as he clasped her in a solid embrace. "You're safe. You'll be safe from now on, Anabelle. I promise."

She nosed farther into Dan's shirt. "Al tried to..." She couldn't finish. Dan looked helplessly at Nora. He'd brought her along just for this purpose.

Nora stepped forward and put her hand on Anabelle's shoulder. "Sweetie, do you need to go to the hospital? Did your brother assault you sexually?"

Gripping Dan's neck as if it were a lifeline, Anabelle shook her head.

"Thank God." Dan's voice was gruff. "All right, I'm going to cuff him and call a black-and-white to come get him. Nora will take you outside to my car."

Still the girl held on. Nora waited, her eyes misting. Finally Anabelle let go. She stepped away and peered up at Dan, then over at Nora.

Nora bit back an outcry. The girl's cheek sported purplish bruises. One eye was swollen shut. Her lip was bleeding.

"We'll need the hospital after all," Nora said, taking Anabelle by the arm.

Dan's hands fisted, and his eyes widened with rage.

Nora nodded to the crumpled heap on the floor. "Call

the uniforms, and take care of him,'' she said with a calmness she didn't feel. ''We'll meet you at the car.''

Dan didn't move.

She touched his hand. ''Dan, for Anabelle's sake, arrest him calmly.''

Drawing a deep breath, he turned to Al Crane. Nora slid her arm around Anabelle's shoulders and led her through the hallway, down the steps and out of her dingy surroundings.

Thank God for Serenity House, Nora thought. It was a place where she—and Dan—could keep Anabelle safe.

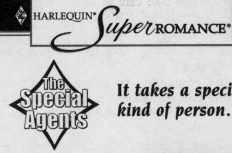

This special volume about the joy of wishing, giving and loving is just the thing to get you into the holiday spirit!

CHRISTMAS *Wishes,*
CHRISTMAS *Gifts*

Two full-length novels
at one remarkably low price!

USA Today bestselling author
TARA TAYLOR QUINN
DAY LECLAIRE

The perfect gift for all the romance readers on your Christmas list (including yourself!)

On sale November 2002 at your favorite retail outlet.

HARLEQUIN®
Makes any time special ®

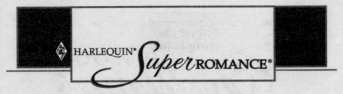

Princes...Princesses...
London Castles...New York Mansions...
To live the life of a royal!

In 2002, Harlequin Books lets you escape to a world of royalty with these royally themed titles:

Temptation:
January 2002—*A Prince of a Guy* (#861)
February 2002—*A Noble Pursuit* (#865)

American Romance:
The Carradignes: American Royalty (Editorially linked series)
March 2002—*The Improperly Pregnant Princess* (#913)
April 2002—*The Unlawfully Wedded Princess* (#917)
May 2002—*The Simply Scandalous Princess* (#921)
November 2002—*The Inconveniently Engaged Prince* (#945)

Intrigue:
The Carradignes: A Royal Mystery (Editorially linked series)
June 2002—*The Duke's Covert Mission* (#666)

Chicago Confidential
September 2002—*Prince Under Cover* (#678)

The Crown Affair
October 2002—*Royal Target* (#682)
November 2002—*Royal Ransom* (#686)
December 2002—*Royal Pursuit* (#690)

Harlequin Romance:
June 2002—*His Majesty's Marriage* (#3703)
July 2002—*The Prince's Proposal* (#3709)

Harlequin Presents:
August 2002—*Society Weddings* (#2268)
September 2002—*The Prince's Pleasure* (#2274)

Duets:
September 2002—*Once Upon a Tiara/Henry Ever After* (#83)
October 2002—*Natalia's Story/Andrea's Story* (#85)

Celebrate a year of royalty with Harlequin Books!

Available at your favorite retail outlet.

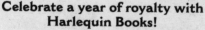

HARLEQUIN®
Makes any time special ®

Visit us at www.eHarlequin.com

HSROY02

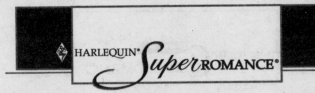
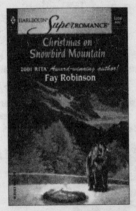